long journey home

long journey home
amber esplin

Bonneville Books
Springville, Utah

ISBN 13: 978-1-55517-928-2
ISBN 10: 1-55517-928-2

Published by Bonneville Books, an imprint of Cedar Fort, Inc., 925 N. Main, Springville, UT, 84663
Distributed by Cedar Fort, Inc., www.cedarfort.com

LIBRARY OF CONGRESS CATALOGING-IN-PUBLICATION DATA
Esplin, Amber.
  The long journey home / by Amber Esplin.
    p. cm.
  ISBN 1-55517-928-2 (acid-free paper)
  1. Teenage girls--Fiction. 2. Fathers and daughters--Fiction. 3. Mormon families--Fiction. I. Title.

PS3605.S64L66 2006
813'.6--dc22

2006017097

Cover design by Nicole Williams
Cover design © 2006 by Lyle Mortimer
Printed in the United States of America

10   9   8   7   6   5   4   3   2   1

Printed on acid-free paper

dedication

To my dear friend and mentor, Diane Smith, and my cousin Rebekah, who helped me find the courage to come home.

o n e

The radio station faded and then crackled with static. Mrs. Owens reached over to adjust the dial. From the backseat of the Owenses' blue LeBaron, Bridget caught a glimpse of a narrow, silver lake and a brightly painted boat with two levels of decks. The highway then veered away from the lake, climbing through a bank of mist to emerge along the crest of a hillside. Mrs. Owens took a second round through the radio stations and finally settled on something with a saxophone playing elevator music. Then she twisted around to look back at Bridget and gave her what she imagined to be a reassuring smile. The fine crow's-feet around her eyes deepened, fanning out toward the line of her short salt-and-pepper hair. "We'll be there soon," she promised.

"Yeah," agreed Mr. Owens from the driver's seat. "Only about twenty miles left."

Bridget smiled back a little stiffly and waited for Mrs. Owens to face front again before extracting a little mirror from her bag. Her "sandy coral" lipstick was holding up well, thank goodness, and she didn't think it was too bright after all, though she had worried about it that morning. She had worried about everything—whether her hoop earrings were too big and her straight denim skirt and sandals were too casual, whether she should have left her hair down instead of spiraling it up into a loose French twist. At least those things she could change if they weren't right. But what if her hair was simply the wrong color, what if she was too tall or too gangly, what if her father didn't like green eyes?

She slipped the mirror back into her bag and stared out the window again, trying consciously to appear calm. She imagined pushing the tension from her chest down into her legs and out the soles of her feet, into her arms and out through her fingertips. "Never let anyone see you out of your comfort zone," her mother had taught her, "even if you live out of it." It was one of the lessons that Margaret Lacey had ingrained in her daughter before getting herself killed in a car accident on the Pacific Coast Highway. Besides that lesson, Bridget had learned never to leave the house without lipstick, never to buy one-ply toilet paper, never to date anyone with longer hair or more earring holes than she had herself, and never to wear polyester underwear. There it was—her complete guide to life.

It was hard to pretend to be comfortable now, though, with the Owenses scrutinizing her with benevolent curiosity. Who could blame them for wanting to know how she would react—she wanted to know herself. She had ridden with them for more than three thousand miles now, all the way from San Francisco to upstate New York, and she felt sure that they had stopped at every historical marker and Denny's restaurant along the way. The trip had dragged on for more than a week already, but all the time their final destination had seemed indistinct.

"Do you remember Phrygia at all?" Mrs. Owens had asked her as they strolled along the boardwalks around Old Faithful in Yellowstone Park. Mrs. Owens's arm had been linked through Bridget's, and if not for that, Bridget would have stopped dead and stared at her. "Phrygia?" she had repeated, puzzled, in the instant before recognition sunk in. *What kind of name is that for a town?* she wondered. But of course, that was where they were going—where she was going, at least. The Owenses would drop her off there and then go on a few miles to Macedon, where their daughter and her family lived.

"Hmm, Phrygia," she had said again. "No, not really. Not much at all."

"Well," Mrs. Owens had replied cheerfully, "maybe when we get there it'll look familiar."

Would it? Bridget considered now. Since Mrs. Owens's question back in Wyoming, she had thought about it almost constantly, trying to sift through the blurred impressions of her early childhood and find one detail, anything at all, that would help prepare her for her return to the place she had lived for the first seven years of her life. Odd, maybe, that she didn't remember more, but when she had moved with her mother to San Francisco it was as if life had started all over again. Everything had been so different that her past in New York had seemed unreal and obsolete. Her father and two younger sisters had ceased to be real humans and had become merely ideas, the way that celebrities seem not to be real people even though everyone knows their names. Bridget's mother never mentioned her other daughters or Bridget's father, and Bridget had never heard from her family once since she left New York, not until two months ago when her mother had died.

Immediately afterward, Bridget had gone to stay with her friend Suzanne in the comfortably shabby three-story town house owned by Suzanne's parents. She had slept on a folding cot in the room shared by Suzanne and her younger sister, with a poster of Freddie Prinze Jr. for a headboard. She had already spent so many nights there that it was as familiar as her own bedroom and twice as homey. It had been easy to imagine that her mother was alive and well back in their own town house, dressed in her white satin robe and fuzzy white slippers and working feverishly over her next novel, which would, of course, be a best seller like all the others. If Bridget could have stayed with Suzanne during her whole senior year, she might never have had to acknowledge that her mother had died. It would have been like one superextended sleepover—cozy, warm, safe, and normal. A year wasn't much time at all; some people had exchange students stay that long. It wasn't too much to expect of Suzanne's parents, was it?

And then the letter had come, the address scrawled in tight, unfamiliar handwriting. Bridget had felt a sense of foreboding as soon as Suzanne's mother handed her the envelope.

"Why don't you go in the den to read it?" Suzanne's mother had suggested gently.

Bridget nodded dumbly and started off alone, closing the door of the den behind her and seating herself behind the wide, cluttered desk where Suzanne's father sometimes worked at home. It was quiet in this room with the door closed, even though from elsewhere in the house she could hear the TV blaring as Suzanne's younger siblings watched afternoon cartoons. She put the letter down on the desk and sat staring at the return address: Gerrick McKenna, 364 Independence Road, Phrygia, New York.

She had suddenly had a flashback of a party her mother had hosted soon after they moved from their cramped apartment into the town house, back when Bridget was about eight or nine. Her mother's first book had just scored a huge success, and their lives had changed so abruptly that they felt like strangers in their new surroundings. As Margaret's novel climbed best-seller lists and garnered nominations for awards in children's literature, her small circle of acquaintances exploded to include a sequined flock of writers, artists, and wealthy connoisseurs, all of whom had descended on the town house one evening in August to drink Margaret's best champagne. Bridget's mother had bought her a new dress for the occasion—black velvet with a long, heavy skirt and a simple bodice, and Bridget had wandered around among the guests, unnoticed until one older woman wearing a beige gown had caught at her arm.

"Who are you?" the woman had demanded. "Are you a critic from the *Times?* They're becoming younger and younger these days, aren't they?" She winked at her friend, a young man with a collar that made Bridget think of clergy, though she was sure he wasn't.

"I'm Bridget McKenna," she had responded matter-of-factly.

"Oh? And how do you know Ms. Lacey?"

Bridget had felt taken aback. She had assumed—unreasonably, she saw now—that everyone knew who she was, as if she sported some sort of label that was universally understood. "She's my mother."

"Ah, I see," said the woman. "Well, that explains it. She could hardly expect you to go to bed amid all this," and she waved her hand in an expansive gesture that included the several brightly lit rooms, the chattering people, and the faint haze of cigarette smoke.

Late the next morning when Bridget had gone down to the airy kitchen to watch her mother make pancakes, she had confronted Margaret with a question.

"Why is my name McKenna, but your name is Lacey?" she wanted to know.

Margaret tucked a strand of copper-colored hair behind her ear and turned her green eyes on her daughter. "You know why, sweetie. Lacey is the name I had when I was growing up, when I was your age. McKenna is your father's name."

"But you're my mother," Bridget persisted. "Mothers have the same name as their children. Why aren't you Margaret McKenna anymore?"

"Because I'm not married to your father anymore," Margaret answered, flipping a pancake with style. Pancakes were the one food she was really good at making.

"Then why isn't my name Lacey?"

Margaret went to the cupboard to get out two plates. They were the new ones she had bought, fine china with a white-on-white pattern and a silver rim. She brought them over to the counter where Bridget was sitting on a stool in front of a bowl of fresh strawberries and a can of fake whipped cream. "It is, don't you remember? What's your name? Say it all for me."

"Bridget Lacey McKenna."

"That's right, and I wouldn't change a bit of it. I couldn't. Maybe sometimes I wish you were just Bridget Lacey—" Margaret paused, setting the plates down and watching Bridget intently. "But I can't make that be. You're Bridget Lacey McKenna; that's who you are. And I'm Margaret Lacey."

Two different people, two separate identities, thought Bridget. And sometimes at Suzanne's house, she imagined she wasn't Bridget McKenna at all, but Suzanne's sister. She wanted to know what it was like to be part of a family, to feel herself melting into a larger whole, like a crooked little stream flowing into a big river. How comforting it would be to lie in bed at night and feel the warmth of belonging in your veins. It was scary sometimes to be a separate, lone entity with nothing to anchor you.

That day two months ago when the letter from her father had come, she had sat staring down at the name—her own name—waiting for the melting feeling to come. Could she go back and be part of this family she had left behind? The name might have been that of a stranger. She couldn't recall a single image of Gerrick McKenna. She opened the envelope slowly, unfolded the paper, and read:

> *Dear Bridget,*
> *I am sorry to hear about your loss. I have been in contact with your mother's lawyer, and it is settled that you are to come to Phrygia as soon as*

arrangements can be made. I have enclosed a check that I hope will cover your needs in the interim. Please contact me at the address or phone number below if you require additional funds. I will send you further information as soon as I have worked out the details of your travel.

Sincerely,

Gerrick McKenna

Was she to call him Gerrick, then, she had wondered. Or Mr. McKenna? She wondered again now, clutching her hands together to keep them from trembling. "Hello, Dad," she had practiced saying in the hotel bathroom the night before. She had stood in front of the mirror, looked herself in the eye, held out her hand, and said it. It was easy enough, of course, when there was only a basket of soap to hear her. She didn't know if she could gaze into her father's face as openly as she had gazed into her own familiar one, which didn't conceal a single mystery. But whatever happened, she had told herself, she had to keep her cool. She had wallowed in enough embarrassment already, begging Suzanne's mother to take her in.

"I won't be any trouble, I promise," she had pleaded.

The memory of her quavering, little-girl voice and the shrill note of desperation that had threatened to end in a squeak made her wince inwardly in humiliation. She had been sitting at the kitchen table watching Suzanne's mother make lasagna for dinner. The scene reminded her of the way she used to sit and watch her mother make pancakes—only it wasn't the same at all because the way the women moved, the way they looked, and the way they filled up their kitchens was so different. This wasn't her own mother, and she didn't belong here. In two days she was leaving with the Owenses, friends of Suzanne's family, and her life in New York loomed before her as a void.

"I'll make dinner every night," she had offered recklessly. "I'll take on an extra set of chores." Anything, anything, if it meant she didn't have to go to the source of that cold letter.

Suzanne's mother had closed her eyes briefly and walked over to take Bridget's hands in her own. The late afternoon sunlight had poured in on them, spreading like honey across the surface of the table.

"Bridget, I think this is best. I think you need to go to your father now."

"Please . . ." It seemed as if all the emotion of her life had flooded into that single word, as if the continuation of life itself depended on the answer.

"You should be with your family," Suzanne's mother had decreed quietly. "You have to go."

Bridget replayed the scene now as a reminder that falling apart didn't help anyone, least of all herself. It had only tainted her departure, which Margaret would have carried off with tragic nobility. Yes, Bridget's mother would have known exactly how to play the strong but grieving heroine, how to let the Owenses stare at her without squirming, and how to present herself to Gerrick McKenna. Whatever she did, whatever she called him, she would make it seem right. But Margaret was gone despite her many talents, and here was Bridget within a few miles of Phrygia. All she could do was push down hard on all the uncertainty and face up to the unknown. And it was only a year. It was a detour, not a derailment. She had always planned to go to Stanford after high school, and that didn't have to change. Even if things went badly, next fall she could go home. She pictured the university's Spanish-style buildings that always made her think of sunshine and guitar music. Just a few months and she'd be back on course.

"This is it!" cried Mrs. Owens.

A big white sign with blue letters read, "Welcome to Phrygia." Below that, a painting of a large hot fudge sundae topped the claim, "Home of the World's Best Ice Cream."

"Well, Bridget, lucky you!" enthused Mr. Owens, whose idea of heaven was a dish of rocky road. Bridget thought she had seen two or three similar signs today alone, but she didn't mention that now. Instead, she flashed the smile she had practiced in the mirror last night and, with Olympian effort, checked her urge to roll down the window and stick her head out of the car like a dog on a joyride. She took in the passing scenery as calmly as she could, noting the old Victorian-style houses in various stages of upkeep and the brief business district that didn't, as far as she could tell without appearing to be too interested, include a single recognizable chain store.

Mr. Owens turned right from the main street and drove on for several blocks, gliding by a series of sprawling lawns and several kids on bikes. Bridget counted three churches before he stopped—abruptly, she thought—in front of a weathered, gray three-story house with a wide front porch and a turret with a pointed roof. Her stomach sunk into her shoes. It was dusk now, but she could see three people on the porch, all of them standing straight and stiff like soldiers at attention. Mr. Owens got out of the car, waved toward the porch in acknowledgment, and headed around to the trunk to get Bridget's luggage. Mrs. Owens got out too and called a greeting. She didn't approach the welcoming party, though, but glanced over her shoulder to where Bridget still sat in the backseat. Bridget would have to go first. They were waiting for her.

Taking a deep breath, Bridget slipped her arm under one strap of the backpack that sat beside her and stepped out carefully, her eyes fixed on the strangers on the porch. As she passed Mrs. Owens, the older woman cupped a hand beneath Bridget's elbow and fell into step a little behind her, letting go when Bridget reached the bottom of the short flight of stairs. A man with dark hair showing gray at the edges waited for her at the top. He was nothing Bridget would have ever connected with the word "Dad." She had imagined someone more like Suzanne's father, a little overweight and balding, with a friendly, capable face. This man might have just come from playing James Bond. His eyes were brown and penetrating, the lines of his face were clean, like those of a marble sculpture, and though it might just have been because he was standing above her, he appeared to be formidably tall.

He stepped back slightly as she mounted the steps, making room for her, but before she could offer him her hand, he nodded curtly. "Bridget," he said in a deep, slightly hoarse voice, "these are your sisters, Lydia"—he indicated the slim, dark-haired girl immediately to his right, who nodded as her father had done—"and Charlotte"—he gestured toward the girl on the end whose hair was a shade lighter than Lydia's.

Bridget's mind went blank, leaving her speechless. What had she rehearsed? She surveyed the faces across from her, finding nothing familiar there, nothing except . . . Charlotte's eyes. Those were her mother's eyes, she was sure of it. Her own eyes.

Charlotte leaped forward impetuously and flung her arms around Bridget. "Call me Charly," she directed breathlessly. Lydia and her father moved slowly out of line and came around behind the pair, locking Bridget in a circle.

"Welcome home," said her father.

t w o

Show Bridget to her room," instructed Gerrick McKenna as he left the porch and strode toward the driveway to help Mr. Owens with the luggage. Bridget looked back at the car uncertainly, clutching her backpack. Through the LeBaron's rear passenger window she could see the silhouette of a small mound of possessions, and for an instant she considered loading herself up further before following her sisters into the house. But when Charly caught at her free arm and tugged her across the porch with an enthusiastic "Come and see, Bridget," she allowed herself to be led through the old-fashioned double doors.

Stepping over the threshold, Bridget felt her stomach twist with anticipation. Would this room trigger a memory, as nothing else had done so far? She wanted to take in everything at once. Her eyeballs seemed ready to bulge out as she stretched her eyelids as far apart as they would go.

"You have big eyes," said Lydia, who had gone into the house first and now stood a few feet away, her hand resting on the knob of another set of doors. As it turned out, there wasn't much to take in yet, for the front doors opened onto a small entryway and the second set of doors, now guarded by Lydia, were closed. A tall umbrella stand painted with white flowers on a blue background and a large mirror hanging over a narrow, dark wood table made up the only furnishings. Bridget met Lydia's eyes in the mirror and noted the coldness glinting out of them. Charly paused to gaze into the mirror as well, and for a moment the three sisters examined their reflections as if the same questions pulsed inside all of them. Was there a resemblance? Was there anything about them that might mark them as something more than strangers? Between Bridget and Lydia there surely wasn't; Bridget was tall and tan with her mother's coppery hair, bleached extra light by California's summer sun, while Lydia was pale and small, what Mrs. Owens might have called "a slip of a girl." Her long, dark hair cascaded smoothly down her back and over the tops of her small arms, and dressed as she was in a white cotton sundress, she might have been a maiden out of a fairy tale. Perhaps Snow White, thought Bridget, and as chilly as the name.

Charly broke the silence first. "C'mon, Bridget, you've gotta see it!" she bubbled, reaching out to link arms with her sisters. She was the link in looks as well, Bridget realized—not quite so dark-haired as Lydia, but not as light as Bridget, and with Margaret's green eyes. Bridget tried rapidly to calculate the girls' ages as she hurried along after Charly. She knew Lydia was the elder of the two and estimated her to be about fifteen, though she couldn't be sure.

"This is the way upstairs," Charly explained unnecessarily as they burst through the second set of doors into a hallway paneled with dark wood. A staircase with a banister the same color as the walls rose up immediately across from the doors. On the left of the staircase, Bridget could see a closed door at the end of a short passage. On the right, a wide archway opened into the living room. Bridget extracted her arm from Charly's, set her backpack down, and stepped slowly through the archway, bracing herself for a flood of memories. A comfortable if mismatched assortment of furniture met her gaze, and she moved farther into the room, trying to know her father from his belongings. In the corner by the high front windows, a leather chair sat under a tall floor lamp with a cream-colored fabric shade and a trim of fine fringe. A large upright piano stood against the wall next to the archway, and a big overstuffed sofa and two pouffy chintz chairs had been grouped across from it as if in preparation for a recital. Beyond them and opposite the front windows, another archway sectioned off a dining area containing a heavy-looking table with fat legs. Bridget reached out and touched the polished edge of the piano. Pictures of Lydia and Charly smiled down at her from gold frames.

"Do you play?" Lydia wanted to know.

"No, I never took lessons."

"Well, we all do," she declared, and Bridget thought that she knew what it must be like to fail miserably at a job interview. She shrugged and smiled. "Cool," she said.

"You've gotta see your room, Bridget," called Charly from the hallway, where she was bouncing up and down on the balls of her feet. "We've been working on it for days."

Bridget walked over to her and stooped to pick up her backpack just as her father and Mr. Owens came hurtling through the doors, propelled by the awkward weight of several suitcases and a big black guitar case. Mrs. Owens followed in their wake, stopping before the stairs to look around.

"You've got a lovely home here, Mr. McKenna," she called as Bridget's father ascended the stairs, and Mr. Owens huffed after him. "Yes, Bridget, this is quite nice," she raved. The high heels she was wearing with khaki slacks and a white sport shirt clicked on the wood floor as she walked toward the living room. "It's a relief we'll be able to see you so well settled before we leave. I've had this ball of anxiety in my stomach ever since Nevada, and I can't imagine how you must have felt."

"Yeah, but let's go," insisted Charly, running up the stairs behind the men. Bridget climbed up after her, expecting to follow her into a room on the second floor. But when she reached the landing she could hear the two men stomping above her, and Charly had already darted halfway up a second flight of stairs that angled back toward the front of the house. The landing at the top of this flight featured a wide window complete with a window seat, but rather than admire the view, Bridget turned into the open doorway on the right and caught her breath.

There was nothing very surprising in the furnishings of the room. A twin-size four-poster bed, a desk, a dresser, and a tall bookcase were made out of the same dark wood that Bridget had noticed in the rest of the house. The bedspread was white and simple, and beside that the room was devoid of decor, an empty canvas ready to be transformed by Bridget's own possessions. It was the wall opposite the bed that drew her attention. She could tell by the way it curved out that it formed the inside of the tower she had observed when they first drove up to the house. Somehow the distinctive shape of the room lent it an air of adventure. Feeling like a character in a movie, Bridget set her backpack down and went over to peer out one of the three windows that together afforded a panoramic view. Through the gathering dusk she could make out the pink and gold line of the horizon.

"What d'ya think?" asked Charly.

"Wow," said Bridget honestly. At the same time, a tiny shiver of foreboding streaked beneath the current of her thoughts. She shook it off and turned to find her father and Mr. Owens watching her. When she met her father's eyes, he looked quickly away.

"Well, I think one more trip oughta do it," said Mr. Owens, and the men tramped back down the stairs.

"I don't know where Lydia went," said Charly.

"She slipped off to do some schoolwork," explained Mrs. Owens, coming into the room and settling herself on the bed. "At least that's what she told me. Goodness, the way they work you children these days, not even letting you have your summer vacation in peace. I'm glad my school days are over."

"I didn't know Lydia had homework to do over the summer," said Charly.

"Maybe she didn't mention it before because school seemed so far away," suggested Bridget. "Come help me unpack, Charly. I've got tons of stuff here, I don't know what I'll do with it all. It didn't seem like so much when it was in my room at home, but when I packed it, it just grew."

"Oh, there's lots of space," Charly assured her. "Look, you've got a walk-in closet." She moved around the bed to the side opposite the entry and opened a door. "It's got its own light, it's so big. It's like a whole separate room."

"Perfect, all the luggage can go in there." Bridget unzipped her biggest suitcase, and she, Charly, and Mrs. Owens began putting clothes into the dresser. Soon Bridget's father and Mr. Owens were back with the last of her things.

"Have you eaten?" her father asked her, looking at her only briefly.

"Yes, thank you, we stopped for dinner before coming on the last few miles."

"Well then, I'll let you get unpacked. Breakfast is at 7:30." He turned to the Owenses and extended a hand. Mrs. Owens came around to hug Bridget while Mr. Owens refused to take the check Mr. McKenna offered to help cover gas and lodging expenses.

"It was our pleasure," said Mr. Owens.

"We'll stop by on our way back through and check on you," Mrs. Owens told her quietly. "I'm sure you'll settle in just fine, but your friends at home will want to know how you're doing."

"Thanks," muttered Bridget, truly grateful for Mrs. Owens's promise and ashamed at her own anxiety over their departure. She blinked rapidly and busied herself arranging clothes in a drawer.

"And don't worry," Mrs. Owens added in a whisper, "like I told you before—I once had some good friends who were Mormons, and they were quite normal."

Bridget glanced at her father and then shifted her eyes quickly back to the drawer. She had managed not to think about that other worrying detail today, that thing about her new family that cast an aura of mystery around all of them, as if they weren't unfamiliar enough. Although Bridget and her mother had not set foot inside a church within the last decade, she knew that her father was religious. And it wasn't just some ordinary religion, either. Sure, she had known a few Mormon kids at her school and they had been nice enough, but . . . everyone knew that they were just a little bit weird.

"We'd better get going," said Mr. Owens. The adults started down the stairs, leaving Bridget and Charly alone.

"Ooh, what's this?" wondered Charly. She had been rummaging in the suitcase, and now she pushed aside some rolled up socks and lifted out a square wooden case. "It's locked."

Bridget came over from the dresser and unlatched the chain she always wore around her neck. On the end of it dangled a small gold key. She inserted it into the keyhole, above which her initials had been carved: BLM. When she opened the lid, Charly sighed in disappointment. The only things visible were two leatherbound books.

"What is this, your portable school desk?" she asked. "Wait, are those your diaries?" she perked up with new excitement. "You write an awful lot. But I guess that means you have a super interesting life."

Bridget picked up one of the books and opened the front cover. "*The Mostly True Adventures of Colin the Superhero,*" proclaimed the title page, "by M. C. Lacey."

"Have you read these?" she asked softly, showing the page to Charly.

The girl sobered instantly. "Yeah," she affirmed. "Mother used to send us free copies just before they hit the bookstores."

Bridget turned a few more pages, not seeing the words but knowing the story anyway. This had been her mother's first book, the book that had changed both their lives. She had written four more after this one, and before she died she had been working on a sixth Colin book, even though she had told her publisher she wanted to stop writing Colin and try something else. "One more," her publisher had coaxed. "Just one more."

"Okay," Margaret had agreed finally. "But this is the last."

In the course of those five novels, young Colin—who wasn't really a superhero, except in his imagination—and his friend Kristy had camped out overnight in the public library, operated a successful pancake-and-hot-dog stand, floated a raft twenty miles down the Eerie Canal, and secretly taken the train to New York City to talk a bigwig CEO out of taking over Colin's dad's business. And with all that, they still found time to dethrone several school bullies and help the police capture a gang of thieves. Colin was lovable and funny and charming, maybe the child her mother had always wanted and never had.

"Did Mom send you anything else?" she asked Charly curiously. She had never known that her mother had maintained any contact at all with her other daughters.

"Yeah, letters, and of course birthday cards every year. Want to see?" Charly bounded out without waiting for an answer and pounded down the stairs. Bridget released the pages she had been holding and felt them *whoosh* against her fingers as they fell back into place. She was looking at one of the first pages now, the dedication page, and the message stood out with sudden poignancy.

"To my little ones, Lydia and Charly, with a prayer for

understanding." Beneath this her mother had written in blue ink, "For my Bridget, who makes my work worthwhile. Love always, Mother."

"Look at this!" Charly burst in carrying a shoe box covered with striped contact paper. Taking off the lid, she dumped the contents onto Bridget's bed, and the two of them gazed down at about a dozen brightly colored cards and several handwritten letters that scattered across the white spread. Charly picked up one card with a rainbow arcing across a blue background under specks of silver glitter. "This was my last one," she explained, handing it to Bridget. Bridget opened it and read. Under the card's printed message "May all your dreams come true," Margaret had written, "My dear Charly, happy twelfth. When I think that you are so grown up, I am filled with awe, but I am excited too to imagine you advancing into young womanhood, gathering rainbows to fill your future with color and light. I believe in you always, my darling, and hope that you will believe in yourself as well. The message of this card isn't an accident. Keep dreaming, and write and tell me about your dreams. You are in my thoughts always. Love, Mother."

Bridget closed the card slowly and looked up into Charly's green eyes.

"What was she like?" asked Charly.

Bridget considered for a moment. "She—she was like this card sounds," she said feebly, overwhelmed by the task of condensing her mother's essence into words.

"She must have been wonderful then," concluded Charly. "She sent funny gifts, though. Sometimes exactly what I wanted, and sometimes something I never would have thought about in a million years." She pried a ball of white cloth out of her pocket and began to unwad it. "See, this was for my birthday." It was a handkerchief, elaborately embroidered around the edges and bearing the initials "CCM."

"Why do you think she chose this?" Charly asked.

"Well, it's pretty, isn't it, and it's . . ." Bridget fumbled for an explanation. "Sometimes she liked old-fashioned things, romantic things, you know."

Charly frowned. "Mushy things?"

"No, not exactly. Not that kind of romantic. She just liked to use her imagination with different kinds of things. Sort of like an actress. She could take something in her hand, study it for a while, and then come up with a whole story about the people connected with it."

"Did she make up a story about a handkerchief?" asked Charly a little skeptically.

"Well—no, not that I know of," Bridget admitted. "But maybe you could. Maybe she hoped you would."

They both stared at the crinkled bit of fabric. "What's your middle name, Charly?"

"Christine. What's yours?"

"Lacey."

"Oh," said Charly. "Lydia's is Margaret."

They stood in silence for a while. "I'll help you put this stuff away," offered Bridget, and she began to scoop up the letters and cards and dump them back into the shoebox.

"Yeah, I guess I should stop bugging you. Dad warned me, he said you'd be tired, and I shouldn't make a pest of myself. But I've tried not to. I really have," she finished earnestly.

"I'm glad you've been here to help me," said Bridget. Impulsively, she draped her arm around Charly's shoulders and pulled her into a brief hug. Charly clung to her for a moment after Bridget let go.

"I'll let you get to bed, though," said Charly, lodging the shoebox under one arm and scampering out of the room. Bridget heard her footsteps on the stairs and then the exuberant slamming of a door. In the quiet that followed, she began to clear off her bed, pausing over the open wooden chest to trace the intricate carvings of leaves and vines that spread around the sides and across the top. This was her treasure box. It was the first present her mother had given her after they left New York, and contemplating the gift now, Bridget thought it might have been an invitation to put down new roots, to create memories that were San Francisco instead of Phrygia. As sturdy and unchanging as the box appeared from the outside, its contents had varied over the years. Its first collections of miscellany had included stickers she had traded for at school and autumn leaves she had picked up from the playground. Later, she had filled it with "best friends" keepsakes, such as a charm that was made to look broken in half and could only be whole if paired up with Suzanne's.

When she had emptied the box the week after her mother's death, it had contained a dried rose from her prom corsage, a note from a guy she had once had a crush on, and, as Charly had guessed, her diary. She didn't recall where she had put those things—they hadn't seemed important anymore. She had to make room for something new, something she didn't understand yet—the thing her mother had left her.

Of course, she had inherited all of her mother's possessions, really; the house would be sold, a few debts would be paid off, and the remainder of her mother's substantial fortune would go into a trust, which among other things would fund Bridget's education. But her mother had specified in her will that Bridget was to have a certain item right away. Lifting out the rest of the Colin books, she could see the real treasure she was hiding in this box. Nothing exciting to look at, she thought, nothing Charly would have wanted to investigate. It was only a bulging manila envelope with the unhelpful label "C & C." Bridget picked it up now and undid the clasp. Inside, the jumble of folded papers rustled as she slid her fingers down into the opening. Her hand closed on one sheet of paper and she drew it out, feeling the way the pen had etched the handwriting into the white surface. She felt it but didn't look at it. Her eyes seemed to have squished closed of their own accord.

The first day after the lawyer had read her mother's instructions and discovered this envelope, Bridget had removed one of the papers inside, puzzled over her mother's bequest. She had skimmed a few lines of writing without unfolding the paper and then, embarrassed, had put it back and extracted another folded sheet. While she had never unfolded any of the papers to read an entire page, she had read enough to know that these were love letters. The handwriting was tight and tall and very even. It might have been her father's—she didn't know. She didn't want to know . . . yet. She stuffed the paper she was holding back into the envelope, piled the books back on top, and fastened the chest with the key. Whatever her mother wanted her to understand from these letters, it could wait.

Once in bed with the light off, she curled up tight and drew the sheet up to her chin, even though the room was heavy with the heat of late summer. She lay in the dark marveling over the mystery of her mother, who had never, as far as Bridget could remember, mentioned Lydia and Charly in the ten years since she had left them and who, through all those long years, had thought of them "always." It wasn't so strange, she supposed, that her mother had kept in touch with them. No, not strange at all. It must have broken her heart to leave them in the first place but that was what she and Bridget's father had worked out.

And it had had to be that way. How could she have taken three little girls to that tiny studio apartment where she and Bridget had dozed uncomfortably in sleeping bags on hardwood floors and tried not to listen to the scuttling of insect bodies whenever one of them turned on the light? She couldn't have known how successful her first Colin book would be or that soon her bank account would rival the annual budget of a small country. By the time that happened, the little girls would have been used to living with their father. She wouldn't have wanted to uproot them, but of course she wrote to them, dreamed of them.

The only thing that really was strange was that Bridget's father had never done the same. He had never written to her in all those years. *Why?* she wondered now, staring up into the unfathomable darkness that hung like a canopy below the high ceiling. Maybe he was as cold as the ice she had seen in Lydia's eyes; maybe he was without warmth or caring, and that's why her mother had left him. She thought of the way he had avoided looking at her, as if he didn't like the sight of her. She lay awake for a long time, thinking.

A car passed on the street below, and Bridget watched the light distorting the shadows as it circled the room. She remembered suddenly the prick of misgiving she had experienced as she had stood at the windows gazing out at the sunset. She knew now what had caused it. She didn't believe that this room had stood empty all those years, waiting for her return. It had to be one of the best rooms in the house. It would have belonged to someone, someone who had had to move out to make way for her. And she thought she could guess who.

t h r e e

In her dream, her mother was leaving. Bridget was nine years old again, leaning against the doorjamb in her mother's bedroom. She met her mother's eyes in the mirror. "Two days," insisted Margaret, sweeping her thick, coppery locks into a bun on the back of her head.

"Only two days. That's nothing. It will go by like that." She snapped her fingers and then picked up a final bobby pin and jabbed it into the roll of hair. She sat at the vanity looking at herself, turning her head from side to side to examine her reflection from different angles.

Bridget stared at her mother's reflection too. She was beautiful, thought Bridget, and dramatic as well in that black felt dress with the empire waistline and long, straight skirt. Margaret called it her "governess dress." To her, every piece of clothing was a costume, and today her smooth, tan skin shone deep gold above the inky black fabric. Somehow, with her simple outfit and austere hairstyle, she made a striking image.

"Mama," Bridget ventured tentatively, "won't they still like your book if you don't go? Won't they still want to buy it?"

Margaret held up a little hand mirror to see the back of her head and then sighed long-sufferingly. "Bridget, I explained to you before. I'm going to have to go to these things. I've got to do my part. What if I just said, 'Okay, no more book signings'? It would serve me right if they did stop buying my book."

Margaret had done several signings already at local bookstores, but this time she was going down to Los Angeles. She was going to be interviewed in a big auditorium, and then afterward she would sit in the lobby and other children's mothers would wait in line to see her while their sons and daughters jerked impatiently at their hands.

"It's too bad Suzanne's family is out of town this weekend," said Margaret. "But it's no problem really. You'll be fine."

Margaret stood up and walked over to the bed, where her suitcase lay open waiting for the final items to be packed. She folded up the burgundy silk pajamas she had worn last night and put them on top of the other clothing. Bridget glimpsed the glitter of sequins before Margaret folded the top of the case over and zipped it up.

"Mama," she said once more, sounding plaintive but not knowing exactly what she meant to ask. She couldn't change anything.

"Oh, for heaven's sake," groaned Margaret, "don't be such a scaredy-cat. I'm not raising you to be a scaredy-cat."

Bridget grew sullen. She slunk away from her mother's door toward her own bedroom. Maybe she was a coward. Maybe anyone else her age would be glad to stay alone for two days. After all, her mother had hinted that she could eat all the ice cream and cookies she wanted, play video games until she was tired of them, and stay up and watch movies until all hours of the night. Suzanne's mother would never let her do anything like that. But things were different at Suzanne's house. There you ate carrot sticks and apple slices for snacks and had dinner at a regular time and went to bed early. At Bridget's house, nothing was regular. There were no rules. So what difference did it make if Margaret was gone? It only meant that Bridget would wander around alone here, without another living soul to talk to. If only Suzanne wasn't out of town!

"Bridget!" Margaret called from down the hall. "I've left the phone number of the hotel next to the phone in the kitchen. If you need help, though, call the Wangs next door." Silence while Margaret waited for a response.

"Sure, okay," Bridget managed finally.

"Bye, love! Wish me luck!"

Bridget heard her mother's feet race down the stairs, and the front door slammed. She lay on her bed for a long time listening to the quiet. "See," she told herself, "nothing will change just because she's gone. It's the same room, the same house." Only it wasn't. Even the quiet wasn't the same. It was wide as an ocean, and the rest of the world was on the other side, laughing, playing, enjoying themselves. Meanwhile, Bridget was stuck on this little island of solitude. She could call out and no one would hear her.

She went downstairs and put in a movie. Music and talk spilled into the room, bringing the illusion of comfort. When the movie was over, Bridget put in another one very quickly, before the silence could wash over her. By the time the second movie ended, it was dark. She'd been stupid not to go back upstairs and get ready for bed while it was still light. She curled up on the couch, willing herself to get over her fear. "What is there to be afraid of?" she asked herself. The upstairs was the upstairs. Nothing new.

She couldn't move. The house was too big—she couldn't be aware of it all at once. All those dark rooms upstairs, all those shadowy recesses where someone might be hiding, and she couldn't check them all at the same time. She couldn't even turn on all the lights at once. All she could do was go from room to room, and whatever might be up there could do that too.

She shivered. Leaping off the couch, she jammed another video into the VCR and turned the volume up high. But now the blaring sound seemed oppressive and unnatural in this quiet world. Even the traffic noises had died down. She lowered the volume again. Then she wrapped herself in the throw that her mother had draped across the love seat and lay down on the couch, waiting for sleep to come and longing for her mother so much that the hurt was almost a physical ache.

*   *   *

Bridget sat up abruptly, staring around at the unfamiliar surroundings and groping in her memory to figure out where she was. Across from her, the wall curved out in a semicircle, and three windows let in the early morning light. *Of course*, she thought, *Phrygia*.

Her chest felt tight, as if a yell or a cry had been ready to come out and was suddenly stifled. She exhaled slowly and then swung her legs out of bed and padded over to the windows. Below her, the little town spread out still and quiet in the clear morning sunshine. She might have been the only one stirring in the whole city. The thought amused her a little, as if all this morning beauty were displayed for her pleasure alone. In San Francisco, someone was always awake. But not here. There was something exquisite and pristine in the stillness, something that made her think of a rosebud damp with dew and closed up tight, with the fullness of its beauty yet to be revealed.

She went to the dresser to find a pair of jeans and remembered her dream from last night. It must have been the unfamiliar bed, she reasoned, that had made her mind so unrestful. Still, why she had called up that particular memory and played it over again, she couldn't understand. Maybe the bewilderment she felt in the face of this change reminded her, deep down, of that first time that her mother had left her alone. But she wasn't nine years old anymore, thank goodness. She'd left that little scaredy-cat behind.

Inching the bedroom door open quietly, she crept across

the landing, past the window with its window seat, toward a door on the other side that she hoped led into a bathroom. It did. She washed her face and applied a thin coat of lipstick. Then she eased herself slowly down the two flights of stairs, wincing at every creaking floorboard, and let herself through the double set of front doors.

Outside, the air washed fresh and clean into her lungs. She trotted across the lawn to the sidewalk and began walking north for no particular reason. On either side of the street, pastel-painted houses with white latticework slept behind curtained windows. After two or three blocks the sidewalk petered out, and she scraped along on the gravel at the side of the road. The lawns weren't quite so formal here, with no line of white cement to define their borders. Overgrown hedges and bushy trees approached the very edges of the street. Finally the houses stopped altogether and gave way to a patch of forest. Bridget could see a wide gap in the trees, and in front of her the road narrowed toward a bridge. She surmised, though she saw no sign, that she had reached the Erie Canal.

She had read about it in the Colin books, and she knew from them and from her mother that part of the canal had long ago been diverted, leaving this section unconnected to the main route. It hadn't been abandoned to stagnate and decay, though, because as a portion of the original canal it was practically a historical monument. Pleasure boats navigated it in the summer, and once—in Margaret Lacey's imagination, at least—a little boy named Colin and his best friend Kristy had floated down it in emulation of the expeditions of the great explorers.

Bridget had wondered, ever since the first Colin book, why her mother had chosen to set her stories in upstate New York. Hadn't she tried to help Bridget forget New York, refused to answer Bridget's questions about the rest of the family, and flung them both into a completely different life? Bridget could only assume that New York held painful memories for her mother and that's why she discouraged Bridget from talking about it. She had asked Margaret once why she didn't set the Colin books in California or somewhere else altogether, and her mother had replied, "Because you should write what you know but not what you are. Otherwise you forget where the fantasy ends and the reality begins." Bridget still wasn't sure she understood what that meant, but maybe Margaret was afraid that if she wrote about San Francisco she'd start expecting to meet Colin at the dry cleaners in Chinatown or down one of the steep, twisty streets. Who could tell? Her mother had created a whole world for herself, and if she understood its laws, who was anyone else to question them?

Finding an opening in the trees, Bridget scooted off the road and into the shelter of the forest, edging carefully down toward the bank of the canal. The undergrowth was not as thick as she had expected, and she moved easily. She appreciated the shifting patterns of light and shadow as the sun filtered down through leaves that rustled and trembled in the cool morning breeze. When she reached the bank she plopped down on the soft earth and stared at the reflections of the trees in the water. She hugged her knees to her chest and rested her chin on them, feeling the questions float to the surface of her mind. Who was Gerrick McKenna? What did he want with her? Had he yanked her away from everything familiar simply out of a sense of duty? What did she owe him? If a stranger took her in and gave her food and shelter for a year, maybe the stranger expected to be paid back. He didn't seem like a parent.

She realized that she knew almost nothing about him. She didn't know what he did for a living, even, or where he had grown up, where he had gone to college. *A daughter should know these things*, she thought guiltily. *But—a father should know something about his daughter, too!* She sensed her own anger for the first time, and it surprised her a little. She was angry that he had abandoned her by ignoring her all those years, and at the same time she was angry that he had taken her back. Well, that settled it, she decided with an ironic smile, he couldn't win.

Her eyes fell closed and she relaxed into the breeze and the warmth of the sunlight. She remembered a TV show that she had watched at Suzanne's house a few months ago. The daughter had done something wrong but was trying to escape blame by explaining that she had no control over the situation.

"It isn't my fault," she said. Her mother didn't buy it.

"It is your fault," she told her. Even though Bridget had sympathy for the daughter, she liked that line; it felt empowering.

"It is my fault," she said aloud now. At least it was partly her fault that she didn't know anything about her father or sisters. She knew that when she first moved to California, she had asked her mother about them, but when she didn't get answers she stopped asking. And eventually, she stopped wondering. "That's my fault," she said again. "And that means I can do something about it." She would talk to her father at breakfast, find out about him. She wasn't going to wait for him to get around to introducing himself.

"What's your fault?" asked a voice. Bridget jerked around to see a boy standing on the bank a few feet away. He was about her own age and had short, sandy-colored hair, but in the first moment of horror at being discovered talking to herself, Bridget didn't register much about him.

"What?" she spluttered.

He grinned. "Guess your guilty conscience kept you from sleeping. What did you do? Rob a bank? Poison your neighbor's poodle?"

Bridget stood up so as to lessen her disadvantage. The boy moved a little closer and they stared at each other across a thin patch of grass. He was close to her own height, no more than two or three inches taller, and his hazel eyes were large for his face. He didn't look at all threatening, but she felt her muscles tighten a little nevertheless. She didn't like being alone in the woods with a stranger.

"I don't believe I've met you," she said.

He held out a hand. "Jeff Iverson," he said. When they had shaken and he had released her hand, he frowned. "I have to say I'm a little disappointed that you don't remember me, though."

"Remember you? Are you sure you've got the right person?"

"Of course," he declared confidently. "Everyone knows who you are."

"Look, buddy," protested Bridget, "you've got me mixed up with some kind of celebrity. I just moved into town. I don't know anyone here."

"I bet you do," he insisted. "You're Bridget McKenna, and I came to your seventh birthday party." He smiled, and Bridget laughed suddenly as some of the tension flowed out of her. "Now, you're right," he continued, "it wasn't fair of me to expect you to remember. Just because I had a gigantic crush on you. . . . But I realize that I looked like a bug back then."

He still sort of resembled a bug, mused Bridget, with his roundish face and big eyes. "I'm not sure I believe you," she said. "Are you sure you were at my party?"

"Oh, yeah. I even remember what I brought you."

"What was it?" asked Bridget curiously, wondering if it would turn out to be one of her familiar possessions.

"A Barbie doll." He shrugged and grinned again. "It was my mom's idea. I wanted to give you a remote-controlled car, or at least one of those little battery-operated four-wheel drives that would climb over sticks and things."

"Hmm, but then I would have had so many of those."

Bridget smiled at his fleeting expression of incredulity.

"True," he agreed. "Barbie was right after all." Actually, Bridget didn't remember ever owning a Barbie doll, though she had played with Suzanne's plenty of times. She wondered what had happened to Jeff's gift.

"Well, Jeff, it was nice to meet you, uh, again, but I'd better be getting home now."

Jeff glanced at his watch quickly, then gave a low whistle. "I'll say. You're cutting it pretty close, aren't you?"

Bridget didn't know what he meant so she only smiled politely and turned away. "Hey!" he called after her, and soon he was climbing beside her up the bank. "I'll walk with you. I guess I didn't explain before, but I live across the street."

"What were you doing out here, anyway?"

"Looking for a green vesinius beetle."

"A what?" Bridget asked, emerging from the trees onto the road.

"A green vesinius beetle," Jeff repeated, falling into step next to her.

"I must have missed that Beatle," joked Bridget. "I knew about John, Paul, Ringo, and George, but not about this other guy."

"Well, it's no wonder," said Jeff, maintaining a serious expression even while one corner of his mouth twitched. "These little dudes get shafted when it comes to publicity. But in my opinion, they're a lot more photogenic than those other guys."

"Is that so? Well when you catch one, be sure to show it to me."

"You can count on it!" He seemed a little too excited about the prospect.

"What did you want with this thing, besides to take its picture?"

"I wanted to study it. Learn about its lifestyle, you

know, its eating habits and behavior and all. I'm going to be an entomologist."

"Oh," said Bridget, fumbling for a suitable response. "That sounds . . . interesting."

"Yeah, I guess you're either wondering what an entomologist is or why anyone would ever want to be one."

"Wrong and wrong," she countered. "I know what an entomologist is—even if I hadn't known it before today, you've made it pretty clear that you love bugs, so I might've figured out that an entomologist studies bugs. And as for why you want to be one, well, it's really none of my business, but it seems like you're perfect for it."

"Hmmm," Jeff considered. "I don't know if that's a compliment or not. So I'll let it go and change the subject. What are your plans for after high school?"

"I'm going to Stanford," answered Bridget automatically. It had been her goal for so long that she didn't even have to think about it. "Eventually I want to go to law school, but I may study English or history for my undergrad."

"Wow, I guess we're in trouble this year," he said, winking. "You're gonna blow the curve for the whole school."

Bridget arched her eyebrow and glanced at him sideways. "I'll do my best," she promised, "but I don't know if I've ever competed with a future entomologist before."

"Be afraid," he told her. "Be very afraid."

They reached the edge of the McKenna lawn, and Bridget turned to face Jeff, trying to decide if she ought to invite him in to breakfast or not. She decided not. "Good to meet you, Jeff," she said. "I'll see you around."

"See you!" he called after her as she jogged toward the rear of the house in search of a back door. "And I hope it won't be another ten years!"

At the very back of the house, Bridget found three cement steps leading up to a screen door. She hurried inside and then froze, convinced for a moment that she had accidentally run into someone else's home. A plump old lady with gray hair pinned back into a bun and a fringe of curled bangs stood in the middle of a big, brightly lit kitchen wiping her hands on her apron. When the screen door banged shut, she looked up at Bridget unconcernedly and put her hands on her hips.

"Well, what did I tell him, I says, 'Mr. McKenna,' I says, 'you try riding in a car for six or seven days and see if you don't take a mind to go out and stretch your legs in the morning.' What did I tell him? And him carrying on like you'd been snatched up in the night by aliens or something." She paused briefly to call out over her shoulder, "Mr. McKenna, she's in here!

"Now, honey, you just tell me what you want to eat and I'll whip it up for you quick as anything, I don't care what he says, some people got to have their breakfast at 7:30 on the dot and some people can wait for quality, that's what I say. My Mr. Prescott, he's just like your dad, got to eat at the same time every day or he starts bellering. Not only that, but he's got to eat the same thing. If that man hasn't had oatmeal every morning of his blessed life—" she fell silent as Bridget's father entered through the swinging door from the dining room and stood towering over the pair. Bridget wasn't short—she was five-feet-five without shoes on—but her father's height seemed intimidating once again. He was dressed in a gray suit, a deep blue shirt, and a silky-looking burgundy tie. She wondered what he would spend his day doing. He looked too dashing to go and sit in an office all day.

"Bridget," he said, fixing his eyes on her for almost the first time, "I believe I told you last night that breakfast was at 7:30."

"Yeeees," agreed Bridget, and she drew out the word while she tried to decide what to call him. She wanted to say "Dad" but couldn't. "Yes, sir, you did. I'm sorry."

"Do you realize that you have not only kept us all waiting, but you have also ruined a peaceful morning by making
us worry?"

"I'm sorry," she repeated quietly. And she was; she had
been thoughtless not to keep a better eye on the time. After
all, he had made a point of telling her last night what time
she was expected at breakfast, and this was her first morning here, their first chance to get acquainted. Still, he seemed
overly upset, she thought. What had she done besides go out
for a morning stroll? She would do that in San Francisco
without worrying, and this was a small town. Weren't they
supposed to be safer? She wasn't even that late. The digital
clock on the stove read 7:36. "It won't happen again," she
assured him, "you have my word."

His eyes seemed to bore into her. "See that it doesn't,"
he said finally. "Now, if you would please join your sisters
and me at the table . . ." he motioned for her to step past
him toward the door into the dining room. She felt a little
nervous as she whisked by him, almost wanting to make a
large circle around him to avoid walking close to him. But
she knew that was stupid.

Charly and Lydia were sitting at the dining room table
before an array of food that looked like a photo from a cooking magazine. Bowls of fruit, a plate of ham, biscuits, and
something that resembled peach pie filled the middle of the
table, and a candle glowed at either end of the untouched
feast. Bridget sat down across from her sisters while her
father took his place at the head of the table. Slowly, the
food was passed around, but nobody touched anything until
everyone's plate was filled. Then the girls watched their
father take a bite before relaxing a little and digging in.
Bridget thought it was the strangest thing she had ever seen.
How could anyone be so formal every morning? Suzanne's
family had regular mealtimes, something that Bridget and
Margaret had never done, but always a friendly sort of

confusion had reigned as kids chattered about their plans for the day or fought over the last of the Froot Loops. This quiet ritual, interrupted only by the clinking of silverware on china, seemed stilted and dreamlike. She hoped things weren't always like this. On the other hand, if all this splendor was for her benefit and she had failed to show up on time, she felt even worse.

After a few minutes Mrs. Prescott blew in through the swinging door, bringing a welcome air of normalcy. "Well now, Bridget, you didn't tell me what you wanted for breakfast. If you'd like something special, you can tell me now."

Bridget smiled up at her. "Everything's wonderful, Mrs. Prescott. This is much fancier than anything I'm used to. This pie is delicious—it melts in my mouth."

"Oh now, that's not pie, love. You don't think I'd be giving children pie for breakfast, do you? That's just a fancy pancake, is all." Indeed, the crust was not really like pie crust, but thick and spongy beneath the glaze that coated the peaches. "Have a dab of cream on it, though, you young ones can afford that, you're thinner than Mr. Prescott's hair, and that's something." She spooned a bit of cream over Bridget's pancake and then added a dab to Charly's and Lydia's plates.

"What did you have for breakfast in California, Bridget?" Charly asked.

"Oh, usually just a piece of toast and some orange juice." Even though her mother's specialty was pancakes, they had rarely eaten those in the morning. Her mother never really got going until afternoon, and then she worked late into the night.

"We're all out of orange juice," announced Lydia, and she seemed personally satisfied by this fact.

"Oh, I've got some over home," said Mrs. Prescott. "I'll just run and grab it."

"No, please," Bridget protested. "I'm fine. This is wonderful."

"It's just next door, I could have been back already." She disappeared through the swinging door.

"Bridget," said her father into the silence. "Do you have what you need for school—notebooks and pens and such?"

"I guess I may need to buy a few things," she admitted.

"That's fine. Your sisters haven't done their shopping either. Why don't you all go today?" He stood up and took his wallet from a pocket inside his suit coat and then laid three twenties and a ten on the table next to Bridget's plate. "That should be enough. You can let me know at dinner if you need anything more." He walked around to the other side of the table to kiss Charly and Lydia on the tops of their heads. Bridget was surprised at the show of affection. He didn't seem the type.

"See you at dinner," he said. He headed for the front door, picking up his briefcase from somewhere by the front windows. "And, Bridget," he said, turning back to face her, "dinner is at 6. Not 6:01, 6. Understood?"

"Yes, sir."

"Good." The double doors closed behind him. Bridget expected talk to break out as soon as he left, but nothing happened. Through the window at the far end of the table she caught a glimpse of Mrs. Prescott jogging across the yard with a carton of orange juice in one hand. She chuckled at the sight, but her spirits quickly slumped. She hadn't asked her father a single question.

f o u r

After breakfast, Bridget went upstairs to take a shower and finish unpacking. The morning had started out quiet, but by the time she turned off the water in the bathtub, the house echoed with the kind of general commotion she associated with life at Suzanne's house. From the first floor she could hear Lydia practicing the piano and striving valiantly to compete with the noise of the vacuum, which meant that Mrs. Prescott had left the kitchen. Charly added to the racket by turning up her radio and singing along with a Britney Spears song. Bridget dried all over with one of the big, fluffy towels she had brought from San Francisco and then got dressed quickly.

"Oops," wailed Charly from one floor below, "I did it again!"

The clashing music almost made Bridget wince, but she decided she might as well contribute her own notes to the cacophony. She unlatched her guitar case and lifted the instrument out gently, sitting down on the edge of the bed with the guitar supported on her lap. She had bought the instrument three years ago from a thrift store with her own money, which she had earned babysitting and doing housework for her neighbors. She hadn't known how to play back then, but her mother had helped her pay for lessons. She still wasn't nearly as good as she wanted to be. She mostly played alone in her room, but she had been brave enough to perform in a school talent show this spring. She had written her own song for it. "I close my eyes, and all I see is your face," she sung quietly, hearing nothing now but the sound of her own instrument. With the next line, her voice poured out round and full:

And all the miles stretched out around you
While I'm alone
In this cold and empty place.
I'll never hold your hand again.

I dream of calling out,
But you'd never hear my voice.
Sound can't make a bridge from heart to heart.
I can't remember
If it was your or my choice.
But I'll never hold your hand again.

After the show one girl had asked her who the song was about. "Ooh, who did you break up with?" she wanted to know. "Who broke your heart that way?" Bridget told her it was just a made-up story, just some sappy lyrics like the ones you hear on the radio. "Fine, don't tell me," the girl sulked. But everyone else seemed to accept that explanation. After all, her mother was M. C. Lacey, the famous writer.

And M. C. Lacey had been in the crowd that day, smiling up at Bridget as, for once, the attention focused away from the famous writer toward the girl who hadn't done much of anything yet. Bridget remembered waiting anxiously offstage and peering out around the edge of the curtain at the packed auditorium. She thought of the way her mother always looked in public, as calm as if she were lounging by the pool. She wished that she could be that way too. In the end, it hadn't gone badly—not at all—because she forgot everyone else as soon as she started to play. The only people in the room were her and her mother, and her mother was pleased. She could tell.

"I've never heard that song before," said Charly. Bridget twisted around to see her younger sister standing by the doorway. The vacuum was still going downstairs, but Charly must have turned her radio off; the only music now was from Lydia, who was still pounding away at a Beethoven sonata.

"I guess you wouldn't have," Bridget responded. "I'm not famous—yet." She grinned, and Charly took that as an invitation to leap onto the bed and take a closer look at the guitar.

"You can really play that thing," she exclaimed. "I know some boys from school who pretend they can play. You know, they carry a guitar around all the time and stand around humming with their eyes closed like they're writing songs."

"What makes you think they aren't?"

"Well, who's ever heard them actually play?" she giggled and poked out a tentative finger to stroke the strings.

"The best thing about a guitar," Bridget told her, "is that it can't really make a bad sound. So even when you're not that good, you can sound okay." She played a few chords, loving the deep, textured timbre of the instrument.

"Sing the rest of the song for me," Charly coaxed. "I think I interrupted you."

Bridget flushed, feeling embarrassed. The song seemed suddenly private.

"C'mon, just a little more."

"All right. But don't ask me who it's all about. There's no real story, I just made it up."

"Sure, okay," Charly agreed. So Bridget strummed a little to warm up and then started back where she had left off.

That day in my car
I just turned and sped away.
The land flowed by so fast, no stopping,

No home place,
No love, no warmth, no place to stay.
I only wanted to hold your hand again.

I kept on going, kept driving,
Wanting nothing but you.
But I searched for you and you were gone.
You'd left my heart,
Left me wondering what was true.
So I'll never hold your hand again.

How could you let go,
Let the shadows swallow me?
If I'd called out then would you have come?
No matter now,
Things are what they will be.
I'll never hold your hand again.

"Oh, I love it!" Charly burst out the moment Bridget stopped playing. "Can you teach me to play too?"

"I don't know, I've never tried to teach anyone. Besides, you already play the piano, don't you?"

"Sure, but only because Dad makes me."

Bridget eased the guitar back into its case and then glanced up at Charly, trying to sound casual.

"Dad's kind of strict, isn't he?" She hesitated only slightly over the word "Dad."

"Strict? Oh, I dunno. He's just funny in some ways. Sometimes he worries over the dumbest things. I guess you thought he was pretty weird this morning, but you shouldn't make up your mind before you know him."

That's sweet, reflected Bridget, *she wants to defend him.* "You're right. I just wondered."

"Did Mom ever—" Charly stopped abruptly and turned away, looking ashamed.

"What?"

"Nothing. Forget it."

"You can ask," Bridget assured her.

"Dad said not to."

"What?"

"He told me not to mention Mom to you." Charly frowned. "I shouldn't have said anything. We talked about it. He said, 'Don't forget Bridget's grieving.' That's the kind of word Dad uses, *grieving*, not something simple like *sad*. I promised him. I said I wouldn't say anything."

They sat in silence until Bridget erupted, "But everyone thinks it's better just to ignore it. Why do they think that? Like I'll feel better just pretending it never happened."

"Well," considered Charly, "I think they just don't want to make you feel worse. That's what Dad meant, I'm sure."

Bridget remembered her first day back at school after the accident. Her mother had died a week before classes let out for the summer, and Bridget had gone to take her finals along with everyone else. But that whole week she was all alone. People stared at her as she approached and then turned away as she walked by, not wanting to risk making eye contact. Even Justin, who had told her a few weeks ago at his senior prom that he loved her, had stared at his feet as she passed.

"It's just—it's not like we can erase her, you know, and it seems like that's what everyone's trying to do. Except in the bookstores, and there they're just trying to make as much money as they possibly can—as usual."

"If you don't mind talking about it," Charly ventured, "then maybe I could ask . . . I just wanted to know more about Mom. Like, what kind of rules did you have? It always seemed like—like she'd be really fun."

"Yeah," Bridget agreed. "She was fun. She bought a huge trampoline that took up our entire backyard—which wasn't hard because it was one of those postage-stamp deals—and we'd go out there and jump together. She could do more fancy stuff than I ever could, somersaults and splits in the air and things."

"Cool."

Bridget stood up and offered Charly a hand. "Hey, c'mon, let's go shopping. Can you believe in all this mountain of stuff I don't have a single pen?"

They went to collect Lydia, who groaned and scowled at the prospect of a trip downtown with her two sisters. "I could just go myself later," she protested. But Charly didn't think that would work.

"Who would help you carry all your stuff then?" Charly asked sweetly. She turned to Bridget and explained, "Lydia has to buy a lot of stuff because she has to coordinate with all her outfits. I mean, if she has a folder in a color that doesn't look good with something, she has to have an alternate folder to carry when she wears that outfit."

"Oh," responded Bridget. She thought of her mother's costumes, her closet with the revolving shoe and purse display. Maybe that stuff was genetic. She smiled at Lydia and told her, "Mom would have approved."

Lydia's eyes flashed. "I don't want to talk about her," she enunciated stiffly.

They left the house in silence and turned in the direction opposite the one Bridget had taken that morning. Across the street, Jeff was out on his front lawn, crouching low over the grass.

"Hey, Jeff!" Charly called, and he glanced up and waved. All three girls smiled and waved back, and the tension seemed to dissipate. After another block, Bridget asked Charly, "What does Dad do for a living?"

"You don't know?" snorted Lydia.

"No," Bridget replied. "I just don't remember, and no one ever told me."

"Yeah, right," muttered Lydia, but Charly cut across her to answer.

"He's a lawyer. He's got an office here in Phrygia. I'll show you where it is. Today he's in Rochester, though. He goes there a lot. He's got an office there too."

"Amazing," laughed Bridget. "I had no idea."

Charly looked puzzled. "What's so amazing about it?"

"Oh, nothing. It's just that I want to be a lawyer too."

Charly giggled. "Not me!" she declared. "I've been to Dad's office. It looks really boring. Just mounds and mounds of folders stuffed with papers. But maybe Dad can give you some tips. Hey, I bet he'd love to have you work for him. He needs help—he's got more work than he can handle."

Bridget wondered how it would be to work in an office with her father, whether he would speak to her or ignore her. "Yeah, maybe," she agreed noncommittally.

"You know what? Lydia wants to be a writer."

"Shut up, Charly," Lydia snapped.

As Bridget had guessed the night before, the business district of Phrygia was made up of small local stores, nothing familiar to someone from out of town. They walked by an ice cream parlor and then a restaurant with a sign in the front window advertising "Clyde's Famous Pizza." Next to that was a bookshop with the latest Colin novel set out among a group of other bestsellers, and beyond that they turned right into Haverley's Drug Store.

Lydia walked ahead of them toward the section with the school supplies, but even without her lead it would have been obvious since a small crowd of kids and parents were currently swarming over the area. The girls made their way down the packed aisles, ducking now and then through a tangle of arms and bodies to pick up a notebook or folder. Lydia would linger in one spot for a long time, apparently deliberating over her choices, and Bridget guessed that what Charly had said about her attempts to coordinate with her clothing was at least partly true. As for herself, she chose her supplies quickly: one small binder for each class, some paper, and packages of pens and pencils. She already had a graphing calculator to use for advanced placement calculus. At the checkout, the harried clerk started scanning the girls' items and then paused to glance up at Bridget. She took a quick breath and narrowed her eyes.

"Well, if it isn't—" she gasped. "If it isn't Bridget McKenna." She set down the glittery purple notebook she was holding and leaned across the counter for a closer look. "Yes, it *is* you, isn't it?" She shook her head in apparent amazement. She was a friendly-looking plump middle-aged woman with short brown hair, and when she moved her head, her glasses slid down her nose. "I'll be darned, I never thought I'd see the day. I never thought you'd be in here again."

Bridget smiled brightly. She'd been fawned over by strangers a few times before because of her mother's books. People at school got used to the idea that she had a famous mother, and besides, a few of them had famous relatives too. But sometimes new acquaintances would get overly excited when they found out about her connection to M. C. Lacey. She didn't know why this woman should take such an interest because she herself must have known M. C. Lacey, or rather Margaret McKenna, but Bridget tried to be gracious anyway.

"It's been a long time," she said warmly, as if she remembered this woman whom she wasn't sure she had ever laid eyes on before in her life. "But it's good to be back."

The woman threw up her arms. "What am I thinking?" she cried. "What kind of welcome am I giving you!" Without warning, she came around from behind the counter and folded Bridget into a deep, soft hug. "My goodness, when I think how we worried over you!" She pushed Bridget back and inspected her from arm's length. Behind them, the other customers stared wide-eyed at Bridget, not complaining over the delay. "And look, you've turned out okay, after all, even if you were raised by a—" She cut herself off abruptly, apparently thinking better of what she had been about to say. "I'll tell you what I'm going to do. I'm going to give you a 20 percent discount."

"That's very nice of you," Bridget thanked her, "but it's not necessary." She hoped the clerk wouldn't argue; she was anxious to escape the scrutiny of what felt like dozens of eyes.

"Of course it is. It's the least I can do, after what you've been through." The woman hurried back around the counter and punched buttons on the cash register. As she scanned the rest of the girls' items, she kept muttering things like "poor Bridget" and "poor little girl." Bridget paid her quickly, and the girls loaded up with two or three bags each and turned to leave. "You're back where you belong, Bridget," the woman called after them. "Don't you forget it."

Once they were out on the street, Charly blurted, "Wow, Bridget, you've got to come shopping with us all the time. Mrs. Haverley never gives discounts! She hates sales! She tried to charge seventy cents for a candy bar until it almost put her out of business. I can't believe it!"

"I can't either," said Bridget.

Charly sobered. "Sorry, I'm doing it again. That stuff she said about what you've been through—I shouldn't be reminding you of it."

"Oh, just be quiet, Charly," interjected Lydia. "You're right, we've all heard more than enough about 'poor Bridget.'" She sped up and walked the rest of the way home five paces in front of them. Bridget was grateful for the reprieve.

Back at the McKenna house, Mrs. Prescott met them in the living room to announce that their father would not be home for dinner. "I could tell he was disappointed," she reported. "I know how he was looking forward to spending some time with you, Bridget, before school starts and things just go crazy."

Bridget smiled. *Yeah, I'll bet*, she thought. "Hey!" she

said, turning to Charly and Lydia. "What if we go out to eat tonight? My treat. That is, if you haven't already gone to the trouble of making something, Mrs. Prescott."

"Oh, I think it's a fine idea. I daresay Mr. Prescott will be glad to see me home a little bit early."

"Go out for dinner? Really?" Charly squealed. "Oh, it's been ages since we did that. Remember, Lydia, the last time was when we were in Rochester with Dad and Natalie and the waiter tripped over your foot and spilled soda all over Natalie's dress."

"Who's Natalie?" Bridget asked.

"She's Dad's friend. You'll get to meet her pretty soon, I'm sure. But Dad's kind of shy about those things." Charly giggled and Lydia rolled her eyes.

"Okay, whatever. Well, you two are the experts on Phrygia night life, so you tell me where we should go."

"There's no place that's good here," complained Lydia, "and we don't have the car so we can't go anywhere else. If you even have a driver's license."

"Yeah, I can drive. But I don't want to go somewhere else, anyway, I want some authentic Phrygian cuisine."

"Gag," was Lydia's comment.

"The best place is Clyde's Pizzeria," volunteered Charly, "and if we're not too full we can order banana splits afterwards. They'll bring them over for you from next door."

"Perfect! Clyde's it is." Bridget stashed her school supplies in her room and spent the rest of the afternoon putting her other things away. At a little before six, she went into the bathroom to comb her hair and reapply her lipstick. The girls were waiting for her in the hall at the foot of the stairs. "Look out, boys of Phrygia!" she whooped, noting that Lydia had bothered to change into a nice white shirt with little speckles of silver glitter.

"What do we care about a bunch of dumb old boys?" Lydia grumbled. "We're not allowed to date until we're sixteen."

"Sixteen?" repeated Bridget. "Really?" She wouldn't have been surprised, though, if their father had tried to keep them from dating until they left for college. Setting the age at sixteen was probably pretty liberal in his eyes.

"Yeah, really," Lydia affirmed. "Because here we actually have morals."

Bridget raised her eyebrows but let the remark pass. Her sisters, after all, were small-town girls who probably had warped ideas about San Francisco.

"Did you date a lot at your old school?" Charly asked as they set off.

"Yeah, some," Bridget said. "But mostly I hung out with people—you know, just casual stuff."

"That's what we do," Charly told her. "People at school talk about going together, but it's not like they're really dating. They just eat lunch together and stuff."

"Dad probably wouldn't like that, either," Lydia warned her sister. "Did you tell him you've been eating lunch with that guy Davey every day?"

Charly giggled nervously. "I might have forgotten to mention it."

"If it's just the two of you sitting at the same lunch table," Bridget volunteered, "I don't see why he'd be upset about it." *Unless he's truly as unreasonable as he seems,* she added to herself.

"Well, it gets complicated sometimes," Charly said, "figuring out what's a date and what's not."

"Does it matter that much?"

"Yeah, because we're not sixteen," Charly affirmed. "So nothing we do better even look like a date."

"Who gets so caught up in rules like that?" Bridget wondered aloud.

Lydia turned to scowl at her. "I told you, we have morals here."

"What's that supposed to mean?"

"Don't you get it? I know you've been inactive forever, but . . ."

"Inactive?" Bridget questioned. "What am I, a volcano? What is 'inactive' supposed to mean?"

"It's our church," Charly explained. "You and Mom didn't go in California, did you?"

"No," replied Bridget warily. She felt both curious and apprehensive, wanting to know more about her family's religion and half afraid of what she would learn. "Is all this stuff about dating from your church?"

"Yeah," Charly said. "It's one of the rules we follow."

"Rules?"

"Yeah," Charly affirmed. "You know, kind of like the commandments."

"Like, 'thou shalt not kill'?" Bridget asked. She couldn't help snickering. "So in your church, you've got the regular list, and then after that you've got 'thou shalt not go out with boys until you're sixteen'? Where did this 'commandment' come from, did God stick his finger out of a bush and carve it on a stone tablet?"

"No, stupid," Lydia answered. "He told the prophet, and the prophet told us."

"The prophet? Like Moses?" This was all getting weirder and weirder.

"Haven't you ever even heard of President Hinckley?" Charly asked.

"No. Who's he—the prophet?"

"Yeah. He's the president of the Church."

"And so he gets to talk to God?" Bridget asked. She couldn't quite keep the amusement out of her voice. "Quite a job." She was surprised Lydia hadn't volunteered for it.

"Yes," Lydia insisted, "it is."

"Okay, okay," Bridget said. She noted that Charly looked hurt. "The point is, we'll ignore all those dumb old boys, right? I just hope this guy hasn't said anything about pizza."

"What guy?" Charly asked.

"This President . . . what's-his-name."

Charly and Lydia exchanged scandalized looks. Finally Charly said, "It's President Hinckley. And eating pizza isn't a problem. But, Bridget—"

"Yeah?"

"Don't talk about him like that, okay? He's wonderful. You'll think so too when you hear him speak."

"Will he be at the church on Sunday?"

This time Bridget's sisters both giggled. "Yeah, right," Lydia said. "Just because everyone's falling all over you, you think the prophet would come all the way here to welcome you?"

Bridget shook her head and shrugged. She hoped they could drop the whole subject for now.

Clyde's Pizzeria wasn't very busy when they got there, but several high school kids sat around in groups of two and four, and in one corner a young couple were trying to keep their toddler from throwing pepperoni onto the linoleum. Bridget looked around at the decor and decided it wasn't quite as impressive as that of the McDonald's two blocks from her home in San Francisco. Brown tables and benches were bolted to orange walls, with a few freestanding tables and several chairs with orange vinyl seat cushions arranged down the center. The walls were just the right shade to make Bridget feel as though she had already been wrapped up in a giant pizza.

Charly and Lydia led the way to a booth on the wall opposite the toddler and slid onto the benches. Bridget sat down beside Lydia. "Should we go up and order?"

"No, Clyde or Mike will come out in a minute."

Soon a genial-looking gray-haired man in a bright red T-shirt and apron appeared through a swinging door in the back and walked over to their table.

"Hi, girls, it's been a while since I've seen you in here," he greeted them. "I was afraid you'd lost your taste for pizza."

"Never!" promised Charly. "But ever since Dad started dating Natalie, he's gone on this health food kick and doesn't want to eat pizza anymore unless it's topped with tofu or something."

"Well, you just explain to your dad that pizza has all the four food groups all in one slice. Now, what else can you eat that you can say that about?"

"I'll tell him, and maybe he can convince Natalie too, so her poor sons don't have to suffer anymore."

"Who's your friend?" the man asked, smiling down at Bridget.

"This is our sister Bridget."

The man's eyes opened wider. "This is Bridget? You don't say! Hey, Mike!" he called toward the back, "come out and see who's paid us a visit."

A young, dark-haired man wearing the same bright red clothing came out from the kitchen and stood beside their table.

"Guess who it is," prodded the older man.

"Uh, Cristina Aguilera," guessed Mike. "Cameron Diaz."

"Oh, you're too young to remember. Hey, Bridget, you used to be one of our regular customers. You loved olives more than any other kid I've ever seen. What do you say I bring you out a large pizza with extra olives, on the house. What else do you want on it? Let's see, you always liked pepperoni better than sausage, I think."

Charly snickered. "We're never going anywhere without you again, Bridget," she said.

"That's so nice of you," Bridget told the man, "but I don't really like olives." She grinned sheepishly. "I must have lost the taste for them—I don't really remember."

"No olives for Bridget?" He frowned exaggeratedly. "It's getting so you can't count on anything these days."

"Clyde, how about you just bring us a medium Canadian bacon and pineapple pizza," ordered Lydia. "That's what we usually get," she told Bridget.

"Clyde," chirped Charly, "what did I like when I was little? Did I always like pineapple?"

"Well, let's see," mused Clyde. "I think you two have always liked pineapple. But this Bridget, she was a real pizza enthusiast. Made my job worthwhile." He winked at Bridget, and then he and Mike went back to the kitchen. When Mike brought out their pizza a few minutes later, he assured them it was still on the house.

"Dad said you've earned it," Mike told Bridget, "after what you've been through."

Bridget thanked him. She never wanted to hear that phrase again.

f i v e

For the next several days, Mr. McKenna failed to show up for dinner. He would call every afternoon around three o'clock and talk to Mrs. Prescott, who would then come and find Bridget to relay the news.

"He's so sorry, Bridget," she would explain. "He's real disappointed. He was hoping to spend some time with you when you first got here."

After two or three days of this, Bridget began to wonder if he was intentionally avoiding her. *Stupid idea*, she told herself. He was just a busy man. But why did Mrs. Prescott have to convey his apologies so ceremoniously, as if Bridget had a special appointment with him that he continually neglected to keep? After all, Mrs. Prescott didn't make such a fuss when she told Lydia and Charly that their dad wasn't coming home.

"Hey, girls," she'd call into the bedroom they shared, "Dad's working late." And without bothering to check whether they had heard her over Charly's blasting radio, she'd canter on down the stairs and go back to dusting the piano.

One afternoon Bridget came in from a bike ride with Jeff to find Mrs. Prescott waiting for her in the kitchen. Bridget started to roll her eyes and then checked herself quickly, determined to listen politely to the regular late-afternoon statement. What good would it do to punish the messenger anyway? But instead of informing her that her father

planned to miss dinner yet again, Mrs. Prescott delivered a
summons. "He wants to talk to you before dinner, so that's
5:45 sharp, in his office."

Careful not to repeat her blunder of the other morning,
Bridget was ready by 5:41. She had washed her face, combed
her hair again, and put on fresh makeup. Her mother had
always taught her that the way she looked was important.
She had to present her best self to the world, and her father
was definitely part of the world. She couldn't imagine right
now that he would ever attain the more intimate level of
family. She wasn't sure where his office was, so she went to
find Mrs. Prescott, who ushered her through the front hallway and around the stairs to the closed door opposite the
front entrance. Mrs. Prescott pulled a key out of her pocket,
turned it in the lock, and let the door swing open.

"I'm sure he'll be right in," she promised, even though
he hadn't actually come home yet.

It seemed a little strange being alone in his office, especially now, when Bridget was more annoyed with him than
anything. She looked around at the walls filled with bookshelves, feeling like an intruder. Nevertheless, she couldn't
help being a curious intruder. She stepped toward one of the
shelves and read some of the titles. Volumes of poetry by
Tennyson, Lord Byron, and Wordsworth suggested that he
might be a closet romantic. *Nah*, thought Bridget. He probably hadn't even really read them. She ignored the fact that
the spines were bent with use. He must have bought them
that way.

On the next shelf up she found a little leather-bound
volume called *Sonnets from the Portuguese*. She'd read the
most famous poem from this collection in her English class
last year: "How do I love thee? Let me count the ways."
She slipped the book off the shelf now and flipped through
it idly with the half-thought of testing her memory of the
poem. Far more interesting, though, turned out to be the

handwriting inside the front cover. "To my darling," it read. "Love always—C." She recognized the writing as her mother's. But why was the note signed "C" when Bridget had never heard her mother's friends call her anything but Margaret? Oh, well, maybe she was wrong about the handwriting. She slid the book back into position and moved slowly toward the huge desk that dominated the middle of the room. Behind this was another row of bookshelves. Something familiar suddenly caught her eye. She hurried around the desk and looked closer. Yes, there it was, the entire Colin collection. Had her mother sent them? She picked one up and opened the front cover, but this time there was no note. Instead, her father had simply written his name: G. C. McKenna.

Nervous and restless, she checked her watch. 5:46. Aha! Who was late now? She wondered if she'd dare mention this fact to her father when he came in. She leafed quickly through some pages of the Colin book and then checked her watch again. Still 5:46. Trying to breathe deeply, she perched on the edge of the big swivel chair behind the desk and began to read somewhere in the middle of the book.

*   *   *

Colin poked his hand into his jacket pocket and rustled the ten-dollar bill with his fingers. "Fat free milk," he muttered, "mild cheddar." After the last time when he'd accidentally come home with a quart of buttermilk, he'd worried that his mom might never trust him enough to send him to the store again. He had to get it right this time, so he repeated the list over and over, trying to picture the items in funny places, like bread hanging in his closet and milk running out of the bathroom tap. If he hadn't been so absorbed in his memory game, he might have noticed the sound sooner. As it was, he had almost passed the main doors of the elementary school when he heard the crying.

Embarrassed, he dodged off the sidewalk and hid behind the big oak tree that he liked to dream about climbing whenever his schoolwork got too boring. He didn't think anyone had seen him, and he hadn't seen anyone either, but he could sure hear someone sobbing. He didn't know why anyone would be here at this time of day. It was 4:30 by now, and school had already been out for two hours. Why had he sneaked off like this, he wondered, when whoever it was might need help? He peeked cautiously around the tree. There, drooping forlornly across one of the cement benches outside the front doors, sat Buster Carmichael. Colin clapped his hands over his mouth in gleeful surprise. Not Buster Carmichael, that overgrown bozo who had pushed Kristy down onto the asphalt playground and called her "Sissy Krissy," not that fat idiot who liked to steal cookies and cupcakes out of people's lunches! Not Buster Carmichael, *crying?*

Colin suddenly wished that Kristy could be here with him. Oh, how they'd laugh, but silently so Buster wouldn't hear them. They'd look at each other and hold their hands over their mouths while they shook with soundless enjoyment. They'd fall over and roll on the ground until as many tears leaked out of their eyes as had ever come out of Buster's. It wasn't quite as fun watching this all alone.

Behind the wailing Buster, the front doors of the school gaped open and two grown-ups, a man and a woman, came out. They must be Buster's parents. Colin eyed them curiously because he had never imagined Buster as having parents. Buster just was. The man and woman didn't look anything like him. They were both wearing dark overcoats and gray suits, the woman's with a skirt, and the man was talking into a cell phone. The woman had her hair slicked back in a tight bun. She looked fierce but sleek, like one of the lawyers in the show his parents watched on TV. She glared down at big, sloppy Buster and sneered.

"Well, this is it, Clarence," she declared. "This is the

last time I'm coming to this school. I've heard enough about your fighting, your troublemaking, and your pathetic grades." She held up a sheet of paper marked with a big red F. "If I get one more call from your teacher or the principal, you're gone. Your father and I have been in touch with that boarding school. They're ready to take you anytime at a moment's notice."

Buster had stopped crying when his parents came out and had tried to sit up straighter on the bench, but now he seemed to crumple down to half his former height, and Colin could hear sobs again, but muffled now.

"Let's go, William." The woman motioned to her husband, and the two of them began walking toward a silver car parked at the curb. Buster got up and followed them, but when he reached out for the handle of the rear door, his mother slapped his hand away. "No, Clarence, you can walk home. Walk home and think. You can either think about fractions or about what you want to take away to school with you. It's up to you." She got in and slammed the door and the car sped away. Buster stared after it, stunned, and then started crying again.

Colin stood and watched with his mouth open, but not because he was laughing. In fact, he didn't feel at all like laughing anymore. Without thinking about what he was going to do, he stepped out from behind the oak tree and approached the boy on the sidewalk.

"Buster," he called. Buster jumped. His head whipped around so that he was no longer staring down the road at the disappearing car. When he spotted Colin, his eyes and mouth twisted up as anger and shame warred across his face. His hands balled themselves into fists, but in the end he couldn't quite hide an expression of anxiety as he tried to stare Colin down. Colin stood his ground.

"Hey, Buster," Colin said, "I thought maybe I could . . . you know, I thought maybe we . . ." How could he explain this to Kristy? What would he say to her if she knew he was about to offer help to Buster Carmichael? "You see, I'm pretty good at fractions. Math is one of my best subjects. If you want, maybe we could study together."

Buster scowled at him. "Get outta here!" he screamed. But he didn't make a move toward Colin.

"Well, you need help, don't you?" The boys stared at each other. Colin realized that his own hands, hidden in his jacket pockets, had clenched up tight. "Come on, you know Mrs. Lyndhart is giving us a test this week. If we work really hard, I bet you can at least get a B. And, Buster, don't take this wrong, but it seems like you don't have much to lose."

Buster must have recognized that this was true because he let his hands relax. He stared at Colin a few seconds longer.

"So you really think you can help?" he asked finally, his voice cracking slightly with barely suppressed eagerness.

"Yeah," said Colin. After all, he was a superhero—it was his job. And that's what he would have to explain to Kristy.

*   *   *

"Bridget?" Bridget jumped at the sound of her father's voice behind her, and the Colin book she had been reading thumped onto the floor. She bent quickly to pick it up and shove it back onto the shelf, and then she shot out of her father's swivel chair and faced him across the desk. He must have come in very quietly, or she must have been very absorbed in reading, because he had apparently been there for a minute or two already without her knowing. Behind him, the office door was closed, and he stood near the desk with his arms folded across his chest, gazing down at her. Would he be angry that she had touched his things? She felt embarrassed that he had caught her reading a Colin book.

Somehow that seemed worse than if she had been reading something else, like Tennyson.

"I'm sorry I'm late," he said in a low voice. He turned toward the corner to the right of the door and dragged a small wooden chair over to the desk. "Please, sit down." She came around and settled nervously on the little chair while her father took his place in his swivel seat and rested his arms on the desk's polished surface. Bridget could feel a pulse beating in her neck and worried that he would see it. Why couldn't she be as calm and unruffled as her mother? Surely Margaret Lacey had never been afraid of this man.

"I thought we might discuss your future," he began, meeting her eyes at first but then glancing down at his own hands. "You're nearly finished with high school. What are your plans after that?"

Well, at least this question was easy. "I'm going to Stanford," Bridget responded. "It's what I've always wanted."

One of her father's eyebrows arched up a little. "Always?"

She blushed. "As long as I can remember, at least."

"And what do you want to study? What are your career plans?"

"I want to be a l—" She froze on the word. *Come on, just say it*, she ordered herself. *No, I can't. I won't.* Somehow it felt like giving in. "I—well, I guess I need to think about it more. You know, take a lot of different classes and figure out what I like."

"That's sounds reasonable," he agreed. His answer surprised her. She couldn't figure out where he was flexible and where he was iron. "But I would've thought since you're so certain where you want to go to school, you'd also know what you want to do in life. Stanford is a good all-around school, of course, one of the best. But there are a lot of other good ones out there, and they all have their strengths and weaknesses. If you have an idea what you want to study, it will help you make a wise choice. You can look at a certain department within a school, see what its track record is."

"Hmm," said Bridget, "that seems like a good idea." *Okay*, she thought, *this is stupid. I know what I want to study. I don't need this kind of advice.*

"I was hoping you might consider some schools around here."

"Uh—" Bridget hesitated. "Yes, well, hmmm. I hadn't thought about that. I'd really like to go back to California."

Her father looked up at her, and the intensity of his gaze added force to his simple words. "California is a long way away."

"Too right," muttered Bridget, seeking escape from her father's eyes by staring down at her lap.

"I'd like you to think about staying around here for college. There are a lot of good schools. I thought we might go visit some this fall, before the application deadlines are past. Oberrath College is one I think might interest you. I went there for my undergraduate years. It's small, but the faculty is excellent. You'd get opportunities for one-on-one association, and that's priceless."

"Oberrath College?" Bridget stalled. "I haven't heard of it." At least now she knew where her father had gone to school. What had her other questions been? She couldn't remember now. Her face felt hot, but she didn't think it was from nervousness anymore.

"Its reputation may not stretch all the way to the West Coast yet, but it's good. You'd get a solid education there."

"I don't know. I mean, I'm sure it's a good school, I wasn't questioning that. But I'd really like to go back to California."

"You need to apply somewhere else besides Stanford. You shouldn't apply to only one place."

"But I'm going to apply for an early decision from Stanford," she explained, trying not to sound impatient. "If I get rejected, I can still make the deadline to apply somewhere else." She hadn't given much thought to what would happen if Stanford didn't accept her, but wherever else she might apply would be someplace in the West, not a school in New York that she had never heard of.

"Just give some schools here a chance," her father pressed. "We'll go up and take a look at them. Don't pass judgment until you see them. Keep an open mind."

Bridget took a breath and met his eyes. "It's just that I know I don't want to stay in the East. I may apply to other colleges, but they'll be schools on the West Coast."

"The West Coast doesn't have a monopoly on good schools. All I'm asking you to do is keep your options open. Is that so unreasonable?"

"It's not unreasonable, but it seems like a waste. Why do all this traveling around when I'm not really interested?"

"Bridget, college is a big decision. I want you to study things out. Get some other applications in before you hear from Stanford so that you're not scrambling at the last minute."

Was he saying he didn't think Stanford would accept her? "Every application costs money," she replied, "and every one wants a different essay. It's extra work to apply to other schools, and it doesn't seem worth it when I can hear from Stanford before I even need to have the other applications in."

"Are you saying you can't do it? You can't fit it all in?"

A spark of anger made Bridget bite her lip. "I didn't say I couldn't."

"All I'm asking you to do is keep your options open," he repeated.

Bridget wondered if witnesses in court felt this annoyed with her father. Couldn't he just leave something alone? "Okay," she acquiesced finally. "I've warned you that I'm not interested, but I guess it wouldn't hurt to tour some campuses." When she got accepted to Stanford, of course, there'd be no question where she'd choose to go.

For now, her father seemed to feel the matter was settled. He exhaled loudly and leaned back in his chair with his hands behind his head. "Great. I'll get our first trip in the works. It's not too far to Oberrath, we can do it in a day. I might just send you shopping with my friend Natalie before we go."

"Shopping?" Bridget questioned. "For dorm stuff? Isn't it kind of early?"

"Shopping for clothes, I mean."

"Oh. Well, I guess if you want. I already bought some stuff before I came out here, though."

"Right," said Mr. McKenna. "But you'll want to be careful how you dress when you're touring a prospective college. Natalie can help you with that."

Careful? She had been careful how she dressed, did her hair, talked, and acted since she came here, and what good did it do? He was never here to see anyway. For all he knew, her clothes were perfect for touring college campuses. Then she noticed the way he was eyeing her pink capri pants and sleeveless white shirt. He certainly didn't approve of this ensemble. She felt embarrassed and irritated at the same time.

"Whatever," she said, just wanting the interview to be over.

"Think about what I've said," he pressed. "I think it would be a good idea for you to stay in New York, or at least on the East Coast."

"I didn't want to come to New York in the first place," she snapped. She immediately regretted the lapse of self-control, but it was too late to do anything about it. She saw her father's face harden, like a sped-up video of molten ore cooling into solid metal.

"Well, but you're here now," he replied quietly. They

stared at each other across the desk until Bridget couldn't stand the silence anymore.

"Yes, I sure am," she said, wincing slightly at the resentment that rang out audibly in every syllable. "I guess we'd better go to dinner. It's 5:59."

"Thank you for pointing that out." He rose and came around the desk; Bridget stood up also and rushed toward the door.

"Bridget, wait," her father said suddenly.

She considered ignoring the request but turned reluctantly to face him once again. With her back against the door, she felt like a suspect cornered by the police.

"There's one more thing I wanted to discuss with you," her father announced. "The weekend is coming up. Sundays are a special day here. There are certain things we don't do, and certain things we always do . . ."

Bridget tensed as she waited for him to continue.

"I know you weren't raised the same way I've tried to raise Charly and Lydia," he declared. "But I'd appreciate it if you'd accompany us to church."

Bridget took a breath while she considered several possible retorts. But underneath her anger, she knew that she didn't really want to make trouble. She had been expecting that he would want her to go to church. She even wanted to go herself, just to see what it was like. It wasn't worth getting worked up about, not like the college issue.

"Okay," she agreed.

"Maybe Natalie can help you find something—"

"I *am* capable of dressing myself," she interrupted impatiently. "Even without Natalie."

He watched her with an expression she could not interpret.

"Yes, I'm sure you are," he said finally. "Very capable."

* * *

Sunday morning Bridget woke up early, opened the door to her walk-in closet, and switched on the light. She stood there staring bemusedly at her bright array of clothing. She didn't like having her father think that he needed to commandeer her wardrobe—or that this Natalie person ought to take charge of it—but the truth was, she didn't know exactly what people wore to church. She thought hard. Suzanne's family sometimes went down the street to the New Life Presbyterian; what did they wear? She had never accompanied them there, but several times she had gone over to see Suzanne soon after they got home. She remembered a couple of times seeing Suzanne's brothers tugging impatiently at ties as they headed for their bedrooms to shed the restrictive clothing. So, shirts and ties . . . but what had Suzanne worn? Probably a skirt of some sort. Maybe it was like going to a wedding. But no, it wouldn't be that dressy, would it? She began sliding hangers around, looking at the familiar items as if she hadn't seen them before, as if something new and interesting and obviously appropriate might turn up magically. Unfortunately, nothing did.

She considered asking Charly for advice. She even walked around the bed and stuck her head out the bedroom door, peering down the stairwell toward her sisters' room. The door was closed and the house was silent. She was over-eager. Breakfast wasn't even on the schedule for another forty-five minutes or so. She walked back to her closet. All she could do, she decided, was choose an outfit and hope for the best. Anyway, how much did it really matter? She had to get over trying to impress her father. She couldn't guess what he would like and what he wouldn't, and she might as well stop trying to figure it out. He would bestow his good opinion or withhold it, and she couldn't help feeling that nothing she did would make much difference. Unless, that is, she suddenly gave up the Stanford idea and announced that she was enrolling in Oberrath College. And she wasn't quite ready for that.

With a new sense of freedom, she selected a knee-length skirt with a small floral print and then a white sleeveless blouse. She laid the clothing out on the bed and surveyed it with satisfaction. Dressy, but not overly so—that should do it. She hummed contentedly as she headed off to the shower.

At breakfast nobody said anything about her clothes, and her father didn't seem any more stern than usual. Charly and Lydia both had on skirts and blouses as well. All in all, she decided, she had to count this as a success.

After breakfast Bridget went upstairs to brush her teeth and then came back down to the living room, expecting to leave for the service soon. Lydia was at the piano playing something unfamiliar, and Charly sat stiffly in one of the chairs, flipping through a magazine with little enthusiasm. Her father was nowhere to be seen.

"What time does church start?" Bridget asked. "I thought Dad had said it was a morning service."

"It is," Charly responded, "but it doesn't start until ten. We usually leave around nine-thirty. We don't even need to leave that early; the church isn't that far from here. But Dad has this thing about making sure we're on time."

"I can imagine. What are you reading?"

Charly held up the magazine. *The New Era*, it said.

"The new era of what?" Bridget asked. "And when did the old era end? Nobody told me."

"What?" Charly asked, scrunching up her face in puzzlement. "That's just the name of the magazine. It doesn't mean anything."

"Okay, whatever. So, what is this magazine about?"

"Church stuff. Kids and church stuff."

"You don't look too excited about it," Bridget observed. "Must not be very interesting."

"Oh, it's all right," Charly countered. "I like to read the fiction stories especially. It's just that it only comes once a month, and I've already read this one."

"Why don't you read something else, then?"

"Can't. It's Sunday."

"You mean all you can read on Sunday is this *New Era*?"

Lydia stopped playing and twisted around on the piano bench. "Of course not," she exclaimed. "That would be dumb. We can also read our scriptures."

"Your what?"

"You know, the Book of Mormon, the Bible, the Doctrine and Covenants—"

"The doctor and what?" Bridget asked.

Lydia rolled her eyes. "Seriously," she muttered, turning back to the piano.

"I've heard of the Book of Mormon. That's like your Bible, right?" she asked Charly.

"No, we have the Bible too. The Book of Mormon is another book. I'll show you." She disappeared up the stairs for a moment and returned waving the thickest book Bridget had ever seen.

Bridget gave a low whistle. "So you can read that, huh? I don't know why you're wasting your time with this magazine, then. That thing's going to take you a while to get through."

"Well, it's not like everyone just reads it all straight through," Charly explained. She handed the book to Bridget. It was bound in burgundy leather that had been engraved with "Charlotte Christine McKenna" in gold letters. Bridget opened the front cover.

"Oh, that's why it's so fat," she said. "It's more than one book."

"Yeah," Charly agreed. "It's all the standard works. It's called a quad."

Bridget smiled and handed the book back to Charly. "Quad? The standard works? I'm going to have to have you write down a glossary for me."

"What's that?"

"It's like a dictionary, but it's specialized. What I need is a Mormon glossary."

"You mean like the Bible Dictionary?"

"Well, maybe that's somewhere to start."

Bridget heard a door opening somewhere, and soon her father strode into sight from the hallway, apparently coming from his office. He had a package in his hand wrapped in gold paper.

"Are your teeth brushed, girls?" he asked.

"Yes, Dad," they chorused.

"Sit up straight, Charlotte," he prodded.

"Aw, Dad, we're not even in church yet."

"What does that have to do with anything? You think sitting up straight is only for church?"

"No, but because we have to spend so much time today sitting on those uncomfortable benches and chairs, I ought to be able to lounge around while I have the chance."

The ghost of a smile crept across Mr. McKenna's face before he turned to Bridget.

"I have something for you, Bridget," he said, holding up the package. "Why don't you get changed, and then you can open this just before we go."

"Changed?"

"Yes. Into your church clothes."

Oh no. Things were definitely about to spiral downward. What could possibly be wrong with what she was wearing?

"Charly and Lydia are already in their church clothes, right?" she hedged.

"Yes. I like them to wear their church clothes all day, but of course I wouldn't expect that of you. I know you grew up differently."

"Well, the thing is, I'm already in my church clothes too."

"In that case, you should have let me have Natalie help you," he said coolly. "I'm afraid what you've chosen isn't quite suitable."

Bridget felt her temper flaring. "Really? What's wrong with it?"

"The blouse is sleeveless."

The answer caught Bridget off guard. She would never have thought of that as a potential problem. "So? I don't see what's so awful about a sleeveless blouse."

"It simply isn't appropriate. The girls can tell you about our standards of modesty on the way to church. For now, you'd better go up and find another blouse." He checked his watch. "We don't want to be late."

"I think Bridget's outfit is pretty, Dad," Charly piped up from the chair. "Don't you love her skirt?"

Mr. McKenna looked startled by Charly's interruption. "I suppose the skirt is fine," he conceded, quickly regaining his composure. "But that is not the issue here."

Bridget cast a grateful smile in Charly's direction and then went upstairs to change. Hadn't she warned herself that she could never impress this man? He could find something wrong with anything! Her fingers trembled a little from anger as she flipped once more through the clothes in her closet. She didn't want to change her whole outfit now, so when she found a light white cardigan, she threw that on over the blouse. Now her arms were completely covered. That had to be good enough—one more step toward "modesty" and she'd be wearing a veil. She laughed suddenly in spite of herself, stopping in front of the mirror to assess her reflection, she imagined her copper hair covered by a nun's habit. Wouldn't he like that!

She had forgotten about the package, but when she arrived back downstairs, he thrust it toward her unceremoniously. She interpreted his silence to mean that her clothing was now acceptable. He checked his watch again while she was ripping off the gold paper, so she didn't bother to remove it neatly, just tore into it and opened the box underneath. A book like the one Charly had just shown her sat on a bed of tissue paper. This one had a navy cover and the name Bridget McKenna engraved in the same style of lettering that spelled out Charly's name. Interesting, though, how Charly's book bore her full name but Bridget's omitted the "Lacey."

"Uh," she began. "Um, thank you." She supposed she had to say that. Anyway, it was a gift. Granted, it was sure to come with strings. Puppet strings, and her father wanted to be holding the controls. A book didn't scare Bridget, though. Her mother didn't approve of being afraid of books.

"When people ban books," Margaret had said once, "they only end up hurting whatever they think they're trying to protect. Because really they're validating those books, they're saying those books are true enough or compelling enough to be dangerous. If they were just the trash people want us to think they are, they wouldn't be worth banning."

Owning a copy of the Book of Mormon wasn't going to make her a Mormon, Bridget mused. Not in the least. Her father wasn't going to have such an easy time making her over into his image of the ideal daughter. So what did it hurt her to be polite about this? "Thank you," she said again, "it's lovely."

At the church the four of them filed in through a lobby with an orange couch and two gold chairs. It reminded Bridget of the pizza place, and suddenly there was Clyde himself striding up to them with a hand outstretched.

"Gerrick, hello," he said, vigorously shaking Mr. McKenna's hand. Clyde had exchanged his red T-shirt and apron for a white shirt and tie. Bridget looked around and decided that was the male uniform. As for the women, they all wore dresses or skirts, many of them definitely exemplifying Bridget's idea of frumpy. She wondered if her mother had ever come here; she wouldn't have fit in.

"And, Bridget," boomed Clyde, now giving her hand the same treatment he had bestowed on Mr. McKenna's. Bridget's arm began to ache. "I'm so glad you decided to come. I didn't know if we'd see you here or not."

"I requested that she join us," Mr. McKenna declared stiffly.

"Ah," said Clyde, as if that explained everything. "Well, don't be nervous, okay? All that stuff about Mormons having horns isn't really true. No, the only thing you've got to watch out for is Brother Neilson's Gospel Doctrine lesson, and the worst that'll do is put you to sleep." He chuckled as if he'd made a good joke.

"Brother? Your brother is in the ministry?" Bridget inquired.

Clyde stopped chuckling and stared at her blankly. "What?"

"What?" echoed Bridget, confused.

"We'd better get into the chapel," said Mr. McKenna, leading the way across the lobby and into a larger room with rows of wooden benches. Bridget understood now why Charly had complained about the uncomfortable seating. Mr. McKenna led them all the way to the front of the chapel and motioned for them to settle on the first bench in the center. He didn't sit next to them, though, but walked on to the bench on the far right. Bridget turned to her sisters. "Aren't men and women allowed to sit together?"

"What?" Charly asked. "What do you mean?"

Bridget glanced around at the benches behind them. Not many people had come in yet, but she could see two or three couples. One pair were even holding hands.

"Why isn't he sitting with us?"

"He has to pass the sacrament."

This only opened up more questions in Bridget's mind, but she decided she could wait to ask them. Maybe it would be better if she didn't try to process too many Mormon quirks at once. She noticed that, as the room began to fill up slowly, more men joined Mr. McKenna on the right side of the chapel. Not long after the service started, these men began passing around bread and water on little trays. Bridget didn't know much about the sacrament, but she thought of the Catholic communion ceremonies she had seen depicted on TV. Nice, she concluded, to have the stuff delivered to you instead of having to go up and get it. *These Mormons are so accommodating.* She would give them a point for that.

After the sacrament, though, the service grew more confusing. She had noticed before that several people, both men and women, were seated behind the pulpit. She had wondered briefly if Mormons allowed female ministers, but she wasn't surprised when one of the men had stood up to conduct the service. She didn't expect this church to be very liberal. But once the bread and water had been passed around, the man who had welcomed the congregation stayed in his seat and one of the women got up behind the pulpit. She began describing how she had met her husband and what had happened in their lives since they got married. Bridget nudged Charly. "Is the regular minister out of town?"

"What?" This seemed to be the response to everything today. Didn't anyone have an actual answer?

"Why is this woman speaking?" Bridget whispered.

"Why shouldn't she be?"

"Who is she?"

"Sister Dawes."

"Sister? Who's sister?"

"What?" Charly asked again.

"Forget it," Bridget conceded.

After a while, the woman's speech did touch on some

religious topics, and when she finished and sat down, a man who turned out to be her husband got up and announced that he was going to talk about faith. He did so for another twenty-five minutes, which Bridget considered a little excessive, but she hated to fault his enthusiasm. She figured he was just filling in for the regular minister, anyway, and didn't have much practice at this kind of thing. The congregation sang a hymn to close the service, someone said a prayer, and then everyone was standing up and stretching gratefully.

"Well, that was interesting," Bridget said. Mr. McKenna had returned to sit with them after the sacrament. He glanced over at her and nodded.

"I think it gave us a lot to talk about at home today," he said. "I'm sure you have questions."

Too bad Charly didn't seem too adept at answering them. She'd rather not have to take them to her father, who was likely to turn any discussion into a lecture on improper clothing or something equally annoying. She nodded noncommittally and surveyed the room. She was grateful when her eyes found a familiar face.

"Jeff," she called, waving at the boy standing near a bench two or three rows behind them. He grinned and waved back at her and then threaded his way through the crowd to come to talk to her.

"Hey, so what did you think?"

"Interesting," she repeated. She thought Jeff might be a good person to go to for clarification, but better to ask her questions when they were alone. "Want to walk home with me?" she invited.

"Sure, if I'm not ready to faint from hunger by then."

Bridget laughed. "Well, how do you feel? Can you make it?"

"I could now, but I can't say for sure about two hours from now. Hey, have you seen all these little kids eating

Cheerios and stuff? Parents of toddlers are so lucky. They can bring snacks and no one looks at them funny, and who's to notice if they snatch a few Cheerios here and there? But me, if I bring snacks, everyone stares. Go figure." He shook his head in mock despair and then winked. Bridget hadn't followed much of this discourse. Her mind had stuck on the phrase "two hours from now."

"Jeff, what do you mean, two hours?"

He sobered a little. "Oh, Bridget, did you think we were finished?"

"You mean we're not?"

"Uh-uh. Sorry to tell you this, but church lasts three hours."

"You're kidding, right?" *Three hours?*

"Nope."

Two hours later, Bridget's mind teemed with so many questions that her head ached at the thought of attempting to sort them out, and Jeff's appetite was demanding attention before he took an extra step, so they didn't end up walking home together. Instead, Bridget rode home with her family. Once inside the house, she went up to the bathroom to freshen up and stood staring at herself in the mirror. She remembered sometimes as a child studying her reflection and marveling at all the things the mirror didn't show: her thoughts, her feelings, her sore throat. If something hurt so bad, how could it not be visible? She considered that now. The girl in the mirror looked slightly dazed, maybe, but nothing about her revealed the extent of her isolation. Today had proven overwhelming. She was getting lost out here, and her year had only begun. And yet the girl in the mirror watched her unconcernedly. Bridget flashed her a smile and pulled out her lipstick. It might not be the answer to everything, but it was the only place she could think of to start.

s i x

On the first day of school, Bridget got up very early so she could have plenty of time to get ready. She went for a brisk jog and then showered and dried her hair, which she decided to leave loose. She had thought about what she wanted to wear and had finally decided on a pinkish coral sundress that brought out the gold tones in her skin. She matched it with a simple gold necklace and tiny gold earrings. She had painted her toenails the night before so that they were the same shade as her dress. When she pulled on her high-heeled sandals with the chunky soles and surveyed herself in the mirror, she felt satisfied with her reflection. Not that she would ever be the beauty her mother had been. But she was pretty enough, she supposed, in an unremarkable way. And today her wardrobe wasn't up for inspection by a group of religious oddballs, thank goodness. She remembered how people had stared at her the day before. True, many of them had eventually come up and introduced themselves, and none of them had actually seemed unfriendly. But she certainly hadn't felt like one of them. Maybe that was impossible, anyway, and she guessed it didn't matter. She didn't intend to be one of them.

She glided down the two flights of stairs with exaggerated dignity and stood waiting at the table until her father and sisters joined her, Charly running down the stairs and only slowing to a walk when she saw that everyone was staring at her. The four of them went through the usual

morning ritual of passing around the food in silence, waiting for Mr. McKenna to take the first bite, and then eating
to the accompaniment of clinking china and Mrs. Prescott
humming in the kitchen. When it was time for him to leave,
Mr. McKenna kissed the two younger girls on the tops
of their heads. One morning Bridget had thought he was
coming around to kiss her as well, and she had stiffened
up and recoiled a little. She didn't know if he had seen her
reaction and thought better of it or if that had never been his
intention at all. Either way, he had never made the slightest
move to approach her since then.

A few minutes later, the girls began the short walk to
school. Lydia was starting high school this year, so she and
Bridget would go to the same building, and Charly explained
that the junior high was just one more block down the road.
"That way it's easy to share the football field and the gym,"
she told Bridget. The high school was a two-story brown
brick building with the date 1925 carved into the stone
above the double front doors. Once inside, Lydia veered off
into the stream of students pouring into the front hall while
Bridget stepped sideways into the office.

"Can I help you?" the secretary asked, still staring at
her computer screen. When she looked over at Bridget, her
eyes widened. "Wow, you're looking very cheerful today."

"I am?" Bridget asked, confused. If anything, she ought
to look lost.

"That dress really lights up the room. Look, I think it's
reflecting on the wall."

The wall still looked white to Bridget. "Um, this is my
first day. I think I'm supposed to meet with the guidance
counselor." The secretary stopped staring at her and got
down to business. Yes, Bridget's records had already been
transferred from her old school, but she still needed to fill
out a few forms and then she could meet with Mrs. Branch
to go over her schedule. Bridget whipped through the

paperwork and waited another ten minutes until an inner door opened and a plump woman in a gray-blue suit ushered her inside.

"Well, then, let's see," said Mrs. Branch as she lowered herself into a chair behind her desk and put on her reading glasses. "It looks like you'll be interested in college prep courses. Is that right?"

"Yes," affirmed Bridget. "I'm not sure what you offer here, but I already had my schedule worked out at my old school and I'd like to take the same things here if I can."

"All right, then, let's see." The woman punched a few keys on the computer and then studied the screen. "I worked out a tentative schedule for you. Let's just see if this works." The printer buzzed and hummed while Bridget and Mrs. Branch stared at it. Bridget felt so anxious to get this settled that she could barely restrain herself from leaping up and snatching the sheet of paper out of the printer, but Mrs. Branch didn't seem to be in any hurry. "All right, now, take a look at that," Mrs. Branch said finally, handing Bridget the printed schedule.

CERAMICS, MR. FARNSWORTH, RM. 217
AEROBIC DANCE, MRS. MOSER, RM. 108
SPANISH 1, MR. MITCHELL, RM. 124
AMERICAN GOVERNMENT, MR. WOMACK, RM. 219
ENGLISH 12, MRS. KELLER, RM. 225
HOME ECONOMICS, MRS. GRAHAM, RM. 104
PHYSICS, MR. WILLIAMS, RM. 116

Bridget gaped up at Mrs. Branch. "Uh—this isn't really what I had in mind," she stammered. Where was the Advanced Placement European history, the Advanced Placement calculus, the Advanced Placement anything? And *ceramics?* Just how was that supposed to prepare her for Stanford?

"Well, you see, so many of our classes were already full when we got your records. I had to squeeze you in where I could. What doesn't look right to you, hon?"

Bridget didn't know where to begin. "Well, I've never taken Spanish."

Mrs. Branch brightened. "Oh, that's fine, I signed you up for the beginners' class."

"But I've already taken German for five years. I was hoping I could go on with that."

"That would be nice, dear, but we don't have a German teacher here. We're lucky to have Spanish and French. We just started our French program a couple of years ago."

Bridget took a deep breath. "Okay. I guess I'll take beginning Spanish. But what about a math class?"

Mrs. Branch began to look distressed. "I saw from your records that you've already taken everything we offer. Our math teacher, Mr. Smith, does everything from algebra to trigonometry, and that's as much as he can handle. We just can't fit a calculus class into his schedule." She shrugged and smiled apologetically. "A lot of seniors like to take things a little bit easy their last year. Just think how nice it will be not to have to worry about math homework every night."

Bridget chewed on her lip and reminded herself that Stanford didn't allow advanced placement credit to be used toward general ed, anyway, so maybe it didn't matter all that much. Even so, she needed to take the most challenging courses available. "Okay, do you have *any* Advanced Placement classes?"

"We have A.P. English, but the class was full." Bridget's face fell. "Now cheer up, Bridget, Mrs. Keller is a very good teacher. You'll learn a lot from her whether you're in her A.P. class or not."

Bridget sighed and looked at the schedule again. "I was already planning to take physics, so that's okay."

Mrs. Branch beamed. "Wonderful! I thought you might

be up for it. Not many are, you know. There are only six people enrolled."

"How many students go to this school?"

"Well, I think our last official count showed 632." Only about a thousand off from Bridget's old school. She had a feeling it was going to make a big difference.

When Bridget said nothing more, Mrs. Branch stood up and held out her hand. "It was a pleasure meeting you, Bridget. Good luck. We'll be getting together a little later in the year to talk about your college applications, and you be sure to let me know if there's anything I can do for you before then."

Bridget opened her mouth to protest at being shoved out of the office this way when none of her concerns had really been resolved, but then she realized there was nothing left to argue about. This "tentative schedule" was all this school had to offer. Bewildered, she put her hand in Mrs. Branch's.

"Now, if you go through the outer office and turn left into the hallway, you'll find the auditorium straight ahead. Everyone's in there for the orientation assembly." She herded Bridget out through the door and closed it behind her. The secretary glanced up as Bridget stepped out into the main office. "It's too bad sunglasses aren't allowed in school," she quipped and then, laughing, turned back to her computer.

Bridget rushed out of the office, but she wasn't sure later if she remembered to turn left or not. She walked through the empty halls without seeing anything, fighting the frustration that had resurfaced again and again over the last few months. Why had her mother had to die at the worst possible time? She hated herself for thinking this. What kind of daughter lost her mother and then worried over the inconvenience of it all? What kind of daughter valued her own goals over her mother's life? Not the kind of daughter anyone would want to have. Only a selfish, shallow person would think like that.

Somewhere in her wandering Bridget passed a girls' bathroom and decided to go inside. She stared at herself in the mirror. Only a couple of hours ago she had examined her reflection with approval. But that just showed again how little a mirror revealed. However innocent the person looking back at her appeared, in reality she was a selfish, shallow person. Because as much as she hated herself for it, she kept thinking that everything would have been so much easier if her mother's accident had happened one year later, after Bridget had already graduated from high school. Then she never would have had to come to this backward school that had hardly heard of calculus, she wouldn't have to listen to advice from the man who had abandoned her for ten years, and she could be home with her friends where she belonged, with Suzanne and with Justin, who would still have been her boyfriend if only . . . if only her mother hadn't died.

She heard a bell ring and then, in the distance, the sound of voices and stomping feet. She pulled out her schedule from where she had jammed it into the small front pocket of her backpack. Ceramics, Mr. Farnsworth, Rm. 217. Taking a deep breath, she pushed the bathroom door open and let herself into the hallway.

"Bridget!" called a familiar voice. Bridget turned to see a crowd of students heading toward her and then, in the midst of the crowd, she recognized Jeff's face.

"Hey!" he waved. "What've you got?"

"Uh, ceramics."

"Oh. I was hoping maybe you'd be in zoology."

"Maybe I could transfer," she suggested, suddenly hopeful.

"Maybe. I think it might be full—Mr. Buys promised a guitar concert every Friday, so a lot of people signed up just for that."

"A guitar concert?"

Jeff grinned. "Yeah. He plays the guitar and sings. Mostly stuff from the 60s. You should hear him do 'Light My Fire.'"

"Yeah, that should put you in the mood to dissect rats."

He laughed and then shrugged. "Well, it'd be better if it were bugs, but diversity is good. Hey, I gotta run. I just wanted to tell you that you look great in that dress."

Bridget smiled as he disappeared back into the crowd. Maybe things weren't so bad. She tried to keep an open mind as she headed for ceramics. In room 217, a youngish, dark-haired man in an apron was placing squishy gobs of wet gray clay in front of all the chairs that lined the single long table. Students filed in gradually and immediately began playing with the stuff with all the gusto of a bunch of three-year-olds building animals out of Play-Doh. Undaunted by the squelching noises arising from the table as the students handled the wet goo, Mr. Farnsworth gave a lecture explaining how to make notches along the sides of two pieces in order to fit them together. Their first assignment was to construct a little house. Bridget made one with a concave roof that looked like it was about to crash down onto the floor. "Good effort," Mr. Farnsworth told her. He promised to bake all the houses in the kiln so that they could paint them over the next few days, and Bridget left feeling like she had just come out of kindergarten.

Aerobic dance was taught by a small, squat woman who informed the girls that her class was the most important one they would take all year because it would make them into new people.

"By next spring you won't even remember how out of shape you were when you first walked in here," she announced. "You'll be healthier, faster, and more energetic. Notice I did not say skinnier. There's more to exercise than losing weight, so you girls who think you can laze around because you're built like sticks, you better understand that you'll have to work in this class. You just wait until you're thirty years old and your adult metabolism kicks in. By then you'll have forgotten almost everything you learned this year, but this class will still be there for you." It already seemed like a decade had passed since Bridget had sat down on the hard gym floor with her legs tucked demurely at her side. Finally the bell brought welcome deliverance.

The next two classes, Spanish and government, were all right—she liked Mr. Womack, the government teacher, and thought the subject might actually prove interesting. Lunch came next, and then it was time for English with Mrs. Keller. When Bridget walked into the classroom, a formidable gray-haired woman in a long gray skirt and blazer confronted her at the door.

"Well?" asked Mrs. Keller, one eyebrow arching up.

"Well—" repeated Bridget uncertainly.

A boy came in behind her, saw Mrs. Keller, and began digging in his backpack.

"You did do the assignment, didn't you?" She waved the small pile of papers she was holding.

"I'm sorry, I'm new and I didn't know there was one."

The boy who'd been fumbling in his bag finally pulled out a piece of paper covered in writing and handed it to the teacher before slinking off to a desk and collapsing in relief.

"Oh, you didn't?" Mrs. Keller's eyebrows drew together and her eyes glittered disapprovingly over her long nose. "Well, I shall have to devise a suitable makeup assignment for you. Please see me after class."

When most of the seats had been filled, Mrs. Keller abandoned her post by the door and walked to the front of the room. She had a commanding presence; unlike some of the other teachers who had had to call for silence, she didn't have to say anything to get people's attention. She glowered down at the class and the class stared timidly back at her.

"Welcome to English 12," she intoned finally. "I am Mrs. Keller, and as I trust you all know by either reputation or experience, I do not tolerate inattention or lack of preparation. Those of you who failed to hand in a completed assignment today have already used up any indulgence I may be willing to offer. See that you shape up from this moment on, because I am not afraid to give anyone a failing grade and keep him or her from graduating.

"Now, I think we are ready to go directly into a discussion of *Lord of the Flies* as soon as we have heard from our new student. New faces are rare around here, and consequently I think it would be appropriate for Miss McKenna to introduce herself. Miss McKenna, please come up and tell us a little about yourself."

Bridget rose slowly and made her way to the front. She disliked improvisational speaking. If she had been allowed to remain at her desk, she could have offered an informal introduction, but this arrangement made it seem as if more was required of her. When she passed the last row of desks, she turned and faced the class, gazing out over the sea of black, gray, brown, white, and denim blue. With her coral dress, she stood out like a hunter in an orange coat, only she wasn't sure that in her case it would keep her safe from stray shots.

"Hi, everyone," she began. "I'm Bridget McKenna. I just moved here from California—uh, San Francisco. I've only been here about a week. Ummm—" What else was she supposed to talk about? She looked for a cue from Mrs. Keller but saw only a stony expression. "I like listening to music and playing tennis . . . " Her voice trailed off and her mind raced as she worried that she might choke from the awkward silence. Finally Mrs. Keller broke in.

"I believe everyone is aware that Miss McKenna is the daughter of M. C. Lacey. We will have high expectations for someone with such an illustrious parent."

Someone in the back snickered and Mrs. Keller's expression sharpened. The sound stopped abruptly. "Well then, thank you, Miss McKenna. Now, everyone, please put your things under your desk. All you'll need is a pen." Mrs. Keller went to her desk and pulled out a sheath of papers from one of the drawers. "Don't be alarmed," she said as she began to distribute the papers, "this quiz is worth only 50 points."

After class, Bridget stopped at Mrs. Keller's desk to get her makeup assignment. "Have you read *Lord of the Flies?*" Mrs. Keller asked.

"Yes, I have, actually."

"Good. Read it again and write an essay. You may choose the topic yourself, as long as it is related to the book. I would say 500 words ought to do it. Have it to me by Monday."

Bridget agreed even though she felt as if someone had just handed her a stack of heavy books. She was turning to leave when Mrs. Keller called her back.

"I know you belong in the Advanced Placement class," she said. "But don't worry, I'm not about to let you get bored. Everyone else may want to go soft on you after what you've been through, but they're not doing you a favor. Do you understand?"

She didn't really know what Mrs. Keller was talking about. "Of course."

"Good. See that you give me the kind of work you're capable of, and everything will be fine."

The final two classes passed by in a blur, and finally the last bell signaled the end of a day Bridget had thought would drag on forever. She was surprised when she came out of physics to find Jeff waiting for her in the hallway.

"Ready to head home?" he asked.

"Am I ever!"

s e v e n

Outside the high school, the afternoon sun shone brightly and gleamed across the windshields and roofs of beat-up station wagons, pickups, and a few shiny new sports cars. "So, what do you think of Phrygia High?" Jeff asked as they descended the front steps and turned down the sidewalk toward home.

"Well—" Bridget hesitated. "Umm, the bathrooms are pretty nice for a school built in 1925."

Jeff laughed. "That's something. Hey, the vending machines aren't bad either. They keep them pretty well stocked. Those huge cookies with the pink frosting make a good lunch in a pinch."

"Sounds like you're a nutrition guru."

"I try," said Jeff.

They crossed a street and turned the corner, and the sounds of students talking and car engines gunning died down. "How was zoology?" Bridget asked. "Did you get a concert this morning?"

"Yeah. Mr. Buys tied a bandana around his head and sang some Simon and Garfunkel songs." Jeff began strumming an imaginary guitar and singing "The Sound of Silence" until Bridget laughed and shoved him gently.

"If people are watching from their front windows, they're going to think you're having a seizure or something and call an ambulance," she teased.

They walked on for another two blocks and then turned

onto Independence Road. Bridget could see Mrs. Prescott out in the front yard bending over a flower bed. At the house on the corner, another woman was trimming an already immaculate hedge.

"Hey, Melanie!" Jeff called to her. The woman turned and waved and then put her clippers down and walked over to the sidewalk.

"Hi," she said. "How was the first day?"

"Not bad," Jeff replied. "But no freshmen ventured into Senior Hall, so I didn't get to rough anyone up."

"Aw, maybe tomorrow," comforted Melanie. She was quite young, maybe in her mid-thirties, and had long blonde hair tied back with a brightly colored scarf. She looked at Bridget curiously with an open friendliness that put Bridget at ease, and Jeff took his cue and made the introduction.

"You remember Bridget," he said. "She just moved back in with the McKennas."

Melanie smiled and held out her hand. "Glad to meet you again, Bridget. We're happy to have you back. I'm Melanie Lanier, you probably don't remember me."

Bridget started to contradict her but then decided to be honest. She shook her head. "I'm sorry, I don't. I haven't remembered much about Phrygia. I guess my memory isn't that great."

Melanie shrugged. "It's funny what we remember and what we don't. For example, I can tell you everything I ate at my fourth birthday party, but I have almost no memory of my baby sister coming home from the hospital just a few months before that."

"It must have been so traumatic that you blocked it out," joked Jeff.

"Right. I must have known even then that she was going to be the one all the boys would be after." Melanie laughed, and the sound came out so carefree and spontaneous that Bridget wanted to laugh too. "Of course," Melanie continued, "I shouldn't have worried, as my own dearest husband came along eventually."

"Melanie and David own this bed and breakfast," Jeff explained, and Bridget noticed the sign for the first time. "Independence Inn, 301 Independence Road," was printed in gold lettering on a black plaque fastened below the mailbox.

"That must keep you busy," said Bridget.

"It does," Melanie agreed. "But never too busy to treat two starving students to an after-school snack. Come on in and have some pastries. I'm trying out a new recipe, and I need some opinions."

Jeff looked at Bridget. "Someone has to do it," he declared solemnly.

In the cool, old-fashioned kitchen, the three of them sat down at the table with a plate full of pastries and three tall glasses of milk. Bridget took a long drink and then looked around at the spacious room. In the light that poured in through two dozen individual windowpanes, the cherry-colored wooden cabinets shone vibrantly. Bridget thought she could detect a faint odor of wood polish beneath the more dominant aromas of cinnamon and baking bread. "I don't know if it's possible," she said softly, "but I think I remember this kitchen."

Melanie studied Bridget's expression before responding, "It's definitely possible. You and your sisters used to come over here sometimes when your mother had errands to run."

Bridget tried to focus in on whatever thread of memory had surfaced, but it had sunk again into her subconscious before she could get a proper hold on it.

"Why don't I remember more?" she asked, suddenly frustrated. "This is the first place that has felt familiar. I always knew I had a father and sisters out here, but I don't know now if I even actually remembered them or if I just created images of them in my mind that weren't real."

"Sometimes we do that," said Melanie. "We fabricate memories without even realizing it. Sometimes you can tell when you reminisce with someone—you don't remember things the same way that they do. Maybe it's because you perceived things differently in the first place, and then you both emphasized different things, chose to keep different parts of the experience."

"I just feel now like I'm trying to live someone else's life," said Bridget. "All these people have memories of me, but it seems like the person they remember is a stranger, not someone I was ever connected to. And they all keep saying—"

"What?" asked Melanie. "What do they say?"

"They say, 'after what you've been through.' I guess they mean my mother dying. But why don't they just say that?"

Melanie offered an understanding smile. Jeff, whose mouth was full of pastry, reached over and rested his hand on Bridget's arm for a few seconds.

"People here have their own memories, whether they're accurate or not," Melanie told her. "They knew your mother before you did. But they didn't know her the same way you did. It's what I was saying before—two people can be in the same room, right next to each other, experiencing two completely different things. Two people can be in a relationship, even, and it's two completely different relationships."

Bridget sighed. "I don't understand that."

"Did you ever like a boy who didn't feel quite the same way about you? Or vice versa? You're as pretty as my little sister that I was just complaining about. I'm sure you've had a lot of guys wanting to spend time with you."

"Yeah, I guess. There have been a couple of guys who I thought were good as friends, but they wanted to be more."

"And maybe they thought you both felt a connection or that they were just responding to your cues, but in fact you never wanted to get that serious. You never felt that connection."

"Yeah, okay."

"So whose experience is true?"

Jeff gulped down the rest of his pastry, finished his milk, and gazed at the women seated on either side of him. "I think we can consider ourselves fed, physically and mentally, and if we chomp down on this serious stuff anymore right now, we're going to end up with indigestion."

Bridget looked at him quizzically. "Mental indigestion or physical indigestion?"

Jeff thought for a moment. "Both."

"Take it from the scientist," said Melanie. "I'll let you two get home to do your homework. I know you're dying to." She winked at them, and Bridget stood up, reluctant to leave the first place in New York that had almost felt like home. "I'm here almost all the time, Bridget," Melanie said as she ushered them out onto the back porch. "If you ever feel like talking . . ."

"Thank you," replied Bridget, meaning it.

Jeff and Bridget said good-bye in front of Bridget's house, and Jeff crossed the street to his home. Mrs. Prescott was still working in the flower beds next to the McKennas' porch. "Hello, Bridget!" she called as Bridget approached. "There's milk in the refrigerator and chocolate chip cookies in the jar on the counter. Help yourself to a snack!"

Bridget smiled. She'd better start jogging every morning or she was going to put on weight in this town. "Thanks, Mrs. Prescott." Once inside, she headed for her bedroom, wanting to put down her backpack and freshen up before thinking of anything else. From the second-floor landing, she saw Lydia hovering in the doorway of her and Charly's bedroom. The usual music boomed out, and Charly lay stomach-down on her bed flipping through a magazine, her knees bent and her feet waving in the air.

Bridget acknowledged her sisters with a "hi." Lydia glared at her, stone-faced, and Charly was too wrapped up in whatever she was looking at to answer. Bridget hurried up the final flight of stairs to her own room and burst through the door with a sigh of relief that quickly turned into a gasp. The place had been torn apart. The bed that she had neatly made that morning was now in disorder; the mattress had slid partway off the box springs beneath. Her dresser drawers were open with clothes spilling out, and a few items were scattered on the floor. She dashed around the bed to the walk-in closet, where half of her clothes were off of the hangers, and her suitcases stood at crazy angles as if flung in carelessly. Furious, she stormed back down to the second-floor landing and confronted Lydia, who seemed to be waiting for her in the open doorway.

"Did you do that to my room?" she demanded.

"Your room?" questioned Lydia. "It was my room for eight years. You've only been sleeping there a few days."

Bridget wanted to reach out and strangle her but resisted. "Did you do it?" she repeated.

"Yes. I had to find something."

"And just where did you think it was? In one of my suitcases? In the pocket of one of my pairs of pants?"

Lydia scowled. "I can't help it that your stuff was in the way. I had to find it."

"And this didn't occur to you before? Like when I was there and could move my stuff for you, or before I came?"

"No. I had to move everything out really fast to make room for you, and I missed some stuff."

"What? What exactly did you have to find that was so important?" Lydia didn't answer. "Show me!" Bridget shouted.

Lydia walked over to a desk, opened one of the drawers, and pulled out what looked like a small sheet of paper. She brought it back over to the doorway and held it up for Bridget to see. It was a half empty page of smiley-face stickers.

"This is what couldn't wait? Well, never mind, I understand. It was either this or a smile transplant since the only expression you can come up with on your own is a pout."

"That's better than a stupid grin," Lydia retorted.

"Then you'd better get rid of those stickers."

"Or I could just get rid of you."

Bridget folded her arms across her chest and tossed her hair back over her shoulders. "I'd like nothing better," she said evenly.

Charly had slid off her bed and turned her music down, and now she came over to stand next to her sisters. "C'mon, Lydia, let's help her clean it up."

"She doesn't need help from us," Lydia snarled. "Didn't you hear her? She doesn't even want to be here."

"Neither do you," Charly declared, "so I guess everyone's even."

Lydia stared at Charly. "Just get out," she whispered finally. She stepped backward into the bedroom, shoved Charly toward the landing, and slammed the door.

Charly and Bridget worked silently for a while in Bridget's room, folding clothes and straightening the bed. Bridget had come up almost shivering with anger, but a few minutes of steady activity and a room that looked close to normal again soothed her until the adrenaline seemed to drain away.

"She could have this room back if she wants," Bridget said to Charly. "I'll share with you if you don't mind."

"She doesn't want it back," answered Charly.

"I think she does."

"No," Charly insisted. "Then what would she have to be mad at you for?"

* * *

That evening when Bridget went down to dinner she found an envelope tucked carefully next to her plate. She drew it out and read the return address with excitement. It was from Suzanne. "It came for you this afternoon," Mrs. Prescott informed her when she saw her with the envelope. "I had the mail still tucked into my apron pocket when you came from school, but it slipped my mind to give it to you then."

Because her father and sisters were now sitting down at the table, ready to eat, Bridget decided to save the letter for after dinner. She ate as quickly as she could in that stiff, formal atmosphere and then rushed upstairs to rip open the envelope in private. "Dear Bridget," she read,

> *Hey chica! How do you like New York? Have you been to NYC yet? Don't forget you promised that you would visit the Metropolitan Museum of Art for me. What's your dad like? Have you been to school there yet? We just started this week, but I'm already behind, can you believe it? I wish you were here to help me with European history. Remember how we were going to dress up this Halloween as French revolutionaries and carry around a little guillotine and a basket of papier-mâché heads? I don't guess I'll do that now that you're not here, but it would have been fun.*
>
> *I saw Justin a couple of times after you left, and we've been hanging out a lot since school started. I think he really wishes he could have had the chance to talk to you after your mom died. At first I told him he was just a wimp, and I was totally disgusted with him, but I didn't understand him at all then—he is so much more sweet and sensitive than we ever knew. He told that me he cried after you moved away and that he's been sleeping with the boutonnière you gave him for prom under his pillow. Isn't*

that romantic? Only just a couple of weeks ago he forced himself to throw it away because he knows he may not ever see you again, and it's just making him hurt worse. I said he should definitely write to you, but he's scared, I guess, that you'll be mad and think he wasn't there for you after the accident. I said you wouldn't be like that, but I don't know if he believes me enough to dare write.

I found out that Anna and Jack are a couple now and Laurie Shepherd broke up with her boyfriend. Sad, huh? But I guess he's up for grabs now. :)

Well, take care and write me as soon as you can!
Suzanne

Bridget read the letter over twice to make sure she hadn't missed anything. She sighed after the second time because she hadn't. Suzanne liked Justin. Well, and what could she do about it? What did it matter? She stared out her windows at the rooftops of the little town. The space between here and California seemed interminable, and the time stretched out longer still. A whole year. She had tried to convince herself that a year wasn't enough time to make any real difference. But she saw now that she couldn't expect to move back to San Francisco next summer and just pick up where she had left off as if nothing had happened. She sighed again and rummaged around in her backpack for the copy of *Lord of the Flies* that Mrs. Keller had given her. She flipped through the pages glumly; she had no interest in reading it again. But there was only one way back to California, she reminded herself. Her acceptance to Stanford would be her only ticket home.

e i g h t

A few days later, the Owenses stopped by on their way to San Francisco. Bridget sat with them at the dining room table while they drank tall glasses of iced tea and chattered on about their daughter and grandchildren. Mr. Owens displayed the pictures from his wallet that Bridget had already seen at least twice before. Finally, when the glasses were emptied, Mr. Owens got to his feet.

"We had better head out soon," he announced. They wanted to make another two or three hundred miles before settling in for the night. Bridget walked out to the car with them. Mrs. Owens gave her a hug.

"I'll tell Suzanne that you look just wonderful. She'll be so pleased."

"Thank you for coming, Mrs. Owens," Bridget said. "Thank you for everything."

"Don't drop off the face of the earth now," ordered Mr. Owens. "Keep in touch."

Bridget nodded. "And I'll see you next year, when I come back to school."

The Owenses got into their LeBaron, and the car started to back down the driveway. Bridget turned back to the house. The sun had gone behind a cloud and perhaps that's why the old gray facade looked especially bleak. Lydia was watching her from one of the front windows. The girl's pale face wore its usual smug expression.

I can't go back in there, Bridget thought suddenly. *I can't stay here.*

She whirled around and jogged toward the Owenses' car, which had pulled out of the driveway now. She could see Mr. Owens shifting from reverse into drive. Mrs. Owens must have caught sight of Bridget because she laid a hand on her husband's arm and motioned for him to roll down the window.

"What is it, Bridget?" he called. "Did we leave something in the house?" He turned to his wife. "Do you have your purse, hon?"

"Yes," replied Mrs. Owens. "It's right here." She held it up.

Bridget felt stupid. *Take me home,* she wanted to shout. *Don't leave without me.* "I'm sorry," she muttered as she drew near the driver's side window, "I only wanted to ask if you would tell Suzanne—" she tried to think of some message that might justify her frantic dash toward the LeBaron, but she couldn't. "Tell her she'll do fine in European history. She's smart, I know she can do it."

"Sure we'll tell her," promised Mrs. Owens. "You two are both so smart. It gives me a headache even thinking about studying European history."

Mr. Owens chuckled. "In that case, just think about ice cream. We'll give Suzanne the message, Bridget."

"Take care," said Mrs. Owens. She held up her hand, and Bridget returned the wave. The car pulled away and sped up as it moved down the street. She stared after it for a long time.

The next morning was Saturday, and Bridget got up early to go jogging while the town was still peaceful and quiet. She needed some time alone and didn't want to worry about getting back for breakfast, so she wrote a note. "I'm out for a jog. Don't hold breakfast for me. I'll be home later this morning." She set it on the dining room table, where at least Mrs. Prescott would be sure to see it when she put out the breakfast things. The freedom felt good. She thought that she might go a long way today, maybe explore some of the back roads.

She jogged for a couple of miles and then slowed to a walk. She was out in farmland now, and she hadn't met anyone yet. After walking for another twenty minutes or so, she passed a pair of ladies out speed walking. Their fists bobbed up and down in front of their chests, and their bodies were bent slightly backward as if their final destination were somewhere in the sky.

"Morning!" one of them called to her.

"Good morning," Bridget responded. Then she was alone again. She looked around at the countryside. It wasn't so different from the land around San Francisco, she thought; both places had low, rolling hills, only some in California were big enough that people referred to them as mountains. She breathed in deeply and concentrated on feeling her lungs expand and the sound of her breath whooshing in and out. Her mother had practiced meditation and had tried to describe it to her.

"It's hard to put it into words," Margaret had explained, "but when you focus on your breath, it's easier to see how transitory your feelings are."

Bridget had never sat down and done it wholeheartedly, but she sort of attempted it sometimes without changing her posture or closing her eyes. She worked now on keeping her mind blank, which she envisioned as a gray, misty void. After a while, the rise and fall of her chest amazed her. She marveled at her own physicality. She wasn't sure why her solidness suddenly seemed so strange, but then she began to think that she perceived herself as an idea, and an idea is perfectly free. When she was little, she had planned her life, and it was as easy as saying what she wanted to happen. "I'm going to be a lawyer," she had declared at about age ten, and she'd had no doubt that those words alone would make it so. "I'm going to marry someone handsome with a good tan and have four children, two boys and two girls." There, it was decreed. Time was all that was needed.

She wasn't such a simpleton now. But maybe she hadn't left those thoughts behind completely. She had a certain picture of who she was, of the kind of life she was supposed to lead, and it was hard to change it. New York wasn't part of the plan, and she almost couldn't believe right now that she was truly tethered here, that her thought alone, that her identity alone could not put her back where she belonged. How odd to crash down into the knowledge that after all she was flesh and blood and couldn't work magic by the sheer force of her will. Or maybe she could change things, but it was so much more complicated and time-consuming than she'd imagined that she wasn't sure she could ever accomplish it.

Out here, alone, she felt that she knew who she was, but she didn't know if that person could exist in this new life. When she thought of her name, she thought of ocean breezes and trolley cars, she thought of barbecues at Suzanne's and of her mother's face reflecting the faint blue light from her computer screen. She didn't want to let go of those images, but she didn't know if she could stand to spend the whole year reminding herself of them, forgetting to live in the present for fear it might spoil the future. She was afraid to change.

She began jogging again, and her breathing became faster. She remembered what old Mr. Wang from next door had said to her once: "You think too much." It was probably true. She didn't want to think anymore.

She finally turned back toward home, but she followed a roundabout route, trusting some instinctual sense of direction to guide her back to Independence Road. She was still on the outskirts of town when she passed a park that she hadn't seen before. She began to cut across it and was approaching the opposite side when she glanced over at the swings. There, a memory. It came sudden and vivid, bringing her up short. She knew these swings as she knew her own bedroom in California. How many times had she flown back and forth through the sky, laughing and clinging to the chains on either side of her? She could picture her mother's face, ten or fifteen years younger. Her mother would stand out in front of her, her arms spread wide, laughing with her. "Be careful!" her mother would shout. "I'm a crocodile! Don't let me bite your foot!" Then she would stretch her arms in front of her with her palms together, one arm on top of the other, ready to raise the top arm and reach for Bridget's shoes as they swung toward her. "Aaaaah!" Bridget screamed in delight, seeing in her mother's arms the snapping jaws of a huge reptile. It had always been easy to pretend when her mother was around.

Bridget moved slowly toward the swings as her mind dove into this memory. She sat down on one of the black rubber seats. They were much lower to the ground than she remembered. She had to curl her legs up very tight beneath her to keep them from scraping on the sand, so it was hard to pump. Finally she gained some height and the movement became easier. The ground whizzed close beneath her for only a fraction of a second before she was climbing again. How old had she been when she learned to pump a swing? she wondered. And then the real question surfaced. If her mother had been in front of her, who had been behind her? Whose were the hands, solid and reliable, that had been at her back to push her skyward once more? They must have been her father's, of course, her young father whose face she didn't remember.

She closed her eyes and imagined the swing carrying her toward her mother. She could see her mother in the Parisian artist costume she had been wearing the day she died, the one with the billowy smock stained—a little too neatly, perhaps—with short streaks of paint.

"Bridget," her mother had been lecturing her, "you have to be willing to try new things. I can't believe how cautious you are. You're like an old grandma." Bridget had stood in the doorway of her mother's room, and a suitcase had lain open on the bed. Her mother was packing for a weekend getaway with her present love interest, whose name Bridget had now forgotten. "I tell you, if some cute boy had invited me to go hang gliding—"

"You're scared of heights," Bridget had pointed out. "He would have had to be really cute for you to say yes."

"Well, isn't this guy really cute?"

Bridget had considered. "He's okay. But I'd rather be with Justin."

Her mother had turned and frowned at her. "Pardon the language, but Justin is an old fuddy-duddy. Justin hasn't invited you hang gliding."

Bridget had frowned back. "Is that the new standard for judging guys?"

Her mother had rolled her eyes, shook her head, and gone back to packing. The message came through clearly: Bridget was hopeless. A few minutes later Margaret was zipping up her suitcase and then racing downstairs and out the front door, calling a careless good-bye over her shoulder. Then, later that day, she had died.

Bridget put her legs down and let her feet drag on the ground. The swing jerked roughly, as if it was angry about stopping so soon. She didn't think she was crying until she reached up to brush a hair away from her cheek. Her face was wet with tears. She hated that final memory, the way that Margaret's critical frown had entrenched itself in Bridget's mind as her most enduring image of her mother. She could never wipe that frown away now; nothing she ever accomplished could put a smile on her mother's face. But would she have been able to do that anyway? How could you ever please someone who didn't need real people, who could retreat into a world of her own making populated with the sort of human beings she wished she knew and didn't? How could Bridget ever compete with Colin—perfect Colin, who tried everything and happened to be good at all of it? And he wasn't even real. How pathetic to be jealous of someone who wasn't even real.

Bridget wiped her face on the sleeve of her T-shirt and waited a few more minutes before starting home. When she turned onto her street, she saw a police car parked in front of the house. Alarmed, she sprinted toward the porch and burst through the double sets of front doors.

"What's wrong?" she shouted to anyone who might be there to listen. She rushed into the living room, and there sat two men in police uniforms. Her father was pacing back and forth in front of them. He stopped when she ran in, and hurried over to her.

"Bridget," he gasped, gripping her shoulders. "Are you all right? Where have you been?"

"I was just out for a jog," she replied. "Didn't you get my note?" He stared at her blankly. "What's the matter?" she asked. "What's happened here?"

The officers stood up. "Hi, Bridget," said the older one, crossing the room toward her and offering his hand. "I'm Sergeant Davies. Good to see you again."

"Nice to meet you," she said, feeling dazed. "Is everything okay?"

"Sure it is," Sergeant Davies assured her. "We were just visiting with your father. He was a little worried about you, that's all. I can see why, now. Such a pretty young lady—it's going to be a full-time job fending off the boys." The officer winked at Mr. McKenna, who didn't acknowledge the gesture.

Bridget blushed. "Why are you here really? It isn't just

about me, is it?" The policemen glanced at each other, and Bridget's stomach sank. "I left a note," she insisted. Her defense sounded feeble even to herself.

"I never saw any note," Mr. McKenna declared to Sergeant Davies. He turned back to Bridget. "Where did you leave it?"

"On the table." She moved toward the dining area as if it might still be sitting where she had placed it. It wasn't. But when she stooped down and peered underneath the table, she spotted a patch of white. She had to crawl partway under the table to pull it out. "Here it is," she said, waving it for them to see. Her father snatched it from her and scanned it quickly.

"So every morning, if you aren't here, we're supposed to get down on our hands and knees and scour the place for a note?"

"It must have slipped off, Gerrick, without anyone seeing it," said the younger officer. "Maybe when Mrs. Prescott brought something out to the table. The swinging door might have let in a gust of air that blew it off."

"Like I said," put in Sergeant Davies, "these things happen. Nothing to worry about. Good seeing you, though. Thought you'd just about moved to Rochester. We hardly see you around anymore."

Mr. McKenna shook his head, apparently speechless.

"Good to meet you, Bridget," said the younger officer.

"Take care," said Sergeant Davies. The two of them let themselves out through the double front doors. Bridget faced her father alone.

"I'm sorry you worried, but I tried to let you know where I was. It isn't my fault that the note slipped off." Her father didn't answer. "I don't see why it's a big deal, anyway," she continued, "for me to be out by myself in the morning. I mean, what do you think's going to happen?"

"Bridget," began Mr. McKenna, speaking low, "you don't

know everything. I'm your father. You're to respect that."

Bridget took a deep breath and shook her head. "What does that even mean?" she said finally. "I don't know what it means to have a father. I don't know how I'm supposed to act." She hesitated, wondering how far she would go. "I've never lived in a police state before."

"Go to your room," her father commanded in a tight, barely controlled voice. "Go until I come for you."

Bridget couldn't remember ever being ordered to her room before. She wanted to laugh. Instead, she surprised herself by shouting, "Who do you think you are?" Before she had gotten the words out, the question seemed obsolete. What she really meant was, *Who do you think I am, one of the daughters you didn't abandon?* She turned away and was going to start up to her room—she had homework to do, anyway—when something urged her back.

"Let me be honest with you," she said, not shouting anymore. "I don't want to stay in New York any longer than I have to. I don't know why you brought me here, I guess you thought you had to. But when the school year's over, I'm going back. So I don't need to tour to all those college campuses, and I don't need to go shopping for new clothes to make me over into whatever you think I'm supposed to be. That's the way it is, and there's no point in talking about it anymore."

"Go to your room," her father repeated. "Today, and tomorrow, and every day after school for the next month."

"I'm going to my room now, but I'm not going to wait in there like a prisoner. And how would you know if I'm in there after school anyway?"

Her father's mouth was clamped into a hard line. She avoided gazing at him directly because the truth was he looked pretty scary. Part of her brain wondered why she kept stirring up trouble when there was enough already, but she was tired of being on her best behavior for this man. She wanted everything out in the open.

Behind Mr. McKenna, the swinging door to the kitchen opened and a woman entered quietly. "Let her go, Gerry," she said softly, almost the way a mother would coax an upset child. "Let it go. It wasn't her fault." Bridget stared at the woman in bewilderment. Who was she? The woman stepped around the table in the dining room and came to stand next to Mr. McKenna. She smiled at Bridget. "I'm Natalie Major," she said. "I don't want you to think I've been in there eavesdropping. I went out onto the back porch so that I wouldn't hear anything, but when I came back in, you two were still going at it. I thought maybe an unbiased third party could be helpful after all."

"I'm sorry," said Bridget, "but who are you?"

"I'm a friend of your father's." She glanced at Mr. McKenna. "I thought he might've mentioned me, but I guess not."

"She's hardly been here a week," he muttered.

"No, it's been two weeks at least," Natalie corrected. To Bridget she said, "Go ahead up to your room and do whatever you were going to do. It's been a stressful morning, but if we can ride it out without doing too much damage, I think things will sort themselves out."

Bridget stared at her, still trying to figure out who she was. Was this her father's girlfriend? Was this the woman who was supposed to take her shopping for college touring outfits? She didn't fit either role. For one thing, she was too casual. She had on jeans with distinct faded spots over both knees. Her light brown hair was long and tied back in a ponytail, and she didn't appear to be wearing any makeup. The truth was, thought Bridget, she would have fit in a lot better in California.

"Go ahead, Bridget," she prodded gently. Bridget turned and went upstairs. She set up her laptop and began polishing her *Lord of the Flies* essay, which she had to turn in to Mrs. Keller on Monday. A few minutes later she was distracted by the sound of something hitting her window. She glanced up but couldn't see anything. A bird must have crashed into the glass and fallen away, stunned. She went back to the essay. The sound came again, so loud that she was surprised not to find the window cracked. She stood up and walked over to look down from her tower. Jeff was standing on the front lawn, waving up at her. She raised the middle windowpane and yelled, "Haven't you ever heard of a telephone?"

Jeff put a finger to his lips and motioned toward the back door. Bridget shook her head and went back to her essay. She wasn't in the mood for games. But the essay was pretty much finished, so after a minute she stood up and walked quietly downstairs. As she eased down the final flight to the main floor, she could hear Natalie's voice from somewhere. She gazed cautiously into the living room, but it was empty. The voice was coming through the partially open door of her father's office.

" . . . not asking you to stop caring about her. Then you wouldn't be you."

"Not this nonsense again!" replied her father's voice, sounding angry. "It's been ten years, I tell you. Of course I don't still care."

Natalie sounded unruffled. "If you'd stop denying it to yourself, that would be half the battle. Why does it make you so angry that you have feelings just like everyone else?"

"I don't have feelings for her. How many times do I have to tell you, you're the one I want?"

"Saying it doesn't make it true," Natalie responded matter-of-factly. "Gerry, you don't know how much I want to be the one you want, and God forgive me, when she died I thought maybe we finally had a chance. But instead it's shown me just how deep your feelings go."

"You're wrong, Natalie," said Mr. McKenna quietly. "I'll prove it to you."

Bridget heard the floorboards creak. She crept away

into the kitchen before one of them could come out and find her listening. Jeff was waiting for her outside the back door. For once she didn't find his pleasant, homely face a welcome sight. "I don't know if this is a good time to talk."

"Why?" he asked sympathetically. "Worried about your father?"

"It hasn't been a great day so far, and I'm in a pretty bad mood. You might be sorry if you talk to me very long, and I'll be sorry for making you sorry."

"I'll risk it," Jeff declared. "Look, I called over here a little while ago, and your dad answered. He told me what happened this morning. I just wanted to see how you're doing."

"What did he tell you?"

"He said you'd gone out without telling anyone where you were."

"That isn't true," Bridget snapped. "I left a note."

"I know," Jeff said simply.

Bridget relaxed. "I'm sorry. I warned you that I might bite your head off."

"No worries, I've still got it. But hey, don't let this get to you. Your father isn't as psychotic as he seems."

Bridget grinned in spite of herself. "So you admit he's psychotic?"

"He's just, you know—after what happened before."

Bridget gazed at him blankly. "Before what?"

"When your mother left."

"How does a divorce make you crazy enough to call the police because your daughter goes out for a morning run? Besides, that was a long time ago."

Jeff stared at her strangely. "Well, it might have something to do with it."

"What?" The two looked at each other. Jeff didn't answer her. "Jeff, it's funny, but sometimes I almost think that you're all hiding something from me."

106

As soon as the words were out, Bridget was ready to laugh at the silliness of the whole idea. But Jeff didn't seem amused. He tried unsuccessfully to shake off his serious expression. "Why would anyone hide anything from you?" he hedged.

"I don't know, that's what I'm asking you."

Jeff looked away, apparently uncomfortable under her scrutiny. "I don't know anything you don't," he insisted.

"Give me your opinion, then. Why does my father act this way?"

"My opinion?" Jeff hesitated, glancing at her and then away again. "I don't know. I'll tell you this. Once he lost some people who were close to him. He couldn't get them back. Maybe he tries too hard now to hold onto what he's got."

Bridget looked down at the grass. She could feel the sun on her neck, and from somewhere nearby came the whirring of insect wings. The conversation she had just overheard replayed itself in her mind. "He's still in love with my mother," she announced to the lawn. "It doesn't make any sense, though. I can't imagine how they ever got together in the first place."

Jeff met her eyes and smiled gently. She didn't know why, but the expression filled her with sadness.

*　*　*

Later that day Bridget walked down to the corner to talk to Melanie.

"Are you too busy?" she asked through the screen door when Melanie appeared on the other side of it. A big red oven mitt covered Melanie's right hand and a dishcloth hung down from where it was tucked into the waist of her jeans.

"Not for you," Melanie assured her. "Come in and tell me if this fudge is okay."

Bridget stepped into the kitchen and felt its warmth encircle her. In this room, the sunlight seemed more golden, more tangible, and almost personal.

"I've had your fudge before," Bridget said, knowing— without having tried to remember—that this was true. "I can already tell you it's delicious."

Melanie looked skeptical. She stood next to the counter, lifting a checked dishcloth from one side of a square pan. "Fudge is tricky. You never know." The rich, tantalizing aroma of chocolate floated out from beneath the cloth. Melanie cut each of them a small piece of fudge, and they sat down at the table to eat.

"I'm not sure it set up just right. Not exactly the right density," Melanie remarked.

"Mmmm," commented Bridget. "Perfect. I think it's perfect. But I admit I have no idea how to make it, so I can't give you any feedback other than that."

Melanie grinned. "Well, that's really the only kind I like to hear anyway."

"My mother was never very interested in cooking," Bridget said. She didn't know why she wanted to confide in Melanie, but it felt good to talk. "I guess she had so many other interests, there wasn't room. Like she just didn't have any passion left to give it."

"And she wouldn't have done anything without passion," agreed Melanie. "She didn't believe in doing things half-heartedly."

"She was so vibrant, so . . . alive. It's hard to imagine that a person like that can die."

Melanie nodded. "I know." They were silent for a little bit, and then Melanie added, "It makes you think about what the essence of a person is. Your mother's gone, her life is over, but her influence will go on indefinitely. Her ideas, her experiences will be part of others' lives. Of course, that's especially true of your mother because so many people read her books. When my father died, he wasn't famous, but it still made me think about the way part of him seemed to stay with us. I started noticing things I did that were like him, things I did that he had taught me. I felt close to him even though I couldn't see him anymore."

Bridget stared down at the table. "I can't imagine ever feeling close to my father."

"Sometimes things we don't think will happen end up happening anyway. You've only known your father for a couple of weeks. You can't decide to give up now."

"Maybe not," Bridget conceded. "But I guess I set myself up with too many expectations. I told myself that I didn't want to come here at all, but part of me did want to."

"Out of curiosity?"

"Yeah. And not just that. I thought maybe I would come here and feel some immediate connection. I always wondered what it would be like to have more of a family. I thought it would be instant belonging."

Melanie smiled, but her eyes were sympathetic. "Families are made up of people. Sometimes maybe we forget that."

"People, as opposed to—"

"As opposed to some kind of perfect beings. Your father isn't perfect. He never will be."

Bridget shrugged. "Okay, of course he's not perfect. But I didn't figure on him being quite like this."

"Like what?"

"So . . . so . . . I don't know. So rigid. So cold. He has to have everything just right."

"Some people place a great deal of value on order. But there is value in order, don't you think?"

"I don't think it matters much whether you start eating breakfast at 7:29 and thirty seconds or 7:31 and ten seconds."

Melanie laughed. "Okay, I agree with you there. Your

father has his little quirks. But I can tell you, he's not a bad man. Try to look beyond the way he's ordered his life. Try to find what's underneath."

Bridget allowed herself a half sigh. "I meant to try, and I haven't really. I guess I got too annoyed. And after today—"

"What happened today?"

"I went out this morning to run. I left a note on the table, but it fell off and no one saw it. So he called the police."

Melanie raised one eyebrow, but she seemed to find it more funny than shocking. "Ah, I warned him. I told him if he wasn't careful, he'd make a fool of himself in front of his oldest daughter."

"When did you warn him?"

"Before you came. He and David and I talked about what it would be like to have you back. He thought he could handle it, but I figured he'd end up doing something like this."

"Why? It's totally unreasonable."

"Not really, if you think about it. Why do people do things that seem unreasonable? Maybe they're acting perfectly logically as they understand the situation. It's just that you understand it a different way."

Bridget shook her head. "There's understanding, and there's wild imagination. Or parental power run amok."

"But think about the background of it. He lost you once. Now he has you back, but only for a little while. It makes him overly cautious."

"If he cares so much about having me back, then why—" Bridget broke off, but Melanie eyed her questioningly.

"Why what?"

"Then why didn't he ever care before? Why didn't he ever write to me?"

Melanie's brow scrunched up. "What? But he did. What are you talking about?"

"What are you talking about? I never heard from him."

"But I know he did," Melanie declared. "He asked my advice on birthday gifts half a dozen times."

"Melanie, I never got a birthday gift from him, not one, not so much as a card." They stared at each other across the table.

"I can't imagine what could have happened," Melanie said slowly.

Bridget took a deep breath. "If you're implying that my mother lied to me and kept his gifts from me," she said as calmly as possible, "then you're just wrong. You've made a mistake."

Melanie glanced away and then stood up and busied herself by polishing a gleaming formica counter. "I wasn't implying that. I wasn't implying anything." She went on polishing and then said carefully, "Even if your mother did interfere with the gifts, I'm sure it was because she thought it was best. Best for you, I mean."

Bridget got to her feet too. "Who do you think my mother was? Can't you see that out of the two of them, it's my father who's the freak?"

Melanie turned to her. "I don't know what happened, Bridget. Neither of us do, we're just jumping to conclusions. But don't throw your relationship with your father away without ever giving him a chance."

"After today it may be too late."

Melanie shook her head. "Not unless you let it be. Look, I know this is a tough time for you. Do you want me to agree that it isn't fair the way things have worked out? Of course it would be better if your father didn't make you work so hard to get to know him. He's the parent, and he should be making more of an effort instead of leaving the burden on you. But in the end, what does all that matter? The circumstances are what they are, and you can let them get worse or try to make them better."

"Sure, that's easy to say," exclaimed Bridget.

"Just try to open up a little corner of your mind where you aren't convinced that your father is a villain."

Bridget looked away. She didn't want to talk about it anymore. There were too many feelings to sort through.

"Thank you for the fudge, Melanie."

"You're welcome." Bridget was almost out the door when Melanie called to her. "Most of the time," Melanie said, "when you think you understand a situation, you don't."

Bridget didn't know what to say to that, so she nodded to show that she had heard and then let the screen door bang shut behind her.

nine

Bridget didn't feel like going straight home, so she walked over to the park she had found that morning. It was empty except for a young family gathered on the playground. The father was pushing his little girl in a swing while the mother sat on a nearby bench holding a baby. From a distance, Bridget could hear the little girl laughing. After a few minutes her father lifted her out of the swing and began to toss her into the air. She flung her little arms out as she flew, and the breeze scattered her hair like a halo around her head. Again Bridget caught the thin, reedy notes of her giggles, and then they mixed with a deeper sound, the father's own laughter.

She didn't want them to notice her staring at them, so she strolled on through the park and turned back to Independence Road. She knew that when she had been that girl's age, she had had a father and a mother, and probably a baby sister too. But she had been a child still when all that had changed. The time she spent alone with her mother had swallowed up everything that had come before, so even though her mother's influence would live on in her, as Melanie said, her father's would never touch her. It was probably true that she had to give her father more of a chance, that she still had to try to get to know him. But she knew that he could never be her daddy now. It was too late for that. Her name might as well be just Bridget Lacey, in spite of what her mother had said.

* * *

At school on Monday, Bridget handed in her essay to Mrs. Keller, and by Thursday afternoon she had it back. The teacher had labeled it with a large red B+, one of the lowest grades Bridget had ever received. The last time Bridget had been unhappy about a grade, her mother had teased, "What's the matter? Did you only get 98 percent?" Actually, it had been 93 percent that time, an A-. She didn't want to argue about the B+ from Mrs. Keller, but she also didn't want to see anymore Bs. The grades she earned this quarter would be the last ones reported to Stanford before the admission decisions were made.

She stopped by Mrs. Keller's desk on the way out of class. "Do you have a minute to talk about the essay?"

The teacher looked up from a stack of quizzes she had been marking in red ink. "Of course," she consented. She took off her glasses and let them dangle from the chain around her neck. Facing her this closely, Bridget thought her nose appeared exceptionally beaklike, and her eyes, without the lenses to distort them, seemed powerful enough to penetrate through any small talk or trivialities.

Bridget got right to the point. "There are no comments on the essay, so I hoped you could give me some specific feedback. Let me know what you thought it was missing so I can do better next time."

Mrs. Keller glared at her, or maybe that was her normal expression. "It was quite good, actually. I was pleased to find a refreshing lack of mechanical problems."

"But you must not have thought it was very good if you only gave it a B+," Bridget persisted.

"Miss McKenna, a B+ is a fine grade. Need I refer you to the grading rubric? A C is for average work. To merit a B+, the essay must be above average."

"I understand. And an A is for something outstanding."

"Naturally."

"Can you give me any advice on reaching that level then?"

"Is that what you expect?" Mrs. Keller questioned, her tone slightly accusatory. "An A?"

"It's what I'd like to get," Bridget assented.

"And have you ever heard of grade inflation?"

"Yes."

"Well, it won't be an issue in my classroom. Your paper was good, but you'll have to dig far deeper next time if you want to approach that level. A trite and formulaic composition does not merit an A. How long did you spend on that paper, Miss McKenna? I know you can do better work than what you gave me."

"But in what way better?" Bridget probed for specifics. "What did you think was trite?"

"The entire analysis was immature and superficial," Mrs. Keller declared. The comment hurt Bridget, but she was determined not to let the teacher see how it had affected her. She focused on keeping her chin set, her head high. "You seem used to getting outstanding marks for above average work. That is not entirely your fault. I suspect your other English teachers gave you your grades on reputation alone, and that was unjust of them. I know your mother's reputation as well as they. I'm going to expect excellent work from you, but I'm not going to give you the grades for it until I receive it. Do you understand?"

"Yes, ma'am," murmured Bridget. She felt deflated as she walked out of the classroom, but by the time she reached the stairs to the lower level her spirits had lifted. After all, she had another paper due Monday. With this one, she promised herself, she would earn her A.

She met Jeff after school as usual but told him she wasn't going straight home. "I've got to buy a present for Lydia," she explained. "Her birthday is tomorrow, and she's having a party tomorrow night."

"I know," said Jeff. He grinned. "I'm invited."

"Do you make it a point to attend all the McKenna birthday parties then?"

"It's my main occupation."

"And what are you giving Lydia?" Bridget asked. "A Barbie doll?"

"Nah, I already used up that idea a few years ago."

"What then?"

Jeff winked. "It's a surprise."

"Oh."

"You sound disappointed."

"Well," Bridget admitted, "I was sort of hoping if you told me what you were getting her, it would give me some ideas. I don't even know where to start."

"I can tell you that," Jeff offered. "Lydia loves to read. I'd start in the bookstore."

So instead of turning toward home, they walked on down to Main Street to the shop where Bridget had seen the Colin book on her second day in Phrygia. For as small a store as it was, it featured an amazing quantity of merchandise; the shelves along the walls reached all the way up to the high ceiling. Bridget found the young adult section and browsed through the titles, but she had no idea what she was looking for. She didn't know what Lydia liked.

After a few minutes she walked over to where Jeff was flipping through *The Secret Lives of Insects*. "I might as well be shopping for a total stranger," she complained. "It's pathetic, but I don't know her at all. I have no idea who she is, if there is anyone under that pouty little face besides a spoiled brat."

"There is," Jeff assured her. "She's just very good at hiding it—amazingly good."

"I can sympathize with her to a point. She's just starting high school—this should be a big year for her. But all the attention gets focused away when this older sister she doesn't even know comes out of nowhere and takes over her room. I'd be upset if I were her too."

"But she's not making things any easier on herself," surmised Jeff.

"No, not at all. If her goal is to make everyone hate her, she's well on her way."

"I know how she can be. Just try not to be too hard on her. Sometimes she acts like she doesn't like people, but it's just that she's afraid they won't like *her*."

"That makes sense," Bridget agreed. "But with me, it's not acting. She really doesn't like me."

"To tell you the truth, Bridget, you never had a chance."

"Why? Because they made her give up her room for me?"

"No, it's more than that. You've got to consider, Lydia's old enough to remember when your mom left."

Bridget pondered this for a little while, strolling back over to the young adult section and from there to the travel section. The salesperson must have noticed that Bridget wasn't getting anywhere because she came over and asked if she could help.

"I don't know," Bridget replied. "I'm looking for something for my sister. She's turning fifteen this week. Do you have any ideas?"

"Hmmm, let me see." The salesperson, a slender woman in her fifties or sixties, glanced around at the various sections of the shop. "Have you thought about giving her a journal?" she suggested. "We sell those as well. Do you know if she has one?"

"I'm not sure. Actually, I don't really know what she has. That's the problem."

Jeff came over to them, carrying a book displaying what looked liked a close-up of a giant frog on the cover. "Hi, Mrs. Stewart."

"Hello, Jeff," the woman smiled. "I thought you might like that." She nodded toward the book.

"Yeah, I think I'll get it."

"Some young men save up for CDs," the woman said to Bridget, "but with Jeff, it's books."

"And his interests are impressively broad," Bridget put in. "They include amphibians as well as insects."

"Does your sister like books on nature?" Mrs. Stewart asked.

"No," Jeff answered for Bridget. "I don't think that's exactly her thing."

"Oh, so you know each other." Mrs. Stewart looked back and forth between them.

"I'm sorry," said Jeff, "I should have introduced you. Mrs. Stewart, this is Bridget McKenna. Bridget, Mrs. Stewart. Her family owns the store."

Bridget began to say "Pleased to meet you," but Mrs. Stewart cut her off. "What? This is Bridget?" she exclaimed. Then she shook her head. "I should have known. You're the image of your mother, you know. It's been a long time, but I should have known."

Bridget glanced self-consciously toward the window display at the front of the store, where a picture of her mother smiled up from the back of the latest Colin novel.

"I never thought there was much resemblance, except for the coloring," she muttered.

Mrs. Stewart followed her gaze. "It's easier for other people to see those kinds of things," she said. Her large blue eyes behind round, silver-rimmed glasses moved back to focus on Bridget. "I almost thought it wasn't right to put that book out there. I'll take it down if you like."

Bridget blinked at her with surprise. "No, I wouldn't expect you to do that."

"I don't like the way the booksellers have made her death seem like a marketing ploy."

Bridget had had the same thought herself, but she didn't think Mrs. Stewart should have to put the book away either.

"You wouldn't believe how many phone calls I've had about it," Mrs. Stewart went on. "From the publisher and her former agent, and then from other bookstores—for the first few weeks, I couldn't sit down for answering the phone. Everyone thought since she had lived here, we should have some big to-do. They wanted to have an event with people who had known her here to answer questions about her."

"I'm sure it would have brought in a lot of business," Bridget said.

"That's the kind of business I don't need," Mrs. Stewart announced. "I'm not going to try to make a profit off somebody's tragedy, and I'm not having people in here spouting their silly opinions about the intimate details of her life. That's nobody business and certainly nothing I ever want to hear."

Bridget wondered what the townspeople would have said about her. Who here had been her mother's friends? Who might Mrs. Stewart have asked to speak about her? She couldn't help suspecting that her mother would have approved of the posthumous attention, even if it all seemed a bit macabre. "I don't think all those people who called you realize that she was a real person. I'm glad you do, Mrs. Stewart."

"Oh, it's different for all of us here. We knew her before she was the famous M. C. Lacey. We're not blinded by the glory streaming from her reputation. We know she had faults. We watched her throw her marriage away. We saw her abandon her little children and put her oldest daughter in danger."

The last part of this speech annoyed Bridget intensely. "She didn't put me in danger," she informed Mrs. Stewart coolly. "I'm fine. We're all fine now."

"Now, yes, but it's in spite of what she did, not because of it. And I'm not going to have people in here pretending she was something she wasn't. She wrote good books, and I'll sell them as long as people want to buy them. But that's the end of it."

Jeff cleared his throat. "So, Mrs. Stewart, do you think you have anything here that Lydia might like?"

*   *   *

On the way home, with a big hardbound copy of *Images of Europe* bumping against her knee, Bridget told Jeff, "I think 'abandon' is a strong word."

"Hmm," said Jeff.

"It implies, well, that she never communicated with them after the divorce, or that she just left them irresponsibly somewhere, like at a bus station. She left them with a parent."

"True," Jeff assented.

"And why should everyone assume that the divorce was her fault? I mean, they know my father. Obviously it couldn't be that easy to live with him."

"Hmm."

"I just don't understand why she ever married him in the first place."

"Maybe he was different then," Jeff proposed.

"Maybe."

"A lot of times a divorce has a big effect on a person."

"Yeah, well, I guess it should. It's a serious thing."

"Bridget?"

"Yeah?"

"Do you remember the day your mother left? Do you remember what it was like?"

Bridget stopped walking so she could face him. "Why?"

"I've just wondered."

"But why? Why are you asking this? What does it have to do with anything?"

Jeff shrugged. "Nothing, I guess."

They started walking again, but the question nagged at Bridget. "Do you remember that day?" she asked. "I want to know why you asked about it."

"I don't really remember it. I remember what happened after."

She frowned at him. "What happened?"

"It was just a shock to everyone, you know?"

"People get divorced all the time. Why should it be such a shock?"

"Do you remember that day?" he asked again.

"Sure, I guess so. I remember the drive across the country. It went on forever. By the time we got to California, I thought I had lived my whole life on that drive."

"But when you actually left. What happened?"

"I don't know." Bridget felt confused and, underneath that, angry. "I don't know why you're asking me this. If you have something to tell me, just say it."

Jeff stared at her for a moment and then shook his head. "I don't have anything to say. People in this town talk too much, if you ask me. You're right, she shouldn't have said that about your sisters being abandoned."

They walked on home and said good-bye as if nothing had happened, but Bridget knew she would never feel quite so open with Jeff again. Not when he kept acting strange, as if her mother had something to be ashamed of. Clearly Mrs. Stewart blamed Bridget's mother for the McKennas' divorce, and when Bridget had gone shopping for school supplies, Mrs. Haverley at the drugstore had bitten back some unkind epithet at the last moment—but they were all wrong about Margaret McKenna. Bridget couldn't believe how judgmental people could be, especially nowadays when women had careers and everything just like men. If her father had been the one to leave, people wouldn't have been so hard on him, Bridget thought, and if he had actually taken one of his children with him, they would have extolled him as a saint. Why did people talk as though only the mother were a true parent and the father some nearly obsolete biological necessity? But on the other hand, she reminded herself, wasn't that exactly what her father had become? A contributor of twenty-three of forty-six chromosomes?

Aside from eating dinner, she spent the rest of the evening in her room working on her next paper for Mrs. Keller.

t e n

That night Bridget lay awake for hours thinking of her mother and their long drive out to California. It had taken on the aura of an epic journey, a legend so colossal that it seemed to block out everything immediately around it. What had that first day been like, the day they left? She couldn't tell if she was remembering it or simply fabricating the sort of details that fit. She tried to probe further back.

When had she found out that her parents were getting a divorce? It must have been upsetting. Why couldn't she pinpoint the exact moment? Had she heard them fighting for weeks or months before? She pictured herself crouched in her room, frightened, listening to the echoes of angry voices. But she wasn't inside that picture, she was observing it from a distance, so she knew she hadn't really lived it.

If she hadn't heard them fighting then, had their split taken her by surprise? How had they broken it to her? Had they sat her down with Lydia and Charly in a sort of family council? She imagined her father gathering them into his office and towering over them from behind his massive desk. "Children," he might have said, "I'm afraid your mother isn't going to be able to live here anymore. She doesn't starch her shirts and she's been late to breakfast twice. I simply cannot tolerate that kind of behavior." He would have been wearing a suit with a silk tie, the way he always was, but her mother would have dressed in something light and floaty. She wouldn't have settled in one of the little wooden chairs either; she would have hovered about by the window like a butterfly, pursing her lips against a whoop of irreverent laughter.

Of course it hadn't happened that way. Her father had probably thought they were all too young for a family council.

What then? Nothing. Everything had been decided without her. They hadn't ever told her, not until it was time to go. Only then did her mother explain, "We're not going to see Daddy anymore."

Was that real? Or a dream? She couldn't tell. She stared up hard into the darkness above her bed as if the answer might be hanging there just out of sight. But there was darkness inside her mind and darkness without, and the only words that came were another question. During those years in California, had her father written to her after all?

No, she told herself. *No, definitely not.* She had never received anything from him, and her mother wouldn't have interfered. She tried to remember exactly what Melanie had said. Something about him asking for advice about birthday presents. Well, that didn't mean anything. He might have thought, once or twice, about sending her something, talked it over with Melanie, and then decided against it. Or not decided anything at all and simply forgotten about it until some other year.

She sat up abruptly and switched on the light. She wanted her mother and there was no use in denying it, no use in trying to push the ache away. She longed to pad quietly into her mother's office and find her curled up in front of her computer, smiling over Colin's latest adventure. "You're up late, sweetie," her mother might have said, because she had kept using pet names like *sweetie* and *precious* even when Bridget was too grown up for them. Sliding out of bed now, Bridget opened one of her drawers and lifted out her wooden treasure box with the leatherbound Colin books on top. She needed to read her mother's words, words that had started out in her mother's mind and, unlike other thoughts, had not been allowed to fade away into nothingness. The thick white pages and black ink were tangible enough, but something intangible hung around them—her mother's essence, maybe her soul.

Bridget chose one of the later volumes, the one where Colin ran for president of his eighth-grade class. She opened up to the page that told about Colin standing at the podium in front of an auditorium full of students. This scene had always puzzled Bridget, because somehow her mother had understood how scary it could be to have a thousand pairs of eyes on you, even though in real life, public appearances had never ruffled her. No, she liked the attention, she had never felt afraid. But all along there had been this secret part of her that knew what it was like to be someone else, that could feel someone else's feelings. Bridget supposed that was what made her a good writer, but she hadn't been just a writer, she had been a person too. There was so much of her that Bridget had never been able to know, but maybe it wasn't too late. As long as she still had Colin . . .

* * *

Colin's mind raced—or at least it would have if it had been capable of functioning at all. He felt as though someone had poured ice water into his ear and frozen everything inside his head. Now his brain struggled to turn over like a car engine in the cold. He willed his mind to think—THINK—but nothing happened. He groped around for an idea, or a sentence, or even a word, but all he could get hold of was a great spreading blank, and everyone knows that you can't hold on to a blank.

A few of the students started to titter. Frozen and helpless, Colin watched as they shifted restlessly in their seats, fanning themselves with notebooks and launching spit wads into the pouffy, permed hair of unsuspecting girls in the next row. He tried to swallow, but someone had coated his mouth with velvet when he wasn't paying attention. His legs shook uncontrollably, but they still supported him, and the podium kept them hidden from everyone except the row of people seated behind him, the teachers supervising the campaigns, his opponents, and worst of all, his own campaign manager, Kristy.

Don't let Kristy see this, he thought. There, a sentence! He had not lost all mental power. He opened his mouth. "I . . ." he began. "I . . . I . . . I would like to tell you why I would be a good choice for president." He had finally said something, but what came next? He couldn't remember why he would be a good president. He really had no idea.

He heard a scraping sound behind him as a metal chair leg slid across the polished wooden floor of the stage. Three quick footsteps followed, and then someone had grasped his hand, the one that hung down behind the podium. Kristy reached out with her other hand to adjust the microphone so that they could both speak into it. Colin felt a pressure against his palm, and then she let it drop.

"Colin is having a hard time with his speech today," Kristy declared, "because he doesn't like to brag about himself. It's the hardest thing for him to do. Unlike some other people," she cast the swiftest glance back at the other candidates, "he doesn't like to talk himself up. In my opinion, that's a good quality in a president. He's not all talk, he's about actually getting stuff done. I've been working with him on this campaign for a few weeks now, and I know he's got some great ideas. I'm going to let him tell you about them now." In that almost-private space behind the podium, she touched his hand again. He could feel the warmth of her skin long after she had taken a step back to give him full access to the microphone.

"Yeah, I've got some ideas," Colin echoed as the warmth

traveled up his arm toward his brain. "I think it's time to let the office of president mean something. I know it's the president's job to make sure we've got some good activities, dances and stuff, and some cool assemblies. That's important. But I think the president can do more than that. Maybe it'd just be small stuff at first, but we could still make a difference. Like, what about meeting with school administrators and getting more choices in the lunchroom? A potato bar maybe." Colin paused, surprised, as a few students broke into applause. "I've been thinking maybe we could set up a committee of students and teachers to maybe—I don't know—help with communication. Like, if a student had a problem with a teacher, they could have someone to go to besides just the principal. The committee could hear them out and try to get things resolved. And if students had ideas or wanted things changed, they could come to me or to the committee and we could work on it." Colin took a deep breath. The words came fast now, so fast he almost couldn't keep up. "I think it's time for all of us to get more involved and take more responsibility for what happens around here. This is like our job, and our parents like to have a say in what happens where they work. That's why there are unions and stuff. This is our school where we come almost every day, so we shouldn't just sit back and let someone else make all the decisions. So if you want to do that, don't vote for me. But if you want to see what someone in this office can do, then give me your vote and get ready for the best year ever!" The room erupted into movement as students jumped up in their seats to whistle and cheer. Colin felt a smile spreading across his face, and when he turned to gaze at his campaign manager, he saw that it had spread to Kristy too.

* * *

Bridget moaned and opened her eyes. Someone had been shaking her roughly. She wanted to tell them to go away, but she was too tired to open her mouth.

"Come on, Bridget, it's late," insisted the nag, who turned out to be Charly. The room was full of sunlight. Bridget couldn't remember falling asleep. The Colin book she had been reading lay open beside her on the bed. The upper corner of one of the pages was bent back slightly, and a little wet smear ran down the margin where she had drooled on it. "Yuck," she exclaimed.

"What?" Charly drew back. "If you mean breakfast, it's not that bad. Sometimes Mrs. Prescott likes to try new recipes, that's all. Mr. Prescott doesn't like her to do it at home."

"What?" grumbled Bridget, confused.

"What?" Charly echoed. Then she shook her head impatiently, bouncing the light brown hair that tumbled loose across her shoulders. "It's late. You've gotta hurry. Dad'll be waiting."

Bridget scooted out of bed and across the hall into the bathroom. The face that stared back at her from the mirror was puffy, and one cheek was distorted with a waffle-weave pattern that had pressed into her skin from her pajamas. She scowled at herself and then splashed cold water onto her face and pulled a brush through her hair. As she rushed downstairs, trying to get dressed as she went, a strange aroma greeted her, and she surmised that it originated from Mrs. Prescott's experimental new dish, which turned out to involve brussels sprouts.

"Brussels sprouts for breakfast?" she could hear Charly saying dubiously. Everyone was sitting at the table already, and Natalie was there too, but no one frowned at her as she approached. Her father was leaning back in his chair and smiling, appearing more relaxed than she had ever seen him. He was holding Natalie's hand.

"Yes," he said to Charly, "I think it's a very . . . nutritious idea, don't you?"

Lydia giggled. "But why today?" she asked. "I thought it would be chocolate chip pancakes. She knows they're my favorite."

"That's what Mrs. Prescott would make if she didn't like you so much. Chocolate chip pancakes aren't very healthy."

"Yeah, not like brussels sprouts." Charly's face scrunched up. "She sure likes us a whole lot."

"Happy birthday, Lydia," Bridget greeted her sister as she pulled out her chair and sat down. "Good morning, Natalie."

Her father cleared his throat and let go of Natalie's hand. Natalie smiled at Bridget across the table. "Looks like this delicious aroma has penetrated to the third floor and brought down another enthusiastic eater." She winked to show that she was kidding, but Bridget remembered Charly saying something about Natalie not letting her kids eat pizza. Bridget wondered if Natalie was really into health food—maybe even brussels sprouts for breakfast.

"Okay, now that we're all here you can tell," prodded Lydia. Everyone already had food on their plates, but no one was eating much. Charly poked around, trying to separate a piece of egg from one of the offending sprouts.

"Wait," said Mr. McKenna. "It isn't time yet. It's only 7:33."

"What are we waiting for?" Bridget asked. "Is Mrs. Prescott going to pop out of a giant carrot or something?"

"Shh," Charly warned. "She's in the kitchen. That's why we all have to be nice."

"That's not it," contradicted Mr. McKenna in a whisper. "I meant every word I said. This is a very nutritious meal."

"Yeah, exactly," agreed Charly, scrunching up her face again.

"We have to wait until 7:41 because that's what time Lydia was born," Natalie explained. "She's not fifteen until then."

Mr. McKenna glanced at his watch. "Seven more minutes of fourteen to go." He picked up a fork and waved it in Lydia's direction like a reporter with a microphone. "Tell us, Miss McKenna, what has this year been like for you? Can you share some highlights with your devoted fans?"

Bridget stared at her father in amazement. She wondered fleetingly if he'd been drinking, but all she could smell beneath the odor of brussels sprouts was aftershave.

"Oh, I'd have to say the biggest highlight was at the end," Lydia responded, "when my father promised me my own car for my sixteenth birthday. Look to the future, I always say."

Mr. McKenna held the fork up to his own mouth and spoke into it. "You hear that, ladies and gentleman? I have always been impressed by this young woman's passion for health and fitness. Not only is she celebrating her birthday with brussels sprouts, she's looking forward to having a new ten-speed bicycle next year. What a superb role model!"

Lydia laughed. "You have brussels sprouts in your ears! The words *car* and *bicycle* don't sound anything alike!"

Mr. McKenna smiled and used his fork to spear one of the sprouts. He put it whole into his mouth and chewed enthusiastically. When he had swallowed, he said, "I suggest we eat. Although Lydia's birthday certainly should be a national holiday, it isn't, and we all have places to go."

An amiable silence took over as everyone made a little more effort to pick out bits of egg. What made things so different this morning, Bridget wanted to know. Was it Natalie? Was it some change in her father? Was this the real him, or was he truly the solemn patriarch he had appeared to be before? She thought of what Charly had told her about him being "funny" sometimes, but nice. She wasn't convinced, though, until she saw more.

At 7:41, Mr. McKenna laid down his fork. "Fifteen years ago this moment, our Lydia came into the world." He spoke the words with such ceremony that Bridget half expected the Gettysburg address to follow.

"Tell the story!" Charly urged.

"It was a dark and stormy night," Mr. McKenna obliged. "The rain had been coming down in sheets for hours. We had barely made it to the hospital when they closed some of the roads. Lydia might have been born in the car somewhere, or here at home. The storm raged on and on. The lightning was intense. The electricity went out, and the hospital had to use its backup generator. The storm just wouldn't quit, and Lydia was taking her time about getting here. Then, suddenly, at 7:41 a.m., Lydia finally showed up. It was amazing. At almost the same moment, the storm died down and a ray of sunshine came out. It made such an impression, we thought of naming her Sunny."

"And thank goodness you didn't!" exclaimed Lydia, rolling her eyes exaggeratedly but unable to keep from smiling.

"Oh, come on, Sunshine, it's what I call you anyway."

"Dad, if you say anything like that tonight," she warned, serious now, "I'll hold it against you the rest of my life. I swear I'll die of the humiliation."

"Well then, I won't have to go unforgiven for very long." He winked, and then as he turned his attention back to his brussels sprouts, his eye caught Bridget's accidentally. Bridget glanced away quickly, embarrassed, but she could feel her father's gaze still on her. She braced herself to meet his eyes again, raising her eyebrows into a question.

"Bridget," her father muttered thoughtfully. "We brought Lydia home to Bridget."

Lydia's eyes darted to Bridget's face, and her expression hardened, but Charly was already begging Mr. McKenna to tell more.

"I used to bring Miss Bridget something every time I came home," he said, not looking at them now but at some indefinite spot on the tablecloth near his plate. "Very small things most of the time, of course, like a pretty leaf or a chestnut. She would come running from wherever she was to meet me on the front lawn or just inside the door, and she'd say, 'What did you bring me, Daddy?' Then I'd tease her and pretend that I hadn't brought her anything because I'd forgotten, and I'd let her look in my coat pockets and open up my briefcase, keeping the present hidden all the time in my hand or somewhere. Whenever she'd find it she'd get so excited. That's why I kept doing it. I've never seen anyone get so excited about something I could pick up off the sidewalk on the way home. Well, no one except . . . At any rate, I'd say, 'Do you like it, bonny Bridget?' and she'd answer, 'I love it, Daddy.' When we brought Lydia home, I thought I'd make a joke on Bridget. I got out of the car by myself, and Bridget came running. I picked her up and she cried, 'What did you bring me, Daddy?' I told her nothing, I'd forgotten. She looked in my pockets and couldn't find anything, so she ran to the car and heaved open one of the doors. She was so little, it almost knocked her down. It was an old Chrysler back then, big as a ship. But Bridget scrambled in and saw Lydia there in her car seat, and Bridget started yelling, 'It's a baby, you brought me a baby!' So I asked her, 'Do you like her, bonny Bridget?' And Bridget said, 'I love her!'"

Lydia twisted up her mouth as if she had swallowed vinegar and stared at Bridget with disgust. Natalie smiled at Mr. McKenna and laid her hand across his on the table, making him tense up visibly. He seemed to come to himself then. Suddenly the stares of his captive audience annoyed him. "It's time I was going," he announced, and his voice had lost something; it sounded hollow. "Happy birthday, Lydia." He took his cloth napkin from across his lap and set it next to his plate, then stood and walked to the front door, neglecting his usual ritual of kissing Charly and Lydia on the tops of the heads.

"See you tonight, Gerry," Natalie called. He lifted one arm in a sort of wave but didn't turn around before pulling the front door shut behind him.

eleven

That morning at school, Bridget painted a ceramic pencil holder that she had made a few days earlier by rolling the clay into long snakes, squishing the ends together, and stacking them. She painted every snake a different color.

"I like it," Mr. Farnsworth commented when she placed it on the shelf to dry at the end of class. "It's bold." He grinned at her, and she smiled back.

Later, while she sat at her desk waiting for Mrs. Keller's class to begin, she pulled out the draft of the paper that she would turn in on Monday and skimmed through it. When she happened to glance up midway through her reading to look at the clock, she met a pair of blue eyes instead. They belonged to the boy who sat in front of her. His name was Matt, if she remembered right. She had only seen the back of his head before and a little bit of the side of his face. Now he was twisted around in his chair, gazing straight at her. He looked different from that angle. She gasped softly, and the paper slipped out of her hand to flutter down onto her desk.

The boy seemed startled for an instant but quickly regained his cool. "What?" he asked in a low voice. Mrs. Keller had come in and was rifling through the papers on her desk. "I knew I was good-looking, but don't faint over it. If you do, though, I'll be here to catch you."

Bridget let her face relax until it felt perfectly bland.

"Thanks, but that won't be necessary," she refused drily. He *was* good-looking, she saw now, with dark hair to go with his blue eyes. A pair of broad shoulders filled out his T-shirt nicely, but she noted these details without much interest. It had been the eyes that struck her. She had seen eyes like that before, blue and intense, only now they were in the wrong face. This wasn't Justin's twin—or Justin himself—staring at her. *You're in New York*, she reminded herself firmly. Podunk, boondocky Phyrgia, New York, and Justin is back in California kissing Suzanne. Or maybe even someone else by now.

"I'm Matt," the boy in front of her was saying. He had turned his face away slightly so that he was looking at her sideways out of the corners of his eyes, which gleamed under long, dark lashes. "I've seen you around."

"Yeah, well, you don't miss much, do you? I've only been sitting back here a couple of weeks."

"What can I say? Nothing gets past me." He winked and turned to face forward as Mrs. Keller walked to the front of the class.

"I hope you've all done your reading," the teacher declared forebodingly as she began to distribute sheets of paper. "At any rate, we shall soon see." A few groans rose up and were cut off by the force of Mrs. Keller's glare. When one of the papers was passed to Bridget, she saw that it was a quiz with about ten short-answer questions. She read through them quickly and wrote down her responses, feeling confident. All the questions seemed straightforward. She had enough time left to check over her work before Mrs. Keller collected all the papers.

After class Matt spoke to her again. "I gave you a couple of weeks to ease into things, you know—enjoy the view of the back of my head before I turned on the full force of my charm."

"Oh, brother," groaned Bridget, but it flattered her to

think that maybe he had noticed her before. She tried to pretend that it didn't because she never wanted to be one of those girls that melts anytime a cute guy so much as speaks to her. She feared if she wasn't careful she might prove to be that stupid.

"Now that you're over the first shock," Matt continued, "we should talk more." He had his head cocked to one side again. Bridget noticed that the writing on his T-shirt said something about a race.

"Do you run track?" she asked.

He raised one eyebrow inquisitively. "Yeah, I do hurdles. How'd you know?" He folded his arms across his chest and widened his stance, obviously proud that she had identified him so quickly as an athlete.

"It's written all over your shirt," Bridget told him.

For an instant he looked embarrassed—actually blushed. She could see a flush of red burning down into his neck. This was the second time that she had caught him off guard. He wasn't really like Justin at all, she decided. His layer of smoothness was too thin. Still, he was working at it. The redness disappeared in a moment. "Right. I don't believe in hiding my accomplishments," he joked. "Well, see you around, Bridget."

"Yeah, I'll be right behind you again tomorrow," she called after him as he strode out into the hallway. She finished gathering up her things and followed him out of the classroom. When she reached her locker, the girl with the locker next to hers asked, "What are you so happy about? Didn't you just come from Keller the Killer's class?"

"Do I look happy?" Bridget wondered, surprised. "I thought I just had my normal expression."

"Not unless your normal expression could be used for a toothpaste ad."

"I was smiling?"

"Yeah," laughed the girl, whose name was Laurie. "Did

you just get a big kiss from your boyfriend or something?"
She laughed some more.

"Nah, I guess I just like to spread cheer. Call me the
morale manager," Bridget told her. She shook her head as
she walked away, maybe trying to shake away the smile. She
had liked Matt's attention, and most of all she had liked his
eyes. It had been a long time since she had looked into eyes
like that—since before her mother died—because Justin
had never looked at her after the accident. Well, that wasn't
exactly true. He had never made eye contact again, but he
had watched her from a distance, across the food court or
from the other side of a classroom. She had felt his gaze
boring into her and had turned to confront him, and he had
always been too fast for her, always turning away at the right
instant to study the back of his hand or the slice of pizza on
his lunch tray. Maybe for the first time in his life Justin had
come up against something he didn't know how to handle.
Funny that that should happen; she was sure nothing less
than death could fluster him. She would swear that he had
never blushed the way Matt did, never in his life. He was too
much in control of things.

She thought about the way he'd asked her out to the
prom. He had convinced eleven friends to give her one rose
each throughout the day—the first guy had come up to her
as she entered the school grounds, others had been waiting outside her classrooms. One approached her at lunch
while she was sitting outside working trigonometry problems. Finally Justin himself had delivered the twelfth rose.
She had already left the building and was strolling along
the Promenade, a long covered walkway that edged along
one side of the outdoor food court. With some imagination,
it might have been the inner garden of a European villa.
Justin had dressed in a tuxedo and slicked his hair back.
She wondered if he had used an entire bottle of mousse. He
knelt down right on the sidewalk, which she thought was

a mistake since it was pretty dirty and the tux was only rented. "Bridget McKenna," he had boomed, taking her hand, "will you go to the prom with me?" She had almost expected his teeth to twinkle the way the hero's teeth did in old movies. The whole scene felt like something played out on a stage, with Justin's voice powerful enough to carry to the far reaches of the theater. He knew how to put on a good show. His dad was an actor who commuted to New York and L.A. and had worked on location on just about every continent. Bridget knew her role in the story, so she smiled graciously and gushed, "Yes, Justin, yes. I'd love to." A handful of students applauded, and Bridget suspected that that thrilled Justin as much as her answer.

It hadn't always been so great sharing the spotlight around Justin, who was the leader at anything he did at school, from drama club to basketball. She wasn't poised and eternally nonchalant like her mother; she didn't always know the right thing to say. But there were those moments of happiness, of belonging, that pulled her in and held her so that she never wanted to let go.

"What are you smiling about?" Jeff asked her when she met him after school.

"Oh, nothing," she said, but then she added, "I just thought of one good thing about being in New York."

"Really? Only one?"

She laughed. "Hey, it's a start."

"Well, what is it?"

"It clears the mind," she replied. "A little distance can do that."

"Sounds good," Jeff agreed. "What were you fogged up about before?"

"Oh, there was this guy . . ." She glanced over at Jeff, at his pleasant, round face and slightly buggy eyes, and suddenly she saw blue eyes instead. "I love you, Bridget," Justin had whispered into her hair, and she had relaxed against him, swaying to the music that filtered tinnily out through the open door of the event center to the parking lot where they stood dancing in the darkness. She had worn a deep red dress, and she remembered thinking it must clash with the row of fire engines lined up at the fire station next door. She had wanted to laugh out loud because she felt so happy and free and someone was holding her close.

"Bridget?" Jeff waved a hand in front of her face. "I thought you said your mind had been cleared. I think it might have up and left the building instead."

She grinned at him. "Sorry. I was just thinking."

"About . . . that guy . . ."

"About fire engines," she said, and she kept laughing in short bursts all the way home.

Jeff came inside with her to help set up for the party. They found Mrs. Prescott in the kitchen arranging strawberry slices on top of a tall, pink cake. Bridget set Jeff up slicing celery and carrots for a vegetable tray and got out the ingredients for a seven-layer nacho dip. A few minutes later the door to the dining room swung out to admit Lydia, who took one look at the cake and cried, "Pink! The cake can't be pink!"

Mrs. Prescott fumbled with one of the strawberry slices and turned to Lydia aghast. "But Lydia, you always have a pink cake. Every year. Why, I've seen a picture of your very first birthday, and guess what color the cake was—pink!"

"That's just it," Lydia moaned, "I'm not a baby anymore! I can't have a pink cake this year. Not this year. What will everyone think?"

Jeff walked over and put a hand on her shoulder. "Come on, Lydia, you know it's going to taste good. That's what will matter to everybody."

"No it won't," Lydia insisted, shrugging him off. "I'm in high school now. They'll all think this is a little kid party."

Mrs. Prescott shook her head. "Now, hon, it'll be the

same friends you've always had. Nothing's going to be that different, and they've always liked pink cake before. I've never heard any complaints. It's always gotten gobbled up pretty quick too."

"But, Mrs. Prescott, this year there will be boys!"

"Boys? Well, what do you think they are, some whole different kind of creature? I daresay they like cake too."

Bridget smiled down at the dip, but Lydia saw her and stalked over to stand next to her. "So you think this is so funny, right?"

Bridget looked at her younger sister and felt something new pierce through her, a pinprick of sympathy. "I was just thinking that Mrs. Prescott isn't far off. Boys can seem like total aliens sometimes. But she's also right—they do like cake, no matter what color."

"The truth is," put in Jeff, "they probably won't even notice the color. Guys don't pay attention to stuff like that."

"Yeah," Bridget agreed quickly. "Just make Jeff turn around—go on Jeff, no peeking. Now ask him what color of shirt I'm wearing today. He's been with me all day, and I bet he hasn't even noticed."

Jeff had turned away good-naturedly. "Uh, I'd say Bridget's shirt is purple. No, wait, blue."

"See?" Bridget said. "Why don't we go pick out some music to put on. We can scoot the chairs and sofa back so that people can dance. It's going to be fun!"

Lydia sighed hopelessly but headed out of the kitchen with Bridget behind her. Lydia had passed through the swinging door already when Jeff stepped close and said softly, "That shirt thing might have been a bad example. How could I not notice that it's green, exactly the same shade as your eyes?"

Bridget glanced up at him with astonishment before following Lydia through the door. She really hadn't expected him to remember.

Up in Lydia's bedroom the girls sorted through several stacks of CDs and chose half a dozen to use for the evening. Back downstairs, Lydia put an Avril Lavigne CD in the player, and Jeff helped Bridget push the furniture aside. By then Mrs. Prescott had filled the table with a tempting spread of munchies, and the pink cake, now topped with fifteen candles, towered regally in the center.

By six o'clock the guests began to arrive. Three or four girls came first and stood around in a circle by the table, taking an occasional tortilla chip and chatting with Lydia about school. When the boys started to show up, they said hi nervously to the group of girls and dove into the refreshments until there were enough guys to form their own group. By 6:30, most everyone had come, and the boys and girls were still hovering in separate groups at opposite ends of the table. Bridget recognized several of the kids from church and figured that a boy-girl party had to be a new experience for them. She was surprised that her father had permitted it and that the other kids' parents had allowed them to come. Of course, not all the kids were Mormons, and maybe Mr. McKenna was sensitive enough to care about letting his daughters fit in with the mostly non-Mormon students at school. Maybe—or maybe he just put an awful lot of trust in Mrs. Prescott as a chaperone.

Bridget observed the guests for a few more minutes and then left her post by the front door and went over to Lydia. "What do you think? Should we get some games going?"

Lydia looked at her pleadingly. "Yeah, we need something."

"Don't worry, the games will break the ice." She raised her voice to address the crowd. "All right, everyone, grab one last chip and come on over to the living room, we're going to play some games." She walked away from the table into the center of the room, drawing the guests with her. "We need a big circle—everyone gather round and sit down on the floor." The boys sat together on one side, the girls on the other, but they had formed a tolerably good circle so she didn't complain.

"Okay, we're going to play Catch the Signal—maybe some of you have played this before. You all choose something to be your signal, something casual and inconspicuous like scratching your nose or tucking your hair behind your ear. Start thinking now about what you might want to use. We all learn everyone's signal and then we pass them back and forth. For example, if I start, and Lydia's signal is playing with an earring, like this, I'm going to look at Lydia and signal her. She repeats the signal to show that she saw me, then she chooses someone else's signal and signals them. What's your name?" she asked a blond boy in a Yankees T-shirt.

"Dave," he replied.

"Okay, say Dave's signal is scratching his chin." She had noticed him doing that earlier, as if he were checking for facial hair. "Lydia scratches her chin to signal Dave. Dave does his signal to accept, then he's got to signal someone else. One person stands in the middle and tries to figure out who has the signal. It's tougher than it might sound! Does everyone have a signal chosen?" She went around the circle until everyone had decided on a signal and shown it to the group, then she stepped out of the circle and let one of the boys be the first person in the middle. He closed his eyes while the others chose someone to get the signaling started. Everything seemed to be going smoothly; people were laughing as they winked and scratched and twitched back and forth without letting the guy in the middle see. It reminded Bridget of passing notes at school, when the whole conversation is all the more thrilling just because the teacher may catch you at any moment.

Bridget went into the kitchen to talk to Jeff and Mrs. Prescott. Charly was peeking out through the swinging door. After a while she reported, "I think they may be ready for a new game." Bridget went back in and got them started on something different. She figured they needed to get better acquainted, so she had them get into a semicircle with two people sitting in front of them. The people in front were each to tell some little-known fact about themselves or some past adventure, but one person told the truth while the other lied, and the group had to guess who was telling the truth. They had a good time for about fifteen minutes and then started to get restless. Bridget was running out of ideas for group games, so she asked Lydia if she wanted to have cake and ice cream and then start the dancing. Mrs. Prescott had been right—no one complained about the pink cake, and several of the kids came back for seconds. *Too bad, though,* thought Bridget, *that they separated out again into groups of boys and girls while they ate.* She hoped the dancing would get them back together.

But when the cake had been eaten, the paper plates thrown away, and the music turned up, no one made a move toward the makeshift dance floor. Bridget poked her head into the kitchen, where Jeff was finishing his third piece of cake. "This is serious," she told him. "Everyone's too nervous. No one wants to be the first one out there."

"Don't worry," Jeff said. He put his plate in the sink and came into the living room. He went straight to Lydia, who was sort of slumped against the wall amid several nervous-looking girls, her eyes downcast.

Jeff stopped in front of her and gave an exaggerated bow. "My dear Lydia," he said in fake, supersuave voice, "may I please have this dance?"

Bridget held her breath, worried that Lydia might be embarrassed, but instead the girl broke into a smile. "Well, yes, of course," she accepted.

Jeff took her hand and led her out onto the dance floor. Pink was singing "Get This Party Started," and the two of them began moving enthusiastically to the music. Bridget couldn't help smiling at some of Jeff's creative moves. Soon another boy had crossed the room and asked a girl to dance, and two friends were right behind him. Five minutes later, the sidelines had been completely abandoned in favor of the dance floor. Jeff kept things going by acting as the DJ.

Bridget's father came home through the back door around 8:30. "How's it going?" he asked Mrs. Prescott, who was cleaning up the kitchen before leaving for home. Bridget stood next to her, making a second batch of dip.

Mrs. Prescott nodded toward the swinging door. "See for yourself."

Mr. McKenna went over to look into the living room. He grinned when he turned back to them. "I was worried," he admitted. "But so far neither of my concerns has materialized. They're not playing kissing games or standing around holding up the walls, too scared to talk to each other."

"Thank Jeff for that," Bridget said. "He got the dancing started."

"Really? Well, he's been hanging around here so long, I knew he'd be good for something someday."

Mr. McKenna seemed to be back in his happy mood from that morning, and Bridget found herself hoping that he would stick around and talk, but soon he was on his way out again. "I'm meeting Natalie," he explained. "I'll see you two later. Keep things under control for me, Bridget, okay?"

"So that means no kissing games?" she teased.

"That's it," he said, tossing a smile over his shoulder at her as he disappeared out the back door.

Bridget put the finishing touches on a second dish of dip and carried it to the dining room table. She scanned the crowd of dancers for Lydia and found her right in the middle, dancing with Jeff again. Lydia wore an expression Bridget had never seen on her face before. The sarcasm and disdain had gone, and without them Lydia looked younger. The uncomplicated happiness that shone from her eyes and the way her cheeks flushed pink from activity reminded Bridget of a small child, a little girl with dark hair and a red mouth running to show Bridget what she had found.

"See, Bridget, a pink rock! See my pretty rock."

Bridget caught her breath. The memory had surfaced without warning, but it sank away again just as quickly, leaving Bridget wondering if it had been real. The song on the CD player ended and the tangle of dancers broke up as people headed over to the refreshment table. Jeff walked over and poured himself a glass of Kool-Aid.

"I'm too ancient to be hanging out with these spry fourteen- and fifteen-year-olds," he complained. "They're wearing me out." A few beads of sweat had gathered at his hairline. He lifted the glass to his forehead to press it against his warm skin. "I'm gonna need a cane pretty soon."

"Maybe my father has one he can loan you."

"If not, there's always Mr. Prescott's walker next door. I think he's got a couple of them, so I'm sure he wouldn't mind if I borrowed one."

"You know, it might be easier if you just sit down for a while," Bridget suggested.

"Yeah," Jeff agreed, but he made no move to leave his place next to the table. "Charly told me you play the guitar," he said.

"Really? When?"

"Earlier tonight when we were in the kitchen. She says you're good."

Bridget shrugged. "I want to get better."

"Maybe some practice would help you."

"I guess it's the only thing that would."

Jeff finished his Kool-Aid and poured himself another glass full. "Why don't you bring it down tonight? It looks like everyone could use a breather." Even though another song was playing now, only a few people had returned to the dance floor. Most of them lingered around the table or had flopped onto the furniture, looking tired.

"I don't know. Just because people are too exhausted to move is no reason for me to inflict my music on them. They won't be able to escape."

The blond-haired boy named Dave came over to get some Kool-Aid. "You play guitar?" he asked.

"Yeah."

Dave turned to his friend. "Hey, Jordan, she plays guitar," he said, jerking a thumb toward Bridget.

Jordan came over to them. "Really? I've been trying to get some money saved up and buy one. What's yours like?"

A few other people caught snatches of the conversation and walked over to hear more. Suddenly Bridget found herself at the center of the largest group in the room. She tried to search over people's heads for Lydia so she could direct the attention back where it belonged.

"Come on, play a couple of songs for us," Jordan urged.

"Not tonight," Bridget told him. "I'm just the waitress tonight."

"Can we just see the guitar?" someone else asked. "Just get it out for a minute?"

Bridget told them no again and tried to back out into the kitchen, but a chorus of protests went up. Finally she relented and went upstairs to get the case. When she brought it back down everyone gathered close to get a look.

"Just play one song," insisted Dave. Bridget decided she would play something short and then put the instrument away again. She could see Lydia now sitting over by the front windows with a couple of girls on either side. The light was dim there and shadows obscured her expression, but Bridget was pretty sure the smile had gone.

Bridget played "Imagine" by John Lennon and then put the guitar back in the case and zipped it up, ignoring the half dozen requests for another song.

"That's it," she declared. "Jeff will get another CD started so you can dance." She carried the guitar back upstairs and stowed it in her closet. When she came back down, at least half the group was dancing again. Jeff was waiting for her on the edge of the room, near the front doors.

"Come out for a minute," he coaxed.

She led the way through the two sets of double doors. Outside, the evening air ruffled the tiny hairs along her arms. She folded her arms against herself in a tight hug.

"You're good," Jeff said.

"I shouldn't have done that. I don't know why I did. It's Lydia's party."

"So? You helped everyone have a good time."

"I shouldn't have taken the attention away from her. I knew while I was doing it that I shouldn't be. I don't know what got into me. I don't even like playing in front of people."

"Really?" Jeff asked. "Even tonight? You didn't look nervous."

"The thing was," Bridget admitted, "I wasn't nervous at all. I got some kind of rush from it. I wanted to stay and play more."

"You love your music. That's all you were thinking about when you were playing."

"Yeah. It does kind of block everything else out." They were silent for a moment, and then Bridget added, "You've been great tonight. Everyone would still be standing around staring at the floor if not for you."

Jeff shrugged and shook his head. "I've had a good time. Your sister is human, you see. I wanted her to have a good birthday."

"It's been interesting watching her today. It's like I keep getting these little glimpses of a person inside who isn't so prickly. I'm going to try really hard to remember the way she looked when she was dancing with you, and the next time I want to smack her, maybe that image will help me keep my temper under control."

Jeff laughed. "How did she look?"

"Sweet and innocent. Vulnerable. She was beaming. Didn't you notice?"

"Maybe it didn't seem so out of the ordinary to me, but you've never seen her like that before."

"No," Bridget agreed. "I sure haven't."

The darkness broke apart as car lights swerved onto the street. An SUV pulled up to the curb and a woman got out. "Hi!" she called to them. "I'm here to get Jordan. Am I too early?"

"It can't be ten o'clock yet, can it?" Bridget asked. "I think everyone's pretty tired, though."

They chatted with Jordan's mom for a few minutes, and then some other parents began arriving. A few kids came out and got on bikes that they had parked in the driveway. By 10:30 the house had emptied out except for the girls and Jeff, who had stayed to help clean up. When they figured they had the kitchen back to Mrs. Prescott's standard, they went into the living room to push the furniture into place.

"I think we're finished," Bridget told him finally. They were all about to fall asleep.

"Okay," he said, stifling a yawn. Bridget, Lydia, and Charly walked with him to the outer set of doors.

"Happy birthday, Lydia." He stooped down and kissed her lightly on the cheek. "Thanks for having me at your party."

Lydia's eyes grew big. "It was my pleasure," she said, sounding dignified. Jeff turned the door handle and stepped outside, letting in a gust of cold air. As soon as the door had closed behind him, Lydia touched the place on her cheek where he had kissed her.

"So," said Bridget, smiling, "how was your first boy-girl party?"

Lydia's dreamy expression dissipated, and she frowned

up at Bridget. "Not bad, in spite of you," she retorted.

"I'm glad," responded Bridget honestly. "Let's get to bed."

t w e l v e

Sunday morning, Bridget came downstairs prepared for the usual morning breakfast ritual, but the table was empty. She pushed through the swinging door into the kitchen to talk to Mrs. Prescott, but the kitchen was deserted. No cheerful humming signaled the start of a new day. Bridget went back into the living room and flopped down in one of the chintz armchairs. She listened intently. Nothing. The house sounded empty. She tried to remember someone telling her that the family would be going some-where early today, but she didn't recall anything like that. Instead, alien abduction kept coming to mind.

After a while, Bridget shook her head to clear it. *Come on,* she told herself. *This isn't* The Twilight Zone. Soon she heard stirring upstairs—a thump and the sound of the water running. Nothing bizarre about that, except that it was already 8:15. Had she missed a time change? No, it couldn't be that. It was still too early in the year.

When Lydia and Charly came down an hour or so later, they were dressed in their Sunday clothes as usual.

"What's going on?" Bridget asked them. "Who called off breakfast? I didn't get the word."

Lydia snickered.

"Oh, we should have remembered to mention it." Charly sounded sympathetic. "The good thing about today is that we get to sleep in. That's what I always try to think about."

"So this happens regularly?"

"Once a month," Lydia said.

"Once a month, you all call off breakfast?"

"Not just breakfast," Lydia informed her. "Lunch too."

"Uh, I don't get it."

"It's fast Sunday," Charly explained.

"Fast Sunday?"

"Yeah," said Charly. "When I was little I thought that meant it was supposed to go by fast—you know, church was supposed to be short and stuff." She sighed. "But that's not it. It definitely doesn't go fast."

"So what is it then?"

"It means we go without food."

"And water," Lydia added.

"Yeah. And soda. And punch. And all that."

"Stop it, Charly, you're only making it worse," Lydia chided.

"You practice ritual starvation?" Bridget said incredulously.

"You don't starve in twenty-four hours," Lydia snapped.

"You feel like it, though," groaned Charly, rubbing her stomach.

"What's the point?" Bridget wondered.

"It's supposed to help you feel closer to the Holy Ghost. And you get stronger, because you're using your willpower over your appetite. Plus, we give the money we would have spent on food to the church to use to feed the poor."

"Oh, so it's a charity thing," Bridget said, struggling to understand. "But why can't you just give money to the poor? Why starve yourselves?"

"Well . . ." Charly began.

"Um . . ." said Lydia.

Then Charly brightened. "It sure makes us feel sorry for people who don't have enough to eat. Man, do I feel sorry for them!"

Bridget heard the door of Mr. McKenna's office open, and soon he appeared in the archway.

"Good morning," he greeted them heartily.

"Morning," the girls responded without enthusiasm.

"What's this? Why these glum faces? I want to see smiles. It's a wonderful day—the Lord's day."

Charly glanced at Bridget with a pained expression.

"And while we're all here together," Mr. McKenna continued, "I have an idea. I think we need to start trying to have family scripture study again. We've really let it go this last year or so. I think this is the perfect morning to get it going. So, let's gather up everyone's scriptures."

Charly and Lydia didn't move at first, but Mr. McKenna only had to say "Girls" once to make them jump up and rummage around for their quads. Bridget walked upstairs for hers, but she wasn't in a hurry. Her family's church seemed weirder all the time. She'd never had a chance to talk to Jeff about it; so many things were happening, she needed more time to process it all. So far, she had avoided discussing it much with her father, although he had invited the full-time missionaries to dinner recently. She had liked having them over because they lightened the usually somber mealtime mood. They were so young, just twenty or so, and they joked all through dinner. She couldn't imagine anyone taking them seriously. After the meal, they had all gone into the living room and the missionaries had had one of the girls read a scripture. Bridget couldn't remember now what it had been about. The missionaries hadn't said much to her directly. A couple of times they asked her opinion on something, apparently trying to feel around for her attitude toward religion. Because she had never thought about it much, she didn't have a lot to offer them, and they didn't press the matter. After they had left, she thought her father had acted disappointed.

When Bridget returned to the living room with her

scriptures, Mr. McKenna motioned her into the hallway.

"We should have talked about fast Sunday before this morning," he said. Bridget guessed this was meant to be an apology, but he made it sound more like an accusation, as if it had been Bridget's responsibility to bring up the subject.

"I won't force you to go without food when you don't share our convictions, but I do ask that if you choose to eat, you do it away from the other girls. It's hard enough for them to get through the day without having to see you eating."

"Of course," Bridget agreed coolly. Why did he have to say things in that condescending way? Why did he make it sound like if he hadn't warned her against it, she would have fixed herself a heaping bowl of ice cream and leftover birthday cake and devoured it with gusto in front of two hungry girls? He seemed to always expect the worst of her.

"All right, then. Let's read."

They went back into the living room and sat down, and then Mr. McKenna led them in a reading of the first few chapters of the Book of Mormon, which recounted an odd tale of two obnoxious young men, Laman and Lemuel, and their self-righteous brother Nephi. Bridget couldn't quite see the point of it all, but finally "family scripture study" came to an end and it was time for three hours of church.

The day dragged on as usual, only worse this time because she was hungry. Out of sympathy for Charly, she had decided not to eat until everyone else did. By four or so in the afternoon, though, she was finding it hard to focus on compassion. Her stomach was sucking up much more of her attention. How could people think they'd end up feeling more spiritual by starving themselves? Another few hours, and all she'd care about would be a big hunk of steak. And she wasn't even much of a meat eater.

She went upstairs to read for a while, but she had a hard time concentrating. Restless, she wandered back down to the living room. Charly lay on the couch, holding her stomach and groaning. Bridget walked over to her and stroked her hair. "Just a couple more hours," she comforted. "Then it will be time for dinner."

Charly moaned again. "It's not that anymore," she whimpered. "My stomach hurts. It's bad."

"If it hurts that much, maybe you'd better just eat something."

"No, no. It isn't that," Charly repeated.

Lydia came in from outside, where she'd been sitting on the front porch. "What's the matter?"

"Charly has a bad stomachache."

"She's probably just hungry."

"No, she says it isn't that."

Lydia came over to the couch and gazed down at her sister.

"What's wrong with you, Charly? Did you sneak too much birthday cake?"

Charly scowled. "I didn't sneak any! Ooooohhhh . . . aarrrr . . . it really hurts!" she wrapped her arms more tightly around herself. Her face was pale and damp with perspiration, and she was trembling.

"I think this is more serious than hunger pangs or too much birthday cake," Bridget told Lydia.

Lydia looked concerned now too. "I'm getting Dad," she announced, hurrying off to pick up the phone. Mr. McKenna had been at the church all afternoon. He had some kind of job with the church that seemed to take a lot of time for a volunteer position, but Bridget was getting used to the idea of a lay ministry. At least she didn't ask anymore why the regular minister didn't give the sermon every week. Mormons liked to work themselves to death, she had concluded. Everyone seemed to do a little of everything, and no one got paid for any of it.

Lydia got her dad on the phone and described Charly's

condition. "I think you'd better come home," she insisted, sounding urgent. "Yes, okay, okay." She hung up the receiver and turned to Bridget. "He's on his way with Brother Devereaux."

"Why is Mr. Devereaux getting involved?" Bridget questioned. She didn't feel comfortable using the terms "Brother" and "Sister," but at least she understood now that these titles didn't refer to literal family relationships.

"Dad's going to administer a blessing to Charly, so he's bringing another priesthood holder." For what seemed liked the millionth time since Bridget had arrived in New York, her sister had offered an explanation that didn't make any sense. But there were other things to worry about at the moment. She went to kitchen and retrieved a cool, damp cloth to wipe Charly's face.

"It hurts," Charly whimpered.

"Dad will be here soon, and if it gets really bad, he'll take you to the hospital," Bridget soothed.

Charly looked frightened at the mention of the hospital. "I don't want to have to go there."

"Don't be scared, it'll probably get better by itself. And if you do need to go to the hospital, the doctors will make you feel better. And we won't leave you alone, we'll stay with you all the time."

Mr. McKenna arrived home a few minutes later, accompanied by a middle-aged, balding man who shook Bridget's hand absently.

Mr. McKenna kneeled down next to Charly. "What is it, sweetheart?"

"My stomach hurts. It's really bad."

"Can you show me where it hurts the worst?"

"It's everywhere," Charly moaned.

"Oh, now, stomachaches are rotten, aren't they, sweetheart, but you'll feel better soon, I'm sure of it."

"But, Daddy, I'm scared," Charly murmured. "Aren't you

going to give me a blessing?"

"Of course I am. Brother Devereaux has the oil right here." Mr. McKenna scooted aside so that Brother Devereaux could reach Charly too. Bridget saw Brother Devereaux extract a small vial from his pocket and pour a drop of something onto Charly's head. Then he put both hands on Charly's head and said a quick prayer. Next, Mr. McKenna put his hands on Charly's head too and began to pray. Bridget thought they'd be better off giving Charly some Pepto Bismol or maybe even bundling her into the car to go to the hospital. She couldn't understand why they were wasting time like this. She gazed at her father, listening impatiently to the words of his prayer. He was using the voice he saved for his most tender moments with the girls, and something had come over his face, a gentleness that made him look less James Bond and more concerned parent. He spoke words of comfort and peace, and Bridget felt her impatience leaving her. In fact, she longed for this moment to last forever because for some reason, she couldn't remember ever feeling so safe.

Over the next few hours, they all sat with Charly, reading to her and talking to try to cheer her up, but she only grew more pale and miserable. At dinnertime, they took turns eating sandwiches in the kitchen. Charly refused her father's offer of ginger ale and dry toast. By bedtime, she was nearly sobbing from pain.

"I'm going to take Charly to the hospital," Mr. McKenna announced finally. "This doesn't seem like the average stomachache. I'm thinking it might be appendicitis."

"I'm coming too," Bridget insisted, remembering her promise to stay with Charly if she had to go to the hospital.

"Me too," said Lydia.

Mr. McKenna carried Charly out to the car, and Lydia and Bridget climbed in to go with them. It turned out that

Mr. McKenna had guessed right—Charly's appendix was swollen and threatening to rupture. The doctors rushed her into surgery, and Bridget, Lydia, and their father sat together in the waiting room until a nurse came to inform them that Charly had been wheeled into recovery. All three stood up to go and see her, but the nurse who delivered the message said that only Mr. McKenna could be with her at first.

"She needs to stay quiet and rest for a while," she explained, "so only one visitor at a time."

When Mr. McKenna had disappeared down the corridor, Bridget and Lydia sat staring at each other.

"That was scary," Lydia admitted.

"Yeah," Bridget agreed. "It came on so fast. And people used to die of appendicitis. Thank goodness Charly wasn't born a hundred years ago."

"Really?" Lydia asked. "People used to die of this?"

"Yeah. But don't worry," Bridget assured her quickly. "Medical care is so much better now, and Charly's going to be fine. She'll be showing off her scar and telling about her adventure."

Lydia considered this for a time. "It's a good thing it wasn't you, though," she said after a few minutes.

"What? Why?"

"If you had died, I mean. It would have been better for Charly to die."

Bridget thought this was a strange thing to say. "Why do you think that?"

"Because you haven't been baptized, have you?"

"No, I guess not. Unless it happened when I was a baby."

Lydia rolled her eyes. "We don't baptize babies. That's dumb."

"Millions of people would disagree with you, but okay, I'm not taking a stand on baptism one way or the other."

"We baptize at age eight."

"Sounds reasonable."

"So you haven't been baptized."

Bridget had been seven years old when her parents had divorced. "No, you're right, I haven't then." She had forgotten by now why they had started talking about this in the first place.

"So it would have been bad for you if you'd died," Lydia reminded her.

"Oh, brother. You aren't one of those churches that condemn all the unbaptized to hell, are you?"

"No, not hell," Lydia said.

"Good."

"Spirit prison. You would have had to go to spirit prison. Someone could have been baptized for you after you were dead, though."

"Oh," Bridget replied. More weirdness. She decided not to encourage Lydia with a response.

"But you would have had to accept the gospel, and you're not doing that in life. So I don't know. You may have had to stay there a long time." Lydia clucked her tongue and shook her head. "It wouldn't have been fun."

"Okay, but I didn't die, and Charly isn't going to either, so I don't know why we're even talking about this." Bridget felt more irritated than she needed to. This whole conversation was irrelevant, after all. She stood up and paced back and forth for a while. Then she realized what was really bothering her.

"So I guess that's where you think she is."

Lydia looked up, startled.

"Who?"

"You know. Mother. She wasn't one of you, either."

Lydia's expression grew dark. "Don't you say that. She was baptized. She and Dad were married in the temple. Know what that means? It means they were married forever."

"Well, but they didn't stay married, did they?"

"That doesn't count. They were married in the temple," Lydia repeated stubbornly. "That means they're still married, even after they die."

"Did Mother know about that little snag?" Bridget questioned coldly. "'Cause if not, she'll be disappointed to find out about it." She couldn't believe how sarcastic she was being, but she was angry—so angry that the feeling pulsed through her as a physical sensation. She understood suddenly what she had been listening for these Sundays in church, the answer to where her mother was. So far, she hadn't found it. But she didn't like Lydia's answer. No, she wasn't going to accept that. Let the Mormons cast off all the unbelievers to this spirit prison place—they didn't know the truth. . . . Did they? She shivered, trying to push away an image of her mother in a prison cell. "It isn't right," she exclaimed. "It isn't true!"

Lydia began crying. Mr. McKenna came back and asked what was wrong. He got no response from Lydia, so he turned on Bridget. "What's going on?" he wanted to know. "Why is Lydia crying?"

"Beats me," Bridget said. It was an honest answer. Lydia was the one who had brought up spirit prison. The malicious little snot, she had made herself cry. And now Mr. McKenna was going to blame Bridget.

"Take her home, please, and stop this arguing. I'm going to stay overnight with Charly." He handed Bridget the car keys. "I don't want to have to worry about you two. You know better than to cause trouble, Bridget."

Bridget opened her mouth to retort, but what could she say? Her head was still spinning.

"C'mon, Lydia," she ordered.

At home, Bridget turned Lydia's words over and over in her mind. She couldn't stand it. All these questions had built up, and she had to know, she had to understand. She needed the one answer that really mattered. She waited as the rest of the night ticked by, and then as soon as she thought Jeff might be up, she picked up the phone and dialed his number.

"Jeff," she gushed too loudly when he answered, sounding groggy. "Jeff," she tried again, keeping her voice more steady, "I know it's early, but can you come over and talk for a minute?"

"Uh, okay. What's up?"

"I'll tell you when you get here."

She met him on the front lawn a few minutes later.

"What is it?" he asked. "You look upset."

"Charly's in the hospital," Bridget blurted. It was the easiest thing to say at the moment.

"What? Is she okay? What happened?" Jeff was instantly sympathetic.

"She's all right. She had appendicitis. They operated, and she's recovering. Dad's with her."

"Aw, that's rough," said Jeff. "The poor kid. We'll have to pamper her good when she gets home, give her all kinds of attention."

"Yeah," Bridget agreed. "We'll take care of her. She'll be okay." The words calmed her a little, but Jeff peered at her in the early morning darkness.

"That's not it," he surmised. "I mean, that's not all of it. What's bothering you?"

"Jeff—" she faltered, not knowing how to begin. "Jeff, my mom . . ."

"What is it, Bridget?" he asked softly.

"Lydia told me about spirit prison," she said, and to her embarrassment, the words spilled out on a sob. "Is that where my mom is, Jeff? Is that all her life means, that she ends up spending eternity in a cell?"

Jeff put a hand on both of her shoulders. "No, no," he promised. "No, it's not like that."

"What, then? What's it like? She never went to church, you know. You must think she was an awful sinner."

"It doesn't surprise me that she never went to church," Jeff said, releasing Bridget. "But I know there was more to your mom than church attendance, or nonattendance for that matter. I know she was a whole person. And I promise you that God knows that too, that He loves her more than we mere mortals even know how to do."

"But that's not what church is all about," Bridget cried.

"What do you mean?"

"It's not about love, it's about sin and punishment and frightening people into goodness."

Jeff shook his head. "That's where you're wrong. That's not it at all. Is that what it sounds like when you come to the meetings?"

"No," she murmured. "But I've only been a couple of times."

"Well, let me tell you, we're nice to people at first but once we lure them in, out with all the scary stuff. Chains and torture devices—just you wait." He shook his head again. "Is that how you think it's going to be?"

Bridget gave him a watery smile. "I don't know. Maybe."

"Sorry to disappoint you. What you see is what you get. A bunch of imperfect people trying to be better, trying to be more loving and more forgiving, like Christ and Heavenly Father. That's it, Bridget, that's what it's about. Not condemning other people."

Bridget brushed at her tears and looked up at the dark sky. "Where do you think she is, then? What happens to people after they die?"

"Look, Bridget, I don't have all the answers. It isn't for me to say. But what I do know is that Heavenly Father *does* have all the answers, and He knows us and loves us and will always do the right thing. And there's no cruelness in

Him. We're His children. Think of it like that. He's a loving Father, the best possible Father."

Bridget focused on Jeff's face. "I don't know if that's a good way for me to think about it," she said. "I don't know much about fathers. And I don't have the greatest relationship with mine."

"But you're working on it. And your dad's only human. Heavenly Father is better than any earthly father. He loves us unconditionally. I don't even think we can really understand that. It's a kind of love we're not quite capable of, no matter how much we try."

Bridget was silent for a few moments, pondering Jeff's words. "This God you talk about, He's unique. He's not the kind of God I've ever heard about before. Are you sure this isn't your own opinion? Or are you just telling me what you think I want to hear?"

"I'm not trying to paint a pretty picture, Bridget. I know we have a loving Heavenly Father. I *know* it. And I don't know exactly what your mom is doing now, but I do know that we have lots of chances, both here and after death, to make progress, to be better. Like I told you, that's what it's all about."

"I don't know Jeff, I don't know. It's all so overwhelming."

"No," he contradicted. "It's simple. You have to let the details go. They don't matter."

"Let them go and then what? What's left?"

Jeff put a hand under her chin and gazed directly into her eyes. "The only thing we really need. Our Father's love."

Bridget backed away and shook her head. "I'm sorry, Jeff. My mother taught me not to accept things at face value. I need to think about things. . . ."

"Yeah, of course, that's what you should do."

She gazed up at the sky again, at the pinpoints of light in the vast carpet of darkness. In the east, the blackness was fading to deep blue. "A father's love, huh?" she said softly. "That would be something."

thirteen

Charly was home from the hospital before long, describing her ordeal to her friends, who gasped in all the right places. The living room filled up with flowers and balloons. Meanwhile, at school, the talk turned to Homecoming and college applications. The game was only a few Saturdays away, and the application deadlines loomed not far beyond. Bridget spent more and more time in her room after school, writing and rewriting essays for Mrs. Keller and her Stanford application.

"We never see you anymore," Charly complained one afternoon when Bridget walked in the door and, as usual, headed straight up the stairs to study. "Don't you ever want to take a break?"

"Maybe next month," Bridget told her. "Or the month after."

Lydia, who had no college applications or even SATs to worry about yet, talked excitedly at dinner one night about the Homecoming festivities. "We're going to paint the window of Nelson's Hardware," she announced. All the high school clubs and associations were painting windows on Main Street the week of the game. "And since we're the French club, we're going to paint the other team's mascot being guillotined."

"Cool!" exclaimed Charly, whose appetite for Mrs. Prescott's mashed potatoes could withstand thoughts of headless eagles without flinching. She crammed a forkful into her mouth and asked, "Whose idea was that?"

"Gross, Charly, you wouldn't be talking with your mouth full of food if Dad were here," Lydia scolded. Mr. McKenna was working late again.

"You were just talking about chopping off heads, and now you're yelling at Charly for being gross at dinner," Bridget joked.

Lydia rolled her eyes. "Whatever. I think it's a great idea, I wish I had thought of it. I guess that's why I'm not the president, though, and Jeff is."

"Jeff?" Bridget repeated. "Jeff from across the street?"

"Yeah, didn't you know? He's the head of the French club."

"I had no idea," she confessed. "I guess he has broader interests than I give him credit for."

"Jeff does all kinds of things," Charly told her. "But you should see his Pepé le Pew imitation sometime. It's so funny, I always ending up laughing so hard I snort."

"That's true," Lydia agreed. "So don't ever let him do it when she has mashed potatoes in her mouth."

*   *   *

Mr. McKenna came home so late that evening that none of the girls saw him, but the next morning he had taken his place at the head of the table by the time they came down. He looked none the worse for what must have been a short night. His hair and clothing were perfectly neat, his face clean shaven, and his expression relaxed.

"Good morning, girls," he greeted them and then they all fell into their usual formal silence. Finally, about halfway through Mrs. Prescott's superb veggie omelets, he looked up and fixed his gaze on Bridget. "It's about time we took some of those trips we talked about to tour college campuses. I thought we should drive up to Oberrath College a week from Saturday."

166

Bridget set her fork down. "I didn't know we were still planning that," she answered slowly. "I thought we decided it was a waste of time."

He arched one eyebrow. "Oh, no," he insisted. "I'm set on our going. There's no reason not to; it's a simple day trip. If you already have plans for that Saturday, we can go another week, maybe even take off on a weekday."

"Isn't that Homecoming weekend?" Bridget asked, more to stall for time than because she dreaded missing the game or the dance.

"No," Lydia replied. "Homecoming is the weekend after that."

"Oh," said Bridget, disappointed.

Mr. McKenna smiled. "Perfect. Then this Saturday I'll send you out with Natalie to shop, we'll go to Oberrath the following week, and you'll be back in town for all the fun."

Her father's insistence that she go shopping with Natalie annoyed Bridget, but she decided not to argue about it now, partly because she was curious what Natalie would select for her. Natalie, whom Bridget had never seen in anything as dressy as a pair of slacks, was being trusted to pick out a proper outfit to impress a bunch of old college administrators? Bridget wondered why her father had delegated the task to Natalie. Did he know something about Natalie's abilities that didn't show through in her own attire, or was he simply palming the job off on her because she was a woman? Bridget would go along with the shopping trip just to find out.

That afternoon in Mrs. Keller's class, Matt, the boy who sat in front of her, turned around to give Bridget a view of something other than the back of his head.

"Hey, Bridget," he said softly as they sat waiting for class to begin.

"Hey."

"So, what's your prediction for the game? Will we take them?"

"Isn't that pretty much a given? I mean, don't they play the worst team possible to make sure they look good?"

"Well, yeah," affirmed Matt. "They're not stupid." Bridget liked that he didn't try to hedge around or make excuses. She allowed herself a half smile.

"That's good to know," she said. "After all those blows to the head."

The low chatter around them died down as Mrs. Keller made her entrance.

"I have here the items you've been waiting for," the teacher announced, waving a thick folder. "Silence, please, as I hand back these papers."

Bridget's stomach churned uncomfortably. She wouldn't allow herself to think about how much she wanted her grade to be an A. Her eyes followed the teacher anxiously until she forced herself to stare down at her notebook. Matt had turned to the front again, and the stiff line of his back suggested that he wasn't too relaxed about this either. Finally Mrs. Keller laid a stapled set of papers face down on Bridget's desk. With a trembling hand, Bridget flipped the sheaf over. A bright red B+ threatened to blind her. She dropped the paper back onto her desk, feeling beads of sweat breaking out at her temples.

Matt twisted back around. "What's the damage?"

"It's bad," Bridget sighed.

"Me too. And I'm not even a football player, you know? No blows to the head."

"Yeah," Bridget agreed. "Me either. I don't know what my excuse is."

She struggled to pay attention for the remainder of the class period. Her mind kept up a running debate: go back to Mrs. Keller and ask for more feedback or let it go and hope she could hit the mark with the next paper? The teacher had written only one comment, and it wasn't very helpful: "I know you can do better work." How did she know, Bridget wondered. She had only written two essays for Mrs. Keller, and the teacher hadn't liked either of them.

She had made up her mind not to speak to Mrs. Keller about the grade—it felt too much like groveling—when Mrs. Keller ended the lesson early and explained that she wanted to read some of the papers aloud. "Because so many of you clearly have no idea how to go about writing a coherent essay, I think some examples of fine work would be in order. I made photocopies of several good models for you to follow. First, there's Amy Jefferson's paper." Amy, a small, quiet girl, flushed red with a mixture of embarrassment and pleasure. "Amy received an A, so listen carefully." She began to read, and Bridget did listen, hoping to glean some clue that would help her figure out what this teacher wanted. The more she listened, though, the more she grew confused. She didn't think it was just ego—that paper wasn't as good as hers. Sure, it was okay, but the analysis wasn't developed as well, the writing wasn't as smooth, and the grammar showed that Amy had missed the lesson on dangling participles. So what was the difference? Why did Amy have an A and Bridget a B+?

She left class that day without speaking to Mrs. Keller, but she could concentrate on little else throughout the evening. Thoughts of grades invaded her dreams, in which Mrs. Keller explained that all grades in her class were based upon the first letter of each student's name. "So you see, Bridget," concluded the dream Mrs. Keller, "you can never have an A because your name begins with B. Your mother should have called you Amy, but there's nothing to be done about it now."

The next day, Friday, Bridget decided she had to know. She had to find out why Mrs. Keller had given Amy an A. As the other students filed out into the hallway after class, she approached Mrs. Keller's desk. "Excuse me," she began. Mrs. Keller, who had been glancing through a stack of recently collected quizzes, looked up and fixed her no-nonsense, don't-waste-my-time gaze on Bridget.

"I need to talk to you," Bridget declared. "If you want me to come back later, after school, I can. I want to understand what I'm doing wrong."

"Wrong?" echoed Mrs. Keller. "Who said you were doing anything wrong?"

"The grade on my paper—"

Mrs. Keller rolled her eyes. "Not this conversation again. I thought I had made myself clear. I do not give out A's like I was throwing saltwater taffy from a parade float. You didn't do anything wrong. Neither did you do anything extraordinary."

"I understand," Bridget replied levelly, "and I wouldn't have come to you again except for what you said at the end of class yesterday. Those papers you read—the one by Amy Jefferson. You gave it an A."

Mrs. Keller leaned back and crossed her arms, glaring at Bridget over the rims of her glasses. "Yes?"

"Did you find it extraordinary?"

The teacher nodded curtly. "Well, as a matter of fact, I did, quite. If you had read Amy's papers from last year, when she took a literature class from me, you would have found it extraordinary too. She has shown such a turnaround, such an extreme level of improvement that I can do nothing other than reward it with an outstanding mark."

"So . . ." Bridget hesitated, trying to decide if she had really caught the gist of what Mrs. Keller had just explained. "You're grading her against her previous performance? Is that it?"

"Isn't that what progress is about? Isn't oneself one's only real competitor, in sports, in life, in everything that counts?"

"But—but how do you establish a baseline?" Bridget

faltered. "How do you compare students? What does a grade mean if there's no absolute value?"

Mrs. Keller smirked. "Bridget, absolute value is a mathematical concept, not a day-to-day reality. We'll never win out over subjectivity, and if we ever did, we'd be sorry."

They stared at each other for a moment, Bridget flabbergasted, Mrs. Keller sardonic and a touch impatient, to judge from the way she kept tapping her fingers against her sleeve. "Do you know how long I've been a teacher?" Mrs. Keller asked suddenly.

Bridget shook her head.

"Much longer than you've been alive, and let's leave it at that. I've seen all kinds of students, and I've seen them grow up into all kinds of people. I've known your father since he first opened his law office. I knew your mother. I've read her books. And I know you can do better work."

"Mrs. Keller," Bridget protested, "I'm not my mother."

"Oh, I know that. She's proven her abilities already, hasn't she? While you have not yet soared above a B+." She unfolded her arms suddenly and picked up the quizzes from her desk. "Well, better luck next time," she said brusquely, dismissing Bridget with a wave of her arm. "I have work to do. And so do you, if you want an A."

Bridget walked home alone that afternoon, telling Jeff she had to stay late to finish something and then starting off on her own after she had seen him a safe distance away. She needed to give herself a good talking to, and you couldn't do that if someone else was trying to carry on a conversation with you at the same time.

Actually, in her mind it was her mother who was doing the talking. "What's a grade, Bridget?" she had often asked. "Should I stamp your forehead with a percentage that tells everyone how smart you are? Do you think if you went around with a 98 percent branded on you, you'd be a better person somehow?"

"Not exactly," Bridget had answered once. "But you can wear a gold medal, or a Super Bowl ring, or a letter on a jacket. This is what I'm good at. School is what I can do."

Her mother never came out and said it, but she didn't think much of school. Once when Bridget was in the eighth grade, she received the first and only B of her middle school career. She came home and showed the report card to her mother, who promptly took her out for pizza and banana splits. A consolation dinner, Bridget thought at first. But no, her mother meant to celebrate.

"Just think, honey, now that you've gotten rid of this perfect record you've been so anxious to keep, you won't have this slave driver beating you up every minute that you're not doing homework. Perfection was too stressful for you. I got tense just watching you study. Now you can relax and really get down to learning—and having more fun."

"I'll do better next semester," Bridget declared stubbornly.

"Better!" Margaret exclaimed. "What's better than this?"

Bridget sighed now, wondering if her mother would be proud of her struggles in Mrs. Keller's class, as if they might make her more lighthearted and fun-loving the way Colin was. But Colin was smart too, Bridget reflected. If her mother had ever written enough books to send him off to college, she probably could have enrolled him just about anywhere. Somehow Colin managed to be everything: smart but not uptight, charming but not manipulative, resourceful but not a know-it-all.

She stared at the street with its pastel Victorian houses and thought of the brown-gold buildings and palm trees that gave the Stanford campus the look of a Spanish villa. She could remember the first time her mother had taken her there, not long after they moved to San Francisco.

Margaret had flung out her arms to catch the summer sun and exclaimed, "See, Bridget, this is the West. Beautiful, romantic, none of that snooty New York stuffiness."

Bridget had gazed around at the buildings that seemed to have come off the set of a movie, and she had thought, "I'm coming here someday. I'll belong here someday." Maybe she had believed that going there would make her beautiful too, like the West that her mother loved so much.

Bridget reached the front door of her father's house, still musing about her mother. "Hey, Bridget!" Charly called in greeting from the living room, where she was playing the piano laboriously under the watchful eye of Mrs. Prescott, who stood off to one side dusting knickknacks.

"Hey," Bridget muttered before heading up the stairs to her room.

"Keep practicing, Charly," she heard Mrs. Prescott say. "You've got fifteen more minutes." And then, just before Bridget closed the door—"Let your sister alone. She has work to do."

Bridget plopped down at her desk, opened her laptop, and sat staring at an empty screen. She could hear the muffled notes of the piano as it started up again. From the street came the distant shouts of neighborhood kids out enjoying what might be the last of the warm weather. Slowly, Bridget pulled the materials from Mrs. Keller's class out of her bag and read the assignment for the next essay. Her mind felt empty. She didn't know what to write. She wondered if her mother's mind had ever felt that way or if it had been constantly full of words and images waiting to spill out onto paper. *It doesn't really matter now,* she answered herself. *I am not my mother.*

*   *   *

The next morning Natalie arrived just after the girls had finished helping Mrs. Prescott clear the breakfast dishes away. Bridget noted Natalie's attire with interest—faded blue jeans and once-white tennis shoes, a lumpy gray sweater, and a blue-and-white-striped scrunchy holding her hair back in something halfway between a ponytail and a bun. She was an attractive woman, no denying that, but she appeared to have stepped out of a Grape Nuts commercial, and Bridget wondered again why her father trusted Natalie to prepare Bridget for the campus tours he was so insistent about taking.

"Ready, Bridget?" Natalie asked.

Bridget grinned and shrugged. "Sure."

They walked out and scrambled into Natalie's red Jeep Wrangler.

"You'll do a fashion show for us when you get back, right?" Charly called from the porch. Lydia had followed them out too.

"I hope so," Lydia yelled, "because it will be the first time we'll be able to look at you straight on without going blind!"

Bridget smiled sweetly and waved at them through the window as Natalie backed down the driveway. *At least I don't worry about how this tangerine sweater matches the car*, Bridget thought. *If I were Lydia, I'd have to go in and change to coordinate better.*

Natalie steered the Jeep out toward the freeway and sped onto the ramp in the direction of Rochester. Neither of them had spoken much for the first few minutes. There had been the standard pleasantries—"How are you?" "Fine." "How's school?" "Fine." But now as they settled into the drive, Natalie broached the subject they both had in mind.

"I guess you're wondering why your father wants us to do this," she said.

Bridget shrugged again. "I've stopped asking questions when it comes to my father. It's just easier not to try to make sense of things."

Out of the corner of her eye she saw Natalie smile. "Sometimes I come to exactly the same conclusion."

Bridget glanced over at her. "Really?"

"Oh, yes. I love your father, but he's an odd man. I won't deny it." She laughed spontaneously. Bridget couldn't help liking the sound.

"So what do you make of all this?" Bridget questioned.

"He's a little uptight about certain things. He wants you to make a good impression at these schools. Of course, even more than that, he wants them to make a good impression on you. He doesn't have much control over that, and it's driving him nuts."

"He's a control freak, isn't he?" said Bridget.

"Only about certain things. Only when he feels he *doesn't* have control. That scares him. It scares a lot of people, actually."

"Why does he care so much about taking me around to these campuses?"

Natalie took her eyes off the road a moment to meet Bridget's gaze. "Well, he wants you to stay around, doesn't he? He's got you back, but it's just for a year and then he loses you again. Unless he can do something about it. And he has to act fast, because the application deadlines don't give him much time."

"But why does he want me to stay around? That's what I don't understand. After so many years of ignoring me, why does it matter now? And Natalie, no offense—I mean, I don't think there's anything wrong with the way you dress. But what does he think you're going to find for me to wear that I couldn't find myself?"

Natalie laughed again. "You need to study up on your clichés, Bridget. Remember, 'don't judge a book by its cover.'"

Bridget raised her eyebrows inquisitively. "Well? So underneath that granola ensemble you have on beats the heart of a straight-laced corporate executive? Or something like that?"

"No, but I do know a little about fashion. It's what I did for a living for a long time. I was a fashion editor in New York City until a few years ago."

This new information left Bridget stunned—and curious for more. "I had no idea. What brought you out to this little podunk town? It must be a big transition after New York City."

"Oh, sure," Natalie agreed. "But I'm used to moving around. It was New York City that was the hardest transition. I'm from a small town in Colorado, see. I lived in the big city for a long time, but I always thought of myself as a small-town girl. I feel more at home in Phrygia."

"Is that why you left the city?" Bridget wanted to know.

"I left for my boys. I have two sons, you know. Their father and I divorced a long time ago, and he moved to Rochester to open a business. I stayed put in New York City. That's where my life was, I thought. But I never saw my children. They were being raised by nannies and sitters. And they never saw their father because he lived six hours away. One day I realized that they were practically strangers to both their parents, and I wasn't going to let things stay that way. I moved to Phrygia later that year. Now they spend time with their father on a regular basis. They're with him this weekend. And when they're with me, they're really with me—not with the nanny. I don't have nightmares anymore that they're going to grow up calling some other woman Mom."

"So what do you do for a living out here?" Bridget asked.

"I'm part owner of the clothing store in town, and I do some fashion design on the side. Low-key stuff, but it keeps us comfortable, and I enjoy it."

"So—" Bridget hesitated. "What's your stuff like?"

"Well, I'm not wearing any of it, if that's what you mean.

I like to design for other people. The world is my canvas," she declared. "Meanwhile, I'd just rather be comfortable in a pair of ratty old jeans!"

"Sounds good," Bridget grinned. "And now—I'm part of your canvas?"

Natalie glanced over at her again. "Don't worry. I'm not going to force anything on you. I think you can choose for yourself. I only hope—"

"What?" Bridget asked.

Natalie began to sigh and then quickly stifled it. "Sorry, I hate to find myself sighing. It seems to happen without my even noticing. All I wanted to say was that I hope you'll give some of these schools a chance. I hope you'll give your father a chance. I know you think you have your future figured out, but right now, while you can, give yourself permission to explore some other options."

This time it was Bridget who sighed, and she let it out long and forlorn. Still, when she realized what she had done, she couldn't help laughing. "I don't know why, but I can't stay uptight around you," she confessed suddenly. She hadn't meant to be so open, but the words had just flown out. She smiled at Natalie a little shyly. "Seems like a lot of people are begging me to give my father a chance," she explained, "but when you say it, I don't feel like you're talking down to me. It's like you know what a hard thing you're asking me to do."

Natalie smiled and shook her head. "I guess that's because I tell myself the same thing sometimes and then I don't always listen."

"But no one can make you do what you don't want to do," Bridget pointed out. "You don't have to give him a chance if you don't want to."

"Yes," Natalie agreed, "but I do want to. I love him. And sometimes I wish I didn't."

They drove in silence for a while until Natalie said, "Hey,

this drive is getting too serious. I was hoping we could have some fun, get to know each other better."

But the things Bridget wanted to know were serious. "Are you planning to marry my father?" she blurted out.

"Oh, goodness," Natalie responded. "There goes my attempt to lighten the mood."

"Well," Bridget persisted. "Are you?"

Natalie stared hard at the road. Bridget faced forward too, letting Natalie take her time while the trees and open fields flowed past.

"It's hard to say how things are going to work out," Natalie said carefully. "I'm only one half of the couple. I can't make decisions for the both of us, so I can't really answer your question one way or the other."

"Okay," Bridget conceded, "if he asked, then. Would you say yes?"

"I respect your right to ask these questions, but can I plead the Fifth for now?"

Bridget turned to stare at her, and Natalie met her eyes sheepishly for a moment before looking back at the road. "It's complicated," Natalie told her.

"Okay." But Bridget wasn't satisfied. "Would you be scared to be that committed to him? Would you worry about this control thing he has? I think I'd be afraid that he'd try to change me, make me over into his ideal. You don't really look like an Easterner, Natalie, for all that you've lived in New York City. You look like you want to go back to Colorado. Do you?"

Natalie shrugged. "Oh, sometimes I think I do. I get homesick periodically for the West. And every time I visit, I ask myself, 'Now, why am I going back to New York?'"

"And what do you answer yourself?"

"Well, there's my boys' father first of all, like I explained earlier. I want them to grow up with him in their lives." Her eyes shifted quickly in Bridget's direction, then flicked back to the interstate. "And I have to be honest with myself. My life isn't back there. At least, my future isn't. Nostalgia is great and all, but you have to go forward, not back. I'm one of those lucky people who can say they had a great childhood. I love the memories I have of growing up, and my times in college and everything. But I can't keep trying to relive them, you know? I have to make new ones, and the new ones are here, in New York, not back home. I visit and get homesick, but then I realize it's just this inner child we all have, the part of us that wants to curl up somewhere familiar and safe and never face the unknown. If we listened to that child, though, we'd be stuck. We'd miss out on so much."

Bridget focused on Natalie's profile. The sun shone in full force onto Natalie's face, revealing all the tiny wrinkles around her eyes and mouth, and Bridget marveled at the way these somehow added to Natalie's beauty. She had heard wrinkles described as "character lines" before, but the term had never made sense until now. "Do you think it's always wrong to go home again?" she questioned steadily.

"No," Natalie answered. "It's different for everybody. All I'm saying is, we can't let fear of the unknown hold us back. Sure, it's tempting to stick with the familiar. At least then we know what we're in for. But there's more out there."

"And that's why I need to consider going to school in New York?"

Natalie shook her head. "I'm not trying to tell you what to do, Bridget. Really, I'm not." At the skeptical look on Bridget's face, she added, "No, I wouldn't believe me either, but it's true. Stanford may be the right school for you. That's why I promise you that the clothes we buy today will fit in either place."

"Seems impossible," Bridget protested. "Seems like fitting into one place means giving up the other."

But Natalie was as good as her word. They hadn't been

in the mall for more than fifteen minutes before Natalie had an armful of skirts, blouses, suits, and slacks for Bridget to try. They didn't look like much on the hangers—they were nothing Bridget would have picked up on her own. Still, when she tried them on and surveyed herself in the three-way mirror, she couldn't help admitting that Natalie knew her stuff. The cuts and colors set off Bridget's tanned skin and slender form. She almost didn't recognize the sophisti-cated young woman staring back at her from the glass. She eyed the flowing gray trousers and pinstriped blazer that both she and Natalie liked best. "I don't know if I can be that person," she said, still surprised by her own reflection.

Natalie met her gaze in the mirror. "Do you want to try?"

Bridget said nothing. She didn't know the answer.

f o u r t e e n

A fter dinner on Sunday night, Bridget dragged herself upstairs, flipped on her computer, and clicked
through the screens to open the file with the Stanford application she thought she was finally ready to submit online.
She read slowly through each page to double-check her
work, hoping she wasn't missing some silly typing error like
spelling her name without a *d*. None of the words seemed
to have much meaning, though, especially when she came to
the essay. The syllables dripped into her mind like a leaky
faucet, repetitive and monotonous. She had already read this
stuff too many times; she was too close to it. She wished
she could have someone with a fresh perspective look over
it just once before she sent it in. If her mother were here,
Bridget would ask her to check it. Though she had always
felt shy about allowing her famous-writer parent to read her
work, she had often subjected herself to her mother's feedback, which was usually brief and to the point.

"Cut out one hundred words and you've got it," Margaret might say, or "Lose this opening paragraph—it does
nothing for me."

Bridget tried now to imagine what her mother might
tell her about the Stanford essay, but her mind was determined to shut down whenever Bridget tried to focus on that
particular topic. All she could do was click on "Submit" and
hope for the best. Or maybe . . . No, she wouldn't ask her
father, even though she had seen him helping Charly and

Lydia with their homework. He was so opposed to her going to Stanford, he probably wouldn't tell her if he found a typo in her application. He'd smile smugly to himself and keep planning their trip to Oberrath College.

A knock at her bedroom door jolted Bridget out of her stupor. She moved her mouse tentatively over the "Submit" button at the bottom of the computer screen, watching the white arrow become a hand with the index finger raised to point at the fateful word. She swallowed hard and pushed the mouse to a more neutral spot. The hand became an arrow again. "Come in," she called.

She had her back to the door and was surprised to hear how slowly it opened. Charly and Mrs. Prescott, the only people likely to be visiting her in her room, usually flung it aside at the first sound of her voice.

"Uh, Bridget?" intoned a deep voice. Bridget stiffened and then swiveled around in her chair. Her father stood just inside the door. Wearing the deep blue silk shirt that brought out a yet-unfaded movie-star tan, he appeared somehow too big for the room. Maybe that was why he looked so awkward.

"Hi," Bridget said because she couldn't think of anything else. "What's up?"

He took another step into the room and thrust his hands into his pockets. "I've just been on the phone with Natalie. She said you two had a good trip yesterday. I didn't get to see you last night because of that client meeting, so I was hoping maybe you could show me now what you bought."

"Oh." Time for inspection with the drill sergeant. Great. "I guess so, if you want." She got up and went into her closet, where the gray pinstriped suit hung inside a plastic garment bag. She removed it from the plastic almost reverently and carried it out into the main room. "Here it is," she said, holding it up so that the pant legs wouldn't drag on the floor.

Her father smiled. "Wow. I knew you and Natalie would be a good team."

"You knew Natalie was a fashion editor from New York. Why didn't you mention that before you sent me shopping with her?"

Mr. McKenna looked vaguely surprised. "Didn't I explain that? I always send my girls shopping with her. She's a lot better at helping them than I ever would be. And they like to go with her because she's so good at finding what they want. I don't know how she does it, but she keeps up with all these teenage trends. She's much better with teenagers than I am." He stopped abruptly, as if realizing that he had divulged more than he meant to. Glancing around the room as if searching for a new subject, he happened to notice the lit computer screen. "What are you working on there?"

Bridget headed for the closet to put the suit away. "Just an application," she said over her shoulder.

"Ah. Just an application, or *the* application?" Without being invited, he walked over and sat down at the desk. Bridget hurried back out of the closet and stared at him stonily. He skimmed the words on the screen and then gazed over at her. "If you like, I could take a look at it for you. It's always helpful to have a proofreader."

"Thanks, but I already asked Jeff to check it," she lied. Actually, she hadn't asked Jeff because every time she mentioned Stanford to him he clammed up and grew suddenly solemn, as if she were talking about a funeral or something. Such a strange boy.

Her father wasn't moving out of the desk chair. "What if I just read your essay?" he suggested.

"Why would you want to do that?"

"I'd like to read some of your work. I bet you're a good writer."

"Why would you think that?" she asked stubbornly.

Mr. McKenna looked nonplussed. "Well, I . . . I know you're good in school," he finished lamely. "You have to be able to write okay if you're going to be at the top of your class, which I know you were at your old school."

They were silent for a moment, Bridget with her hands on her hips, staring impatiently at the computer, Mr. McKenna with his eyes on his shoes.

"May I please read your essay, Bridget?" he asked finally.

She let her hands fall from her hips and turned them palms upward in a gesture of acquiescence. "Okay, I guess, if you insist." She moved over to stand next to him and clicked back to the screen with the essay, and then she retreated to the bed and sat watching him read it. He seemed to take a long time. Maybe he read it twice—she suspected he did from the way his head tilted gradually toward the bottom of the screen and then back to the top and back down. Finally he looked over at her.

"Excellent," he pronounced. "This is excellent work, Bridget. Are you thinking of being a writer someday?"

She shook her head. "I'm not my mother."

"No. She couldn't have written something this mature at your age." He must have noticed the flash of anger that stirred across her face, because he added hastily, "She developed in other ways and on a different time frame. You're both extraordinary."

Bridget tried to relax, though it was always hard in his presence. "Well, thanks for looking over the essay, and thanks for the compliment." She hoped he would leave now, but he sat there still, filling up her little swivel chair and blocking her access to the computer. After a minute or so, Bridget heard the phone ring downstairs. Soon Charly was calling, "Bridget! Bridget, it's for you." This finally roused Mr. McKenna, who stood up and stepped toward the door. "I'll let you get that," he said by way of dismissal. Bridget followed him downstairs. In the living room, Mrs. Prescott was telling Charly, "I swear, my ears are still ringing. I don't know why with such young legs you can't just run upstairs and deliver your message in a normal voice."

Bridget picked up the receiver from the end table where Charly had left it.

"Hello?"

"Hey. Bridget?"

"Yes, this is Bridget."

"Hey. This is Matt." Matt? It took a moment for this information to register. "You know," he went on, "from Killer Keller's class."

"Sure," she said. She smiled into the phone because her mother had always told her that smiling would make her voice sound friendlier. "How's it going?"

"Good. Did you finish that essay she wants on Wednesday?"

"No, I've been trying to get something else out of the way. I'll have to get on it tomorrow night."

"Yeah, me too." He paused, and she wondered if he was about to ask for help with the paper. She didn't really want to tutor him. She'd found that when guys asked for that kind of help, what they actually wanted was for her to do their work for them. Like she had time to waste on that.

"Hey, I was wondering," he began, "have you heard about this Homecoming Dance coming up in a couple of weeks?"

Bridget laughed. "Yeah, I think I've heard something about that."

"Well, I was wondering if you'd want to go with me. To the dance."

Bridget's smile grew genuine. "That sounds good, Matt. I'd like to go."

"Really?" he asked, his voice suddenly high with excitement. "I mean, cool," he said in a more even tone. "I'll get with you later to talk about the details."

"Okay," Bridget agreed. "See you in class."

"Yeah, see you." They hung up, and Bridget turned to

find the entire household watching her. She flushed deep red. "What?" she asked.

"So, what was that about?" Mrs. Prescott demanded bluntly. "Charly said it was a boy."

"Do I know this boy?" her father asked.

"I don't know," Bridget replied. "It was just a boy from school."

"What did he want?" Charly inquired.

"He wanted to borrow my notes," she answered soberly. Then, without meaning to, she broke into a smile. "Okay, okay. He wanted to ask me to Homecoming."

"I knew it!" Charly exclaimed, bouncing up and down with enthusiasm. "We'll have to go shopping for a dress. Dad, you'll let Bridget borrow one of your credit cards, right?"

Mr. McKenna looked stern. "Only if I get to meet this young man. I take it this isn't Jeff?"

"No, it's someone from English class," Bridget told him.

"Hmm," said Mr. McKenna. "Well, hmm. It looks like you've got two exciting weekends coming up."

"Two?"

"Yes. Homecoming in a couple of weeks, and next Saturday—best of all—Oberrath College!"

As soon as she could break away from her captive audience, Bridget went back upstairs, sat down at her computer, and clicked on "Submit."

*　*　*

Saturday morning dawned overcast and chilly. At breakfast Mr. McKenna asked Bridget if she had a warm jacket.

"I should have had you buy a few more things when you went with Natalie," he declared. "There's a big difference between the climates of New York and California when it gets to be this time of year."

"I'll be fine," Bridget assured him. "San Francisco can get pretty cold, and it's not like it's winter coat weather here yet."

Still, when she came down wearing the suit under a long sweater with a sash around the waist, her father eyed her ensemble skeptically.

"That's the warm jacket?" he asked, nodding at the sweater.

"It's thick," Bridget insisted. She pinched a fold of it between her fingers so that he could see how substantial it was. He shook his head and went over to the phone.

"Natalie?" he said after a moment. "We've got a clothing emergency. Can you bring over a jacket to go over Bridget's suit? It's cold today, and she'll freeze to death in what she's got on."

When he hung up the phone, he turned back to Bridget. "She'll take care of it."

Bridget grinned. "Well, thanks, Grandma," she teased. Natalie arrived about twenty minutes later with a three-quarter length wool coat in charcoal gray, and the three of them gathered up the travel snacks that Mrs. Prescott had packed and stepped out into the brisk autumn morning. Little white puffs of air floated up from their noses as they hurried to the car. Mr. McKenna gave the motor a few minutes to warm up and then cranked up the heater.

"We've been spoiled by this Indian summer," he said. "Days like this prove that winter's just around the corner."

Bridget snuggled into the coat and leaned her head against the window. The approach of winter meant that she was nearing the halfway point in her year in New York. Once again, she counted the days since she had submitted her Stanford application and tried to figure out how many days she had left to wait before receiving a decision.

Her father merged onto the interstate toward Rochester, but after a few miles he exited onto a two-lane highway going north. Apparently Oberrath College wasn't near any booming metropolis, Bridget reflected. Maybe the college town was even smaller than Phrygia. What would her father expect her to do there for four years? Study, she guessed. She wondered if everyone at Oberrath had good grades.

They had driven for an hour or so when the sun came out. Bridget gazed at the landscape of rolling hills that still showed the last of summer's green. The sun on her face was warm through the glass. *It is beautiful,* she thought, *but lonely.*

Shortly after ten o'clock, they arrived in the college town of Swansea and drove straight to the campus, which was built up around a hill topped with a bell tower that seemed to stand at the center of everything.

"That's Old Margaret," her father told her, gesturing toward the bell tower. "She keeps the students on schedule."

He drove right up to the top of the hill and maneuvered into a parking space in a tiny lot between the tower and an ancient-looking brick building with Gothic windows. Bridget got out of the car and took several long steps to stretch her legs. Facing away from the Gothic building, she could gaze out for what must have been miles, and in the hazy blue distance she could make out . . . the ocean.

"That's Lake Ontario," her father informed her, following her gaze.

"Oh." She hadn't realized how much a Great Lake could resemble a sea. It appeared to stretch on interminably.

Mr. McKenna checked his watch. "Let's go on in," he said. "I set up a meeting with an admissions officer for 10:30, and we're only a few minutes early." He led them into the Gothic building, which despite its appearance turned out not be a church but rather the main administration center. Her father led them through a series of dark-paneled hallways to a suite of offices with windows opening on the tower and the uninterrupted view beyond.

"Good morning," he said to the receptionist. "I'm Gerrick McKenna, and this is my daughter Bridget and my friend Natalie. We're here to meet with Miss Brighton."

"Of course." The receptionist picked up the phone and dialed a couple of numbers. "Miss Brighton," she said, "your ten-thirty is here." A few moments later a young woman in a black business suit came out of one of the inner offices.

"Welcome," she said, extending her hand to each in turn. "Please, come on back and have a seat." They followed her to the office she had just vacated and settled into leather chairs that faced a window overlooking one side of campus. Bridget could see students traversing brick-paved sidewalks as they made their way between buildings that mirrored the old-fashioned style of the administration center. Miss Brighton came around the vast oak desk that stretched between the McKennas and the window and sat down in a leather chair that reminded Bridget of a throne.

"Welcome to Oberrath," Miss Brighton said again. She directed her next comment to Mr. McKenna. "I understand this is your alma mater. It must be good to be back."

Mr. McKenna broke into a smile. "Yes, it is. It's been too long. I'm glad to have an excuse to visit again."

Miss Brighton returned the smile, glancing significantly toward Bridget. "Well, maybe you'll have lots of excuses to come next year." Her gaze swept across all of them and then settled on Bridget again. "Let me tell you a little about Oberrath College, and then I'll be glad to answer any questions." She began describing the advantages of a small university—the low student-to-faculty ratio, the chance to work closely with professors, the numerous extracurricular opportunities, all the factors Mr. McKenna had already laid out.

"It's a wonderful place," she told them. "The four years you spend in college are so formative, and here you can experience things and participate in things that a big college could never offer you. We believe in developing the whole person, not just training for a career, though of course that's important. But why not train for your whole life while you're at it? At Oberrath, you can major in math and at the same time play the lead in a student production or sing in one of our choirs. You can row for one of our intramural canoeing teams or play soccer or basketball. There are almost limitless ways to enrich your experience here as well as the rest of your life."

When she had finished her speech, she chatted with Natalie and Mr. McKenna for a few minutes and then asked them to leave so that she could interview Bridget alone. After she and Bridget discussed Bridget's grades, SAT scores, and various school activities, Miss Brighton reaffirmed what a great school Oberrath was.

"Bridget, I'm impressed with what you've told me," she announced finally. "I think I can assure you without hesitation that you would not only be accepted here but would be offered a good scholarship. I hope it's something you'll consider. You and Oberrath could be a good fit for each other. Have you filled out an application yet?"

At this point Bridget felt a pang of guilt. "No, I haven't," she admitted. "I'm afraid we may have been wasting your time this morning. My first choice is Stanford, and I'm waiting for an early decision from them."

"Ah," said Miss Brighton. "Well, it never hurts to keep your options open. Let me get you an application and a general catalog on the way out. This is a wonderful school, Bridget, and as good as Stanford is, I don't think it can give you as meaningful an experience as Oberrath can."

"Did you go to Oberrath?" Bridget asked.

Miss Brighton grinned. "Yes, I did, so I know whereof I speak. I went elsewhere for graduate school, so I have some experience with other places too. I feel very fortunate to be back here now. It's a place I really believe in."

Bridget studied the young woman's face, which had glowed animatedly as she delivered what must have been her standard spiel. Either she was a good actress or she really liked her job.

"I can tell," Bridget said.

"Keep us in mind," Miss Brighton prompted. "I hope you'll at least do that."

Bridget was surprised to hear herself promise, "Okay. I will."

* * *

It was lunchtime when the three of them emerged from the administration building, and Mr. McKenna led them to the student center, where they found a food court that appeared to offer every imaginable kind of fast food and a few other choices as well. Bridget and her father each ordered a slice of pizza and a soda at Pizza Hut and then met Natalie at a table in a far corner by a window. Natalie had piled a paper plate high with lettuce, tomatoes, raw mushrooms, bean sprouts, and tofu. To Bridget, it actually looked pretty good and she almost regretted her pizza as she picked up the slice and noticed the grease stains marking her own paper plate.

"Do you like to cook?" she asked Natalie.

"I do," Natalie replied, "but unfortunately I like it better as a hobby than as a practical skill. I love trying new recipes, but I'm not always enthusiastic about actually putting a meal on the table every night, you know?"

"Sure," Bridget grinned. "I think I'd be the same way. I was just thinking, you probably have a lot of good tofu recipes." She nodded toward the white chunks of bean curd topping Natalie's plate. "Are you a strict vegetarian?"

Natalie shook her head. "I was for a while. I eat some fish now and then, though, and I cook meat for the boys.

See, that's my laziness. I found it hard to be too strict about limiting meat when I became a working mom. I try to keep us all eating healthy, but once in a while I give in to the quick-and-convenient factor."

"That is to say," Mr. McKenna broke in, "that once in a while she becomes human and eats like the rest of us." He winked at Natalie, and she smirked back.

"You know what your father and I are sitting here thinking about each other," Natalie said, speaking to Bridget but watching Mr. McKenna. "How can the other person eat that?"

Bridget glanced at her father inquisitively. "It's true," he agreed. "What kind of a lunch is that? It looks like you went grazing in the pasture and then found some packing peanuts and sprinkled them on top."

"No," Natalie protested. "Those peanuts are usually pink. Or teal."

"I've seen white ones," Mr. McKenna insisted.

"Well, eating packing peanuts may be just about as healthy as what you're about to down," she argued. Bridget set her pizza back on her plate, not because of what Natalie had said but because the flirtation going on before her fascinated her.

"I'm a man who appreciates flavor," Mr. McKenna declared.

Natalie rolled her eyes exaggeratedly. "Do you like tofu?" she asked Bridget.

"Yeah. I mean, it's true it doesn't have much flavor on its own, but that's the beauty of it, right? You can put it in almost anything, and it just adds this nice texture."

Natalie smiled. "I can tell you're one of us—a connoisseur."

Bridget laughed. "Not really. But my mom liked to eat a lot of it." She broke off suddenly, feeling awkward at the mention of her mother. Natalie pretended not to notice, and

Bridget didn't look at Mr. McKenna.

"It's great stuff," Natalie agreed. "So versatile. Not at all like that garlicky mound of grease there."

"Are you referring to me or my pizza?" Mr. McKenna asked calmly, and all three of them laughed.

After lunch Mr. McKenna took them on a tour of the campus. He led them toward the outer perimeter where the dorms rose up between grassy courtyards edged with bicycle racks.

"Here it is!" he exclaimed at one point, stopping before a caramel-colored building with carved wooden double doors. "Prince Trevor Hall. I lived here two years, before some friends and I got an apartment off campus."

"Who was Prince Trevor?" Bridget wanted to know.

Mr. McKenna frowned. "Never found out."

"No one," Natalie guessed. "Who would give a name like Trevor to royalty?"

Mr. McKenna poked at her ribs. "You're pretty bossy today, aren't you? First you don't like our lunch choice, now you're criticizing the taste of dead kings and queens."

Natalie put on an air of offended dignity. "Someone's got to keep you in line, Gerry. I see what being back here does to you."

"Oh, what's that?"

"Reminds you of when you were young and frisky, doesn't it? Puts you right back in the days of parties and panty raids."

Bridget let out a short guffaw. She couldn't imagine her father ever participating in a panty raid—not that she wanted to imagine such a scene.

"Please!" Mr. McKenna scoffed. "I worked very hard here for four long years."

"Four years *is* a long time," Natalie agreed. "Long enough to find a few minutes for mischief here and there."

Mr. McKenna sighed and shook his head as if to say that

the whole argument was beneath him. "Come on in and I'll show you around a bit," he invited. They had to wait until someone else approached the doors and used a keycard to unlock them, and then they followed the student inside. Mr. McKenna led them downstairs toward a room emitting a low hum. "Best room in the place," he told them, swinging open the door and gesturing for them to enter. Bridget walked through the doorway to see rows of washers and dryers interspersed with long tables. Here and there, a few students sat bent over textbooks or typing on laptops. The scent of fabric softener tickled Bridget's nostrils as it wafted over from a nearby set of dryers.

"The laundry room?" Bridget questioned. "This was your favorite room?" *Oh brother*, she thought. *His favorite thing about college was white starched shirts.*

"Yes," her father responded. "I used to spend hours here."

"Don't get the wrong impression," Natalie said. "It wasn't about the laundry."

"No. This was the best place to study. Quiet, away from everything."

"Yeah, really quiet," Natalie agreed. "Back then, this was a men's-only dorm. These machines were never running."

Mr. McKenna smiled. "A sexist comment, perhaps, but true. Since it became coed, it's not as quiet. But at least it's white noise."

"In fact," Natalie went on, "did you ever actually do laundry here, Gerry?"

Mr. McKenna's eyebrows shot up. "Of course. What do you take me for?"

"Hmm. So, you pretty much kept your sheets washed once a week, right? Or at least once a month."

"Uh, right. Of course."

"Really? Which one?"

"What do you mean?"

"Exactly how many times would you say you washed your sheets during the two years that you lived here?" Natalie glanced at Bridget and winked.

"Oh, I don't know, it was so long ago. How do you expect me to remember details like that?"

"Well, I just don't expect it's that high a number, so I thought maybe the two or three times were memorable."

"Two or three times? Ha!"

"Well, then?"

Mr. McKenna turned to Bridget. "Why don't I show you the building I worked in as a janitor? I'd love to go in there and not have to scrub the toilet."

"You worked as a janitor?" Bridget repeated, her eyes widening with surprise.

"Oh, yes. I didn't just step into a law office right away, you know. I was a junior before I had a chance to do any internships, and even though those *sounded* more impressive, they sometimes weren't that far removed from the janitor gig, to be honest. In fact, you do a lot of grunt work as a lawyer. I sometimes feel I haven't progressed far from my employment roots even now."

"Show us the building you kept sparkling clean," Natalie teased, "since clearly your sheets weren't."

"Sheets aren't supposed to sparkle," Mr. McKenna informed her. Bridget followed them out into the sunlight and back across several courtyards to the main campus. It turned out that her father had been on the janitorial team assigned to the Beckman Science Center. "A few times a year, someone had to climb up and try to dust that dinosaur," he said of the large skeleton that hung before the building's tall front windows.

"Didn't they bring in scientists for that?" Bridget asked. "You know, people who would know how to take care of the bones without damaging them?"

"Nah, these bones aren't real. This is just a model."

"Sounds like an exciting job," Bridget teased.

"Oh, yes, it was. But the best part was the uniform. They gave us these orange jumpsuits to wear over our clothes so we could keep clean enough to go straight to class after work."

"Orange, eh?" said Natalie.

"Yeah. Don't ask me why. I swear they got them at a discount from the prison system. Come on, I'll show you the best bathroom."

"This is what you brought us all the way up to this campus for?" Natalie asked. "To look at a bathroom?"

Mr. McKenna, who had started off in front of them, turned back to survey them. For the first time in his sparring with Natalie, he appeared genuinely bewildered. "I'm sorry, I guess I am wasting our time."

"No," Bridget countered. "These are important things. Part of what life is like here. I mean, you can talk up the school's programs all you want, but when you're really here and you've gotta go, what's more important? The opportunity to row for the canoe team or the great bathrooms in the Beckman Science Center?"

Mr. McKenna looked hurt. "This is an amazing place, Bridget," he proclaimed gravely.

Amazing? After all, it had transformed her stiff, cold father into a different person, one who laughed and teased and liked to be teased back. "Yes," Bridget heard herself agreeing. "It is."

*   *   *

"Just one more stop," Mr. McKenna told them later that afternoon as they strolled across a brick-paved courtyard in the direction of the setting sun. He glanced at his watch. "I told him we'd check in with him about now. I hope we can catch him." He led them through a Gothic-style wooden door into a lobby that seemed dimly lit, as if the many lights in sconces along the wall couldn't muster enough will-power among them to relieve the gloom of the wood panel-ing. With Natalie and Bridget in tow, Mr. McKenna fairly bounded up two flights of stairs to emerge in a hallway with walls painted a noncommittal shade of light gray and floors lined with white linoleum. Here fluorescent lights hung from long silver fixtures. While the construction and deco-rating crew seemed to have meticulously avoided endowing the space with any hint of personality, the inhabitants of the hallway had plastered it with yellow, orange, and purple fliers advertising, Bridget noticed, everything from study groups to poetry readings to a department-sponsored trip to London and Stratford-on-Avon to experience Shake-speare "in his native environment."

"Welcome to the English Department," her father announced. "Now, if nothing's changed . . ." He strode off down the hall, peering now and then at name plaques and occasional photos that identified the occupants of various offices. Bridget and Natalie trailed after him, neither quite matching his pace because they kept stopping to stare at professors' portraits and peruse the notices, comics, and lit-erary quotes stuck to their doors.

"Here it is," Mr. McKenna called. He raised his hand to knock, but before he could do so the door swung open and a tall man with a fringe of white hair and a white beard burst out into the hallway.

"Gerrick!" He boomed. "You're really here! I wondered if I'd missed you. I was forced to go out for a bite to eat a while ago. Not that Thomas Hardy isn't fascinating as always, but he couldn't quite make me forget my stomach today." He embraced Mr. McKenna heartily, slapping him on the back, and Mr. McKenna returned the gesture with an enthusiastic laugh.

"That's one thing I always liked about you," Mr. McKenna exclaimed. "You were proof that a person can appreciate good literature without having to be one of those airy, starving-artist types."

"Nah," agreed the other man, "let the gifted writers starve, that's why I'm not one of them. I'll take my nice cushy office here in the safe haven of academia." He stepped back now and turned toward Natalie and Bridget, smiling and extending his hand. "Well, are these beautiful ladies to be my guests as well?"

Bridget thought she saw her father's chest puff out slightly. "Owen, this is my good friend Natalie Major and my eldest daughter, Bridget."

The man called Owen took Natalie's hand, but instead of simply shaking it he bowed low to bestow a light kiss. Next he did the same with Bridget's. "I am charmed," he declared soberly. "Or, in that lovely way the French have of putting it, enchanté. Please come in and be comfortable."

He herded them into the office, which turned out to be larger than Bridget had expected. Still, she doubted that the professor could have crammed another item of furniture or even another book into it. Owen motioned the two women into green leather armchairs and offered Mr. McKenna the wooden swivel seat behind the desk. He settled himself on one corner of a table piled with a mess of papers that appeared, from the alternating typed lines and scraggly handwriting across the top sheets, to be a recent set of student exams. Next to these ordinary professorial trappings sprawled two crumpled pieces of flannel fringed with yarn. Bridget eyed these curiously while the others talked. When another round of pleasantries ended with a pause in the conversation, Owen followed Bridget's gaze and grinned.

"Would you like to try these?" he invited, picking up the nearer of the flannel pieces and fitting it onto one hand. Short tufts of yellow yarn now sprouted from each of his fingertips, and a large pink nose and mouth and two button eyes covered his palm. Noticing the black and white pattern of the flannel, Bridget judged the hand-puppet to represent a cow. She reached for the other puppet and found it to be a horse with a chocolate-colored yarn mane and the same black button eyes.

"Go ahead," Owen coaxed, "try him on." Bridget slipped her hand inside the puppet and wiggled her fingers.

"Was he helping you study Thomas Hardy?" she asked, smiling.

"Oh, yes. As a matter of fact, I get all my best ideas from these two." Owen winked and lowered his voice conspiratorially. "Don't let the department know, though, who should really get credit for my last publication."

Bridget laughed and looked down at the puppet. She wondered why it didn't embarrass Owen to appear so un-academic in front of a former student—even more, in front of a potential future one. But it was she who suddenly felt self-conscious with the puppet on her hand; she took it off and set it back on the table beside the half-graded tests.

"How old are your grandchildren now, Owen?" her father was asking, as if he saw nothing odd in addressing a man with a Holstein cow on one hand.

"Five and six," Owen replied.

"Ah," said Mr. McKenna, "both in school, then?"

"The younger one, Ben, is in preschool this year. He starts kindergarten next fall."

"Got them both reading yet?" Mr. McKenna inquired.

"Sure, they both took to it a couple of years ago. Look here, I've got a recent photo around somewhere. You've really got to see it." He stepped over a pile of file folders to rummage around on his desk and then stepped back, beaming, holding out a picture of two small children standing on a beach. The wooden frame had been decorated with seashells, and "We love Grampa" was scrawled across the bottom in purple crayon.

"The boy resembles you," Natalie remarked. "What did

you say his name was? Ben, I think?"

"That's right," Owen agreed. "They thought of naming him after me but decided to be more merciful. He looked even more like me when he was a baby. He had a fringe of hair just like mine and almost as white." He shook his head and chuckled. "He's got such a well-shaped head, though, I can imagine how jealous everyone would have been if it hadn't gotten covered up. I deal with that kind of envy everyday." He sighed dramatically. "Yes," he went on, handing the picture to Mr. McKenna and settling back on the table, "it's not everyone that can have my kind of good looks." He winked at Bridget again. "I'll tell you the real truth," he offered, his eyes twinkling. "It's not these puppets that give me all my best ideas, it's those two kids. Smartest pair of munchkins I've ever met, and I'm not just bragging them up. I never brag about them, actually. I'm afraid to. The department might give them both a professorship and kick me out to make room for them. I try to keep it all hush-hush that my Lucie can quote Shakespeare better than I can. And Ben's reading stuff that flummoxed me in high school."

"Well, they're bound to be bright," said Mr. McKenna. "It's in the genes."

"Aw, shucks, Gerrick, you don't have to say that," Owen protested. "I'd put in a good word for your girl even without your flattery."

"I hope so, because there's not much more where that came from." Both men laughed, and Owen finally removed the cow puppet and put it back on the table.

"It's sure good to have those nippers in here, but my students are going to tar and feather me when they find out I still haven't finished grading their exams."

"We'll let you go, then," Mr. McKenna replied, rising to his feet. "Then you can get some work done before you have to face the mob."

"No, no, don't rush off," Owen countered. "We've hardly

had a chance to visit. And I've only just met these two lovely ladies."

"You're a charmer as ever, Owen, but we won't keep you."

The professor argued a few more times that they ought to stay and chat, but finally Mr. McKenna said, "Hopefully we'll be back before too long," and both men glanced significantly at Bridget. Sensing Bridget's discomfort, Natalie placed a hand on Bridget's shoulder. "Yes, Gerrick," she agreed, "we should come up here to visit more often. This place has the most interesting effect on you." Together, she and Bridget turned to go, but Owen called them back once more.

"Bridget, I did want to say one thing in all seriousness," he declared. Bridget doubted whether that were possible, but she stopped walking to listen.

"Your father tells me your goal is Stanford, and I can't stand here and say that Stanford isn't a great school or that you shouldn't try to go there. But the one thing I can tell you, and this is coming from an old professor who's seen the inside of academia for more years than you've been alive, is that ultimately there's more to life than school. You just remember that and you'll be fine."

*　*　*

Riding home that evening, Bridget rested her cheek on the car window and shut her eyes against the glare of oncoming headlights. Exhaustion had relaxed her body into limpness, but her mind refused to give in to sleep. Images crowded through her head, mental snapshots of her father taken at various moments throughout the day—standing outside his old dorm, the breeze rustling his hair so that for an instant a strand or two had been out of place; devouring pizza with the kind of gusto she expected from Charly; laughing—actually laughing—so that the lines deepened around his eyes and transformed his face into that of a man who had lived.

"It's nice that Owen can bring his grandchildren into the office with him," she heard Natalie say from the front seat. "Nice that he wants to spend time with them like that."

"Mmm," came her father's reply.

"I loved working with my grandfather. Of course, it was different with him, no office to take us to and no papers for us to mess up. Did I ever tell you that I first drove a tractor at the age of eight?"

"Really? A sort of tractor prodigy, were you?"

Natalie laughed softly. "Not exactly. My brother was way ahead of me. He started driving at six."

"How did he reach everything?" Mr. McKenna wanted to know.

"My gramps rigged up these sort of stilts so that my brother could work the pedals."

"Mmm," Mr. McKenna remarked. "I think it's safer being the grandchild of an English professor."

"Maybe. Did you get to work with your grandfather? Or your father?"

"Sure, all the time. In the family business."

"Tell me about it," Natalie coaxed.

"Some other time."

They road in silence for a while, hearing only the hum of the engine and the otherworldly swishing of cars passing by.

"I know so little about your childhood," Natalie said finally. "I don't want to force you to share."

Mr. McKenna didn't answer right away. A minute, maybe two, lapsed in silence again. "I'll take you to meet my father," he suggested suddenly. "I'll show you where I grew up."

Bridget, who had been only half listening to the conversation, now focused intently on her father's words. Had he just said that she had grandparents, or at least a grandfather, a living one who she could meet and talk to? Her mother's parents had died when she was young, and her mother had told her—or maybe she had never said it exactly, but Bridget had always believed that all of her grandparents were dead.

"I'd like that," Natalie said.

Her body now tensed, Bridget waited for something more, some detail about her grandfather, some statement that Mr. McKenna meant to take her to meet him too. But he didn't say that. Instead he said, "I used to have Bridget in the office with me sometimes. Her mother would bring her in while she went out to run errands or something. Bridget was so cute, sitting at the desk sorting papers—my little secretary. I let her answer the phone a couple of times. She was better at it than some that I've paid to do the job."

"Did you pay her then? A quarter per phone call maybe?"

"No, the poor kid didn't know what she was worth," Mr. McKenna joked. "I would have given her a dollar per phone call if she'd asked for it. But we always went for ice cream on the way home."

"Ah, you can't beat that."

"Yeah." Mr. McKenna paused before adding, "Her mother stopped bringing her in after a while."

"Why? Did you ask her to stop?"

"No, I never did. She stopped because . . ." he paused again. "Is Bridget asleep back there?" he asked softly. Bridget shut her eyes quickly in the darkness, longing to know whatever he meant to divulge. She heard Natalie twist in the seat to look back at her.

"Yes," Natalie assured him. "I think she fell asleep an hour ago."

"Her mother stopped bringing her because—" Mr. McKenna was keeping his voice low so that Bridget had to strain to catch each word. "Because she thought Bridget was becoming too much like me. That I was having too much influence over her."

"What? Why?" Natalie sounded flabbergasted. "Why wouldn't she want Bridget to be like you? Successful and smart—what could she have against that?"

"There was more to it than that. Margaret was successful and smart, but she was nothing like me. She thought Bridget was becoming—I don't know, too organized, too rigid. All the things she hated about me."

"She hated your being organized?"

"Yeah. She hated my day planner, for one thing. Said she couldn't compete with it."

"Hmm. I'm beginning to understand."

"What's that supposed to mean?" Mr. McKenna sounded irritable now.

"It is a pretty formidable foe," Natalie told him. "I don't know if anything else really commands your full attention."

"Don't be ridiculous. I know there's more to life than my day planner. I can't argue with my day planner and then kiss it and make up, now can I?"

"I should hope not!" Natalie exclaimed, her voice expressive even in a whisper.

"Look, I know what Margaret hated about me." Mr. McKenna had grown serious again. "In the end it wasn't the day planner or the briefcase or the suits from Brooks Brothers. All those things she complained about, they really had nothing to do with it. What she hated was that—

"Yes?" Natalie prodded when it seemed that he wouldn't go on. "Tell me, Gerrick. You can say it."

Her father drew in a breath and then said flatly, "She hated that I grew up."

* * *

By the time they reached home that night, everyone else had already gone to bed. Mrs. Prescott, who had come over to stay with Charly and Lydia, snored contentedly on the couch beneath a knitted afghan. Bridget felt groggy even though she had never managed to fall asleep. She muttered good night to her father and Natalie and then headed upstairs to her room, where she slipped quickly into her pajamas and climbed under the covers. But even here, sleep wouldn't come. She considered getting a Colin book to read, but instead she padded over to her wooden box and took out the manila envelope with the letters. Who were "C & C"? she wondered. Then she shook her head in frustration. Every time she looked at this envelope, she came up against the same questions—questions and no answers. She was tired of that. She needed to understand why her mother had given her these letters. Chewing anxiously on her lower lip, she undid the envelope's clasp and pulled out one of the folded sheets of paper. She opened it slowly and deliberately, trying to ignore the quickening of her pulse. Why should she be afraid to read it? What difference could it possibly make? She needed to get to know her mother better; surely that's what Margaret had had in mind when she willed the letters to Bridget.

But the truth was, she admitted to herself, she didn't want to know. What if these letters were from someone other than her father, some lover that Bridget had never known about? What if her mother had been unfaithful during her marriage and everybody in this town knew it? Maybe that's why their faces clouded over when they spoke of her. It was obvious that she hadn't been well liked, or at least that she hadn't left on good terms.

Bridget took a deep breath. Whatever was in these letters, her mother had wanted her to know. And they could be innocent; they could all be from her father. What if they were? Somehow Bridget found little comfort in that possibility. She didn't want to find out that her mother had been unfaithful, but she couldn't imagine reading the private love missives that might have passed between her parents. Maybe if they were both dead—no, not even then. She could never imagine her father penning a love letter. It seemed too personal even to think about it.

Her mother had been asking too much of her. She was always doing that. She didn't hide her disappointment with Bridget's awkwardness, with her fear of large crowds, with her cautious, deliberate ways. Yes, disappointment, that's what Bridget meant to her mother. But knowing that hadn't fixed her. She still hated having people stare at her when she spoke in public or first walked onstage to play her guitar. And she just wasn't ready to read these letters. To know her parents as people—that was asking too much. She tucked the envelope back in place, flopped into bed again, and finally slept.

f i f t e e n

Charly was eager to go shopping for Bridget's Homecoming attire. She had brought it up at breakfast nearly every morning since Matt had called and invited Bridget to the dance. Other times she peppered Bridget with questions. "What color of dress do you want, Bridget?" she asked several times a day, and Bridget gave her various answers, partly because she didn't know for sure and partly because it entertained Charly to envision gowns in a rainbow of colors. On the Monday morning before the dance, Charly hung around outside the bathroom while Bridget applied her makeup and fixed her hair.

"Only six shopping days left," Charly reminded her, "and that's with Saturday, which shouldn't really count because that's the day of the dance. You don't have time to shop that day."

"Well, the dance isn't until evening," Bridget countered. "Matt's picking me up at 7:30."

Charly looked disgusted. "But you have to get *ready*," she emphasized.

Bridget laughed. "Just how bad do you think I usually look? Do you think I need all day to get presentable?"

"C'mon, Bridge, you know what I mean. This is special. You'll spend extra time on your hair and stuff. You could even go in to the salon and have them do it for you. They're really good with updos and French braids and things like that."

"Hmm," Bridget replied. She had stuck a couple of bobby pins between her lips as she swept her own hair into a French twist.

"Plus, at the salon," Charly continued, "they could do your makeup. And you could get a manicure and even a pedicure. Yeah, 'cause you might wear open-toed shoes. And you could get your nails painted the same color as your dress."

Bridget poked the bobby pins into her hair. "That may be overdoing it a little," she said. "It's not like I'm going to dye my shoes to match my dress. That's so old-fashioned. Can you imagine? Say, a sea green gown, sea green shoes, sea green toenails. Ugh! I'm not going that route."

"Okay, so no sea green," Charly replied amiably. "But you could still get a pedicure and all that other stuff. So you just better block out the whole day on Saturday."

"Sure, and I'll set my alarm for six A.M. too," Bridget teased.

"The point is, Bridget, when are you going to buy your dress? Everyone else already has theirs."

"How do you know this stuff?"

"I just do. Didn't you go to dances in California?"

"Yeah," said Bridget, thinking of Justin's prom. "But I knew where to find things there. There was this little thrift shop on—"

"*Thrift shop?*" Charly wrinkled her nose. "Couldn't you afford something from a real store?"

"Yes, but a real store would never have the kind of vintage treasures you could find at this place," Bridget explained patiently.

"What's vintage?"

"You know, from the past. Sort of like antiques, only in clothes."

Charly looked scornful. "You mean old-fashioned? Why is that any different from sea green shoes?"

Bridget laughed. "You've got a point there. All I can say

is, there's a world of difference."

"I think you better take me shopping with you," Charly advised seriously.

"Great," Bridget joked. "Isn't there *any* member of this family who trusts my taste in clothes?"

But she did take Charly along when she finally drove to Rochester on Wednesday afternoon. As Bridget flipped through the clothing racks at the bridal and formal shop in the mall, she couldn't help wondering how much like Justin Matt would turn out to be. Was image as important to him as it was to Justin? Justin had always cared about appearances, and when Bridget had chosen her prom dress, she had done it as much because she knew it would appeal to Justin as because she liked it herself. In fact, now that she thought about it, that dress seemed to characterize her whole experience with Justin. She tried to remember what they had talked about when they were together, what the substance of their relationship had been. She couldn't recall a single meaningful conversation, now that she thought about it. Instead, she remembered holding his arm and smiling as they glided through crowds at all the right parties, the way people would step aside and peer at them admiringly—or at least at Justin. Funny, she mused. She had faulted Justin before for being superficial, but she saw now that she had been as much to blame. Had she tried to penetrate through the reputation, the glitter, the suaveness, to the person underneath? And when he had told her he loved her, had she really believed him? Or hadn't she known deep down, all along, that it was merely part of the script? Justin's whole life was like a movie, and he knew what it took to be the leading man. He had the role down well. Meanwhile, she had enjoyed going along for the ride. *That's all it was*, she thought. *And that's all I've lost.* Her hands slowed and then grew still, one resting on a strapless gown with purple sequins, the other on a satin slip dress. Bridget stared at the gowns without seeing them. She knew, had known for a long time maybe, that there had never been anything real between her and Justin. And yet . . . *And yet it still hurts*, she acknowledged. *It's stupid, but it hurts.*

"Bridget, there you are," Charly called, coming toward her through the maze of formalwear. She had three or four dresses draped over one arm. "What are you doing, it's getting late! Did you find anything over here?" Bridget shook her head no, but Charly had barely paused for an answer. "Here, try these on," she commanded, flinging the gowns over Bridget's arm. "Hurry, I can't wait to see them on."

"Yes, ma'am," Bridget giggled, relieved to be brought back to the ordinariness of everyday things. Charly was right, she had to get moving. She had a dress to buy.

"Which one do you think Matt would like?" she asked Charly as the two of them threaded their way to the dressing room.

"Oh, I don't know, they're all great. I have an eye for these things," Charly asserted, sounding very important.

"Do you now? Wonderful." Maybe she did too, because when Bridget stood before the three-way mirror in the last of Charly's picks, she had to admit that they all looked good.

"Do you know what colors Matt likes?" Charly inquired, trying to help Bridget choose.

"No," Bridget answered. "But it doesn't really matter, does it? Because *I* like this one best."

*   *   *

The day of the dance, Bridget couldn't help catching some of Charly's excitement. Even Lydia wanted to be in on the preparations, and she got so interested in inspecting Bridget's dress and discussing the best hair and makeup choices that she kept forgetting to wear her usual smirk. Bridget decided to follow Charly's counsel and go to the salon for a manicure and pedicure, even if she didn't need her nails painted the same color as her dress. Charly and Lydia approved of the shiny, clear polish that coated her French manicure.

"You're going to look so glamorous!" Charly exclaimed.

Lydia helped Bridget pick out some dangly diamond earrings, and both Charly and Lydia watched in admiration as Bridget applied her makeup and curled her hair, twisting it into an intricate upsweep. Finally it was time to put on the dress, a midnight blue satin two-piece gown. At 7:20, the three of them stood before the mirror, smiling in satisfaction at the results of the day's handiwork.

"You look pretty good," Lydia commented, which Bridget accepted as positively glowing praise.

"I couldn't have done it without you two," she said, wrapping an arm around each sister and pulling them close.

"Careful," Charly warned, "you'll crush your hair!"

Bridget laughed and herded her sisters downstairs to wait for Matt to arrive. They found Mr. McKenna pacing in the living room, but he sat down quickly and picked up a newspaper when he saw the girls coming down.

"Bridget," he boomed, setting the paper down and standing up again when she came into the room, "you look nice. I'd forgotten—it's the Homecoming dance tonight, isn't it?"

Charly frowned. "You didn't forget. I heard you talking about it with Natalie this morning."

Mr. McKenna looked sheepish. "Oh, well, yes . . . I guess it had just slipped my mind for a moment."

The doorbell rang a few minutes later, and Mr. McKenna, Lydia, and Charly all jumped up to answer it. "Oh, let Dad get it," Lydia decreed, tugging Charly back to the living room. "You know he's been waiting around to interview this guy." She and Charly both snickered.

"Poor Matt," Charly said. "I hope he has his future

planned out through retirement."

"Yeah," agreed Lydia, "and he better be planning on a well-paying career."

"He better not have a single speeding ticket,"added Charly.

"Or a parking ticket," continued Lydia. "And he better read the *Wall Street Journal* and be good at investing money."

"And he better not expect to stay out past ten!"

"Ugh," was all Bridget could say, and then Mr. McKenna was showing Matt through the second set of double doors.

"Just step into my office for a moment," she heard her father say. "Don't worry, I won't keep you long."

Bridget waited to hear the office door shut and then turned to her sisters. "I thought you two were joking."

Lydia guffawed.

"This is Dad's first date," Charly pointed out. "He's nervous. Plus, we've seen the way he is with our friends. And the way he talks about us dating."

"Yeah, it's scary," Lydia said. "Honestly, I don't think we're going to get out much before college. That's why I'm not going anywhere too close to home!"

Ten or fifteen minutes later, the office door opened and Matt emerged, looking a little ruffled.

"Well, ah, Bridget, are you ready to go?" he asked from the hallway. He hovered close to the doors as if anxious to make his escape. As Bridget walked toward him, though, he regained a little composure. "You look spectacular," he told her, grinning.

"Be home by twelve, Bridget," her father ordered as she and Matt walked out the doors. "Twelve on the dot, you understand!"

Bridget enjoyed herself during dinner, feeling more relaxed than she usually had with Justin. She didn't have to keep wondering how many people were watching them.

She and Matt talked pleasantly about school and then about music and movies. When they had finished eating, they went on to the dance, which was being held in the high school gym. At Bridget's old school, dances were always held somewhere fancy, like an elegant hotel. Still, there was a certain charm to basketball hoops draped with streamers, she decided. She smiled at Matt. "At least I can't smell the locker rooms," she said.

"Coach had us scrub them out," he told her.

"Really?"

"Yeah. Can't you smell the cleaner?"

Come to think of it, there was a certain odor in the air, something that reminded Bridget of bug spray.

"Hmm. I'm not sure what's worse," she said, and they both laughed.

"Should we walk around for a minute before we dance," Matt suggested, "and see who's here?"

"Okay." They stopped and talked to some of Matt's friends for a while, and then Bridget spotted Jeff onstage behind a long table of CDs.

"I need to say hello to my friend Jeff," she said, stepping quickly toward the stage. "Aren't you dancing tonight?" she called to him when she was close enough. "Being the DJ at Lydia's party is one thing, but you should take a night off once in a while."

He grinned at her. "Nah," he declined. "I just can't get enough of serving my fellow men. And women." He winked at her, but she didn't have time to talk anymore because Matt was pulling her back toward the dance floor. Soon she had forgotten about Jeff as she moved to the music.

"You're a good dancer," Matt said.

"Thanks," she replied. "So are you." But she wasn't prepared for the way he pulled her close when the next song, a slow ballad, came on. He held her tightly as they moved across the floor.

"One does have to be able to breathe, though," she informed him, "in order to dance well." He got the hint and released her a little.

"Sorry," he said. After a minute he added, "It's just that you look so good tonight. Well, every day actually. I have to admit, I've been watching you for a long time."

"Do you have eyes in the back of your head?" she joked.

He grinned. "Just about." Soon he was holding her tightly again.

"Matt, I'm serious," she warned. "That's too tight."

He let her go. "Okay, okay. Why don't we go for a walk and get some fresh air?" Outside, the sharp night air smelled of winter, but it was a relief to be away from the press of dancing couples. They chatted easily as they walked up and down in front of the high school a few times.

"Let's go back inside now," Bridget said when they had traversed the sidewalk for the third time. "I'm ready to dance some more." She liked dancing, but she was also a little worried about Matt's intentions and didn't want to spend too much time outside alone with him. *Am I becoming my father?* she thought fleetingly. But no, she assured herself, she just wanted to be smart.

Only she hadn't been quite smart enough. Suddenly Matt was pulling her close again and pressing his mouth hard against hers. She struggled against him and finally managed to shove him away.

"Stop it!" she yelled at him. He approached her again but she punched him hard in the stomach, and when he had recovered enough to look up at her from his doubled-over position, his face showed embarrassment.

"I'm sorry," he said for the second time in the last hour. "I don't know what came over me."

"I think they're called hormones," Bridget said. "Ever heard of them?"

"It's just that you look so good. You know, irresistible."

"Okay, fine, apology accepted. But let me help you resist me." She turned on her heel and walked off, leaving him with his arms wrapped around his stomach.

Back in the building, she wandered aimlessly for a while. Adrenaline had made her face flushed in spite of the cool air outside, and at first she felt proud of herself and powerful. Her mother certainly would have approved of the right hook that knocked Matt down to half his height. After a few minutes, though, she began to wonder what to do next. She didn't want to go home yet. Her father was sure to ask questions if she arrived this early and alone, and the last thing she wanted to do was tell him what had happened. She'd never be allowed out of the house again! She finally decided to go and talk to Jeff.

As she headed up to the stage, she saw Matt come in from outside. He met her eyes and then ducked away sheepishly.

"Can I join you?" she asked Jeff as she approached the table where the music and equipment were laid out.

"Yeah, but where's your date?" Bridget looked around and spotted Matt standing a little awkwardly near a group of his friends.

"Oh, he's one of those unfortunate suitors that I've had to leave whimpering in the bushes."

Jeff's eyebrows shot up. "Oh?"

"Yeah, he was slightly overeager, so I told him I'd see myself home."

"Ah." He was quiet for a moment, and then he asked, "Seriously, though, are you okay?"

"Yeah, I'm fine." She thought about it for a minute. "Disappointed, I guess, because I was having a good time, you know, and thinking maybe we could go out again. Just for fun. It's not like it's a big tragedy."

"I should've known Matt would be the type," Jeff said angrily. "I should've warned you."

"Why should he have been the type? Does he have a reputation or something?"

"No, it's just . . ."

"What?"

"You know, he's one of those jock types, popular, thinks he can have his own way."

Bridget shook her head. "That's just a stereotype. It's not like being athletic and popular automatically makes you unable to control your hormones."

"Or unwilling to."

"Right. Whatever, let's just forget it."

"Hey, I know it's not what you had planned for the evening, but how about saving me a dance a little later on? You can't waste that dress."

She smiled. "I think I can do that." Anyway, she didn't want to go back out onto the dance floor as long as Matt was still lurking around. She stayed with Jeff for the rest of the evening, and a little before midnight he found someone to take over for a couple of songs while he danced with Bridget.

"What time do you have to be home?" he asked after the second dance.

"Midnight. Or I turn into a pumpkin."

"I figured," he said. "Pretty good, though, I thought maybe your dad would want you home by eleven."

"I think Natalie talked him out of that."

"Thank goodness for Natalie then! Come on, I'll walk you home."

"Don't you need to stay and help put the equipment away? I can go home by myself. It's only a few blocks." She thought she had seen Matt leaving a while ago, so she didn't think she'd have any problems from him.

"It's late," Jeff protested. "I'll come back and get the stuff put away. Come on, it won't take long, but I don't want to send you off on your own."

They walked the few blocks to the McKenna home, but

Bridget hesitated to go in. She could see her father's shadow through the front window. She had dared to hope that he wouldn't be waiting up for her. Of course, that had been a pretty unrealistic wish.

Jeff looked over at her. "Hey, how about some hot chocolate before you go in to face the Inquisition?"

"Great, are you going to conjure some up out of your sleeve?"

Jeff motioned toward his own house, where light still glowed in a few of the windows. "In case you've forgotten, I live across the street."

"Well, then. Shall we?" She accompanied him gratefully across the McKennas' lawn. She was surprised to find Jeff's mom waiting up when they stepped quietly into Jeff's kitchen. Mrs. Iverson had wrapped herself in a pink bathrobe that matched the pink curlers in her hair.

"Bridget, welcome!" Mrs. Iverson greeted her, spreading her arms and folding Bridget into a soft hug. Bridget had met Mrs. Iverson at church a few times and had noted the woman's resemblance to her son, with her round, friendly face and large eyes. "It's good to see you again," Mrs. Iverson said.

"Hey, Mom," Jeff said. "We could really use some hot chocolate. Got any available?"

"Of course. Sit down, relax, and I'll whip it up in a moment."

"Oh, Mrs. Iverson, please don't go to any trouble," Bridget objected. "We can make it ourselves."

"Oh, it's no trouble," she insisted. "I don't let Jeff loose in the kitchen much. He tends to come up with interesting combinations."

"Interesting?"

"Creative, imaginative, all that good stuff, but best kept secret." Mrs. Iverson winked at them and then busied herself over the stove.

"As a matter of fact," she continued, "it's good to have a friend of Jeff's stop by."

"Your house is probably overrun most of the time," Bridget guessed. "I know Jeff has lots of friends."

"Hmm, now what did I do with those marshmallows? Jeff, will you check in the pantry and see if I put some marshmallows in there?" his mother requested.

"You don't have to ask me twice when it comes to marsh-mallows," Jeff said, standing up and leaving the kitchen.

Mrs. Iverson glanced over at Bridget and said quietly, "The truth is, Jeff does have lots of friends. Everyone likes him. But he doesn't have any close friends, do you know what I mean? He's so nice all the time, and I wouldn't change that because that's how we've raised him to be. But sometimes I think he gets taken for granted. He has so much to offer, but people just take, take, take and never think of him."

"Mom," Jeff called from the pantry. "Any idea where those marshmallows might be?"

"No," Mrs. Iverson called back, "but I'm just sure I put some in there somewhere." She turned back to Bridget. "Jeff just lets it happen. Like tonight. I wanted him to dance. It's his senior year, and I wanted him to go to at least one dance and actually *dance*."

"He did dance tonight, Mrs. Iverson. We danced for two songs."

Mrs. Iverson smiled. "I'm glad to hear it. Thank you, Bridget."

"Mom," Jeff called. "I just can't find them."

"Oh, Jeff," she called back. "I'm so sorry, but here they are in the cupboard after all."

Jeff reappeared in the kitchen doorway and sat down next to Bridget again. He shook his head sadly. "Mom, I hoped your mind wouldn't be the first thing to go. Isn't hearing supposed to go first?"

Mrs. Iverson shrugged. "Sorry," she said again as she

topped two steaming mugs with marshmallows and carried them over to the table.

Bridget's tension eased as the warm liquid streamed into her. "This is wonderful," she told Mrs. Iverson. By the time Jeff led her back through the living room to walk her across the street, she felt fortified enough to face her father. She had even relaxed enough to take in details of the Iversons' home, like the large picture of Christ that hung prominently over the piano. Jeff followed her gaze, and once they had stepped outside, he asked, "So, uh, how are you feeling about the Church now that you've been coming for a while?"

"That's quite a conversation opener. Do you use that as a pickup line?"

"Sorry," he apologized. "You don't have to answer if you don't want to."

"No, it's okay." Bridget considered for a moment how to sum up her ideas. "I'm feeling . . . I'm feeling like it's one more aspect of my family that I need to accept, and maybe it won't be as hard as I first thought. I like what you've said about your beliefs. I like the way they work in your life. You were right, I needed to forget about all these details, the cultural stuff and the words I don't understand. I see that the people at church are good people."

"That's great," Jeff said. "But . . ."

"Is there a but?"

"I was sure I heard one."

"Oh, well," Bridget hesitated. "I'm still me, you know?" she said, wanting him to understand what she wasn't sure how to express. "And maybe I'm more willing now to work to accept my family as they are. But I want the same from them. I don't want to have to be remade in order for my father to accept me. I want him to care about me the way I am. Does that make sense?"

"Yeah," Jeff said, shrugging. "That's what everyone wants."

They stared at each other for a moment in silence.

"And he does care," Jeff went on. "I'm not gonna argue that he has funny ways of showing it, but he does care."

"I don't know," Bridget said. "He seems to be all about rules." She laughed ironically. "Kind of like the Church, I guess. They both seem pretty rigid about dating and stuff."

"Maybe that's it. Your father is a lot like the Church. Or I mean, he's like other people in the Church."

"What's that supposed to mean?"

"He has rules but it's because he cares. And under all that, he's just trying to do the best he can."

Bridget looked toward the front window, where her father's shadow still sat waiting.

"I guess so," she said. "Anyway, here goes." She left Jeff on the lawn and went inside.

s i x t e e n

Bridget was hoping to spend a quiet weekend at home now that her Stanford application was in and the trip to Oberrath and the Homecoming dance were both over, but her father announced at breakfast the next Thursday that they'd be taking a family trip on Saturday.

"You haven't made any plans with Matt, have you?" he asked. Bridget had managed to avoid answering too many questions on the night of the dance, explaining that Matt had dropped her off quickly and then left to go to an after-dance party with his friends. Bridget, of course, couldn't accompany him to the party because of her curfew. Her father had seemed to accept this and hadn't pried too much since then.

"No," she said now, "I don't have any plans yet. But where are we going?"

"I thought you might be interested in seeing your grandfather."

"Really?" Charly piped up. "We're going to see Gramps?"

"Yes," Mr. McKenna affirmed calmly. "And Natalie will be coming with us. He's been anxious to meet her."

"Cool!" whooped Charly.

Mr. McKenna eyed her sternly. "Charlotte, may I remind you that we are at the table."

"Sorry," said Charly, sobering quickly.

"Will you take us out on the pond?" Lydia asked.

"Yes, if the weather's good," Mr. McKenna promised. "I

haven't been rowing for a long time. But it's getting late in the year. It won't be long before the pond is better for ice skating than boating."

"I'll throw my skates in just in case," Charly said.

"I think Dad was exaggerating a little," Lydia told her. "It takes ages for the pond to get solid enough to skate on."

"I know," Charly answered. "But still . . ."

Later that day Bridget asked Charly, "Does your grandfather—I mean, *our* grandfather—does he ever come to visit you?"

"Not anymore."

"What do you mean?"

"You'll see. He can't really get around much since the stroke."

"Oh," said Bridget.

Charly brightened. "But he's still fun. You'll love him."

"And our grandmother?"

"She died a long time ago, when I was little."

Friday night it snowed, and Saturday morning the girls woke to find a white skiff coating the grass and turning the trees to lace. Bridget ran outside in her pajamas to get a closer look. Charly followed, dancing around the lawn in her slippers.

"Isn't it great?" Charly cried. "This means it's time to start counting down to Christmas!"

"It's so beautiful," Bridget marveled, reaching down to touch it. Her fingers traced thin patterns across the surface. Impulsively, she lay down on her back and moved her arms and legs back and forth to make a snow angel. Dampness seeped instantly through the thin cotton of her pajamas, and when she stood up, she saw only mud and grass where her form had been.

"It's not deep enough," Charly explained. "But just wait till we get a couple of feet! You know, once in a while it even gets bad enough that they cancel school."

Bridget wondered if the family trip would be canceled, but after breakfast the girls piled into the car along with their father and Natalie. During the two-hour drive to the town where Mr. McKenna had grown up, Natalie kept asking about his childhood, but he mostly gave short, non-committal answers. Finally he said, "I'll give you the complete tour when we get there."

"And you'll take questions?" Natalie prodded.

"I didn't say that."

Preston turned out to be almost a mirror image of Phrygia, except it was a bit more rural. It hadn't snowed there yet, and a few trees still bore traces of fading autumn colors.

"Did you live here all your life until college?" Bridget asked her father.

"Yes," he replied. He glanced back at her. "Not quite as exciting as San Francisco, is it?" She couldn't tell if he was being sarcastic or not. She had a feeling he didn't much care for San Francisco. She longed to ask him more questions, to find out where he had worked for his first job, what he had done for fun here, what school had been like (small, for one thing). But if Natalie couldn't pry the information from him, she was sure to have no better luck.

They drove through one end of the business district, which appeared to be even smaller than Phrygia's, and pulled up in front of a pleasant-looking gray stone building with the sign "Stoneybrook Retirement Home." Inside the lobby, Bridget noted the unmistakable smell of nursing homes—a combination of medicine, stale urine, and old age—but the lobby had been attractively decorated and the carpeted hallways lined with paintings of nature scenes, which gave off a friendly air. Mr. McKenna led them to a room halfway down one hallway and knocked on the door before opening it gently and poking his head inside.

"Poppy," he called softly. "Are you awake? I've brought

you some visitors." Bridget thought she heard a low response from inside the room, and then her father swung the door open wider and motioned for the girls and Natalie to step inside. The room was larger than Bridget had expected, with a small kitchenette to the right of the doorway and a living room sectioned off from the sleeping area, which was screened from full view by a three-quarter-height wall. A man sat on a sofa with a blanket across his lap. Maybe it was this hint of invalidism that suggested frailty at first glance, or it might have been the fluff of white hair that seemed too fine to lie flat against his scalp. A closer look revealed that he had once been strong. His shoulders were still broad and well filled out, and when he stood, wobbling unsteadily on his cane, he rose to a height as formidable as his son's.

"Gerrick," he cried, reaching out to them all. "Girls, come and see me." Charly rushed over and embraced him, and he stooped to let her kiss him on the cheek. Mr. McKenna approached more slowly, guiding Natalie toward his father with his hand on the small of her back.

"Poppy," said Mr. McKenna, "this is my friend Natalie."

"Natalie," the old man addressed her. "I'm so glad to meet you."

She offered him her hand. "And I've been looking forward to meeting you for a long time," she replied.

"I hope this will be the first of many visits," he said. Bridget thought she saw his eyes twinkling. "What's this word *friend*, son? You ought to say what you mean. Didn't I teach you to be straightforward?"

Mr. McKenna came as close to squirming as Bridget imagined was possible, but he quickly diverted the old man's attention, turning back to his eldest daughter to beckon her forward. "And here's Bridget, Poppy. I've brought her back to you."

Bridget moved toward the old man slowly, but when she had come close enough, he held out an arm and pulled her against him briefly. His chest felt hard beneath the soft wool of his sweater. His whiskers scratched against her temple. "Bridget," he whispered. "Bridget." He let her go and stood watching her intently, as if trying to memorize every detail. "It's been much too long. We were all so worried . . ."

"Worried?"

"Yes. Three days it was, and we never slept the entire time, we were waiting by the phone feeling helpless—"

"Poppy," Mr. McKenna interrupted. "That was a long time ago. But she's back with us now."

The old man smiled. "Yes, she's back. Welcome back, Bridget. Welcome home."

Bridget gazed into her grandfather's eyes, which were deep-set amid wrinkles collected throughout decades of living. She glanced around at the others in the room, her father poised stiff and straight as usual, Lydia seated on an ottoman twirling a strand of dark hair, Charly still hovering close to her grandfather's side. Natalie had found a collection of photographs to study on a shelf in the corner. Bridget was no longer a stranger among these people. After all, this was her family, this was what she had wanted for so long, and her grandfather was inviting her into the circle, telling her she fit in here. But something in her didn't want to be welcomed, something kept pricking her with the thought, *This isn't your real home. Home is California. Home is where you have to get back to.* She didn't say that out loud. She only returned her grandfather's smile and said, "Thank you."

"This is where you belong, you know," he affirmed, and for a moment Bridget wondered if he could read her thoughts, if he sensed the stubborn part inside that refused to be drawn into this New York life. She almost wanted to explain that she didn't belong here at all, not any more than her mother had, but she didn't want to start an argument. She hoped that they could get past this awkwardness, this too-close-to-truthness, and talk about something else so that everyone could enjoy the day.

"I'm excited to meet you . . . again," she said finally. "I was always jealous of kids who had grandparents."

He chuckled. "Grandparents and grandchildren are some of the best things in life, it's true." He grew serious again and reached out for Bridget's hand. "But you've missed out on many things, and it wasn't your fault. No matter. You're back where you belong now."

Bridget was glad a couple of hours later when her father proclaimed that it was time to go. "We've tired you out enough for one day, Poppy."

"No, no," the old man objected. "I'm not tired a bit. If *you're* tired, Gerrick, just admit it, don't blame it on me."

"Well, some of us aren't as spry as we used to be, Poppy," Mr. McKenna said.

"I'm sorry to hear that son. Have you thought about adopting my morning routine?" He turned to Natalie and Bridget and explained, "I lift weights every morning. Keeps me toned." He held up one arm to demonstrate. "Feel that bicep."

"Poppy, no one needs to feel your muscles."

"It's true, Mr. McKenna," Natalie said. "I can see that bulging bicep from here."

The old man grinned and looked up at his son. "I like this girl, Gerrick. Don't let her get away, now, will you?"

Bridget's father, who had risen to his feet and begun drifting toward the door, paused and gazed down at Natalie. "Well, that's up to her, isn't it," he said softly. Natalie met his eyes, and the two exchanged unreadable expressions.

"Dad, are you going to take us out on the pond?" Lydia asked into the silence.

Mr. McKenna let his eyes slide from Natalie to his daughters. "Yes, I think the weather's good enough."

"Let's go then," Lydia insisted, jumping up. "Bye, Gramps." She stooped to kiss the old man and then bounded toward the door with Charly in tow. Soon they were all back in the car, with Charly and Lydia chattering excitedly about going boating on the pond. Mr. McKenna, Natalie, and Bridget sat silently, each with their own thoughts. Bridget struggled to remember her grandfather's exact words . . . *three days*. What had he said about three days and waiting by the phone? What had he meant? Maybe he had been talking about something that had happened when she was a little girl, but she wanted to know more.

At one point during the drive back through town, her father met her eyes in the rearview mirror. "Poppy does pretty well," he said to her, "but maybe you gathered, he does get a little confused sometimes. Ever since the stroke."

"What was he talking about when—" Bridget began.

"Nothing," her father said firmly. "Nothing."

They passed through a residential neighborhood and then continued out beyond the sign marking the city limits. Fields began to flow by, and a few scattered houses broke up the landscape. After a while, Bridget spotted several buildings that were grouped together, one of which was obviously a house, another of which appeared to be a shop of some kind. She was surprised when Mr. McKenna slowed the car and pulled into the driveway of the house. It towered above them, a rambling Victorian that various owners in various eras had added on to so that now it displayed a hodgepodge of styles, with wings sprawling out from the main house like chicks gathered around a mother hen. Bridget found herself liking the house. It impressed her with an unapologetic frankness, as if it had given up trying to be a beauty and decided to focus on the comfort of its inhabitants. She thought the windows along the front even resembled a smiling face.

"What is this place?" she asked. "Who lives here?"

"Your uncle Mitch lives here now," her father replied. Then he twisted around in his seat to look at her. "This is where I grew up."

They all climbed out of the car, and a middle-aged, dark-haired woman threw open the front door and hurried across the grass to greet them.

"So you made it!" she called. "I was starting to get a little worried."

"We visited with Poppy a bit longer than I expected," Mr. McKenna explained.

"Oh, I'm sure he loved that," the woman said.

Mr. McKenna made the introductions. "Annie, this is my friend Natalie. Natalie, my sister-in-law Annie. And Bridget you've met before, Annie, but I bet you wouldn't recognize her."

"Oh, wouldn't I?" Annie contradicted. "I'd know those eyes and that copper hair anywhere. Welcome home, Bridget," she said, wrapping Bridget in a quick embrace. "Let me take a good look at you. I'm sorry we haven't been over to see you before now, this season has been so busy with the shop and all."

"Well, that's good to hear," said Mr. McKenna. "Business is good?"

"It sure is. And even after all this time, our reputation is still spreading. We're starting to get orders in from Pennsylvania and New England."

"Wonderful!" Mr. McKenna replied.

"Mitch is in the shop right now doing some finish work. Come on in." She led them across the lawn to one of the other buildings that Bridget had noticed when they first arrived. A sign identified it as the McKenna Fine Cabinetry and Furniture Shop. Inside, an array of gleaming wood furniture filled the front room of the shop. Bridget let her eyes explore the intricately carved rocking chairs, dining tables, baby cribs, benches, and other assorted items. Impressed, she reached out to touch the etched surface of a nearby coatrack.

"This is beautiful stuff," she commented. "Your husband makes these?"

"He sure does, he and his apprentices. And they do it all by hand. You don't find much furniture made like this anymore." Annie led them through the display room to the work area in the back, where a man bent over an old-fashioned-looking rocking horse.

"Mitch, they're here," Annie said. The man straightened up, brushed a few wood shavings from his front, and reached out a hand.

"Hey, Gerrick, girls, good to see you. And this must be Bridget. Wow, you've grown up into a knockout." He chuckled. "If I know you, Gerrick, and I do, I'd say you've been walking the floors at night devising ways to keep the guys away from this one."

"Don't give him any ideas," Bridget warned, smiling. She studied her uncle's appearance with curiosity, noting how his eyes and the shape of his face resembled her father's. His jaw was more square, though, and he was stockier all over. He wouldn't look right in a James Bond movie, but she could easily picture him in an advertisement for some sort of outdoor gear, like fishing supplies or something.

"And this must be Natalie," Uncle Mitch continued. "It's about time you all came to visit us, Gerrick. Haven't you and Natalie been seeing each other for a couple of years? You must be getting serious now that you're finally getting around to introducing her to the family. Should we watch for a wedding announcement soon? Give us some notice, will you, so I can arrange to have someone cover the shop."

"Mitch, have some tact," chided Annie. "You know Gerrick likes to be a man of mystery."

"That's true," Natalie put in. "Often he's a mystery even to me."

Mitch shrugged. "That's my brother. If you ask me, he thinks about things way too much. He needs to think less and do more. Take some action." He slapped his brother on the back.

Mr. McKenna appeared unperturbed. "If we asked you? But nobody did, Mitch."

They all went up to the house to visit for a while, and Annie showed Bridget pictures of her and Mitch's three children, all of whom were off at college. Bridget encouraged Annie to talk about her kids, though Charly and Lydia had clearly heard their list of achievements recited before and didn't take much interest. To Bridget, the idea of cousins was novel and fascinating. She would have listened to Annie all day.

After a while Lydia reminded her father that he had promised to take them out on the pond, and he said he'd better do it before they ran out of daylight. Mitch was too busy to come with them; he had to get back to the shop, and Annie declined the invitation to join them. "It's cold out, Gerry," she declared. "Don't keep the kids out too long. And stay out of the water!"

Mr. McKenna, Natalie, and the girls tramped across the backyard and down through a wooded area to a clearing where a large pond shone silver in the afternoon sunlight. Mr. McKenna led them to a shed built on the edge of the pond and dragged out a canoe, which he proceeded to launch into the water.

"Come on," he called to them, "hop in."

"Are we all going to fit in that?" Bridget asked skeptically.

"Sure we are," Charly assured her. One by one, they stepped gingerly across a couple of feet of shallow water to climb into the canoe, and then Mr. McKenna, who had positioned himself in the middle, began rowing hard out toward the center of the pond. The canoe glided swiftly over the glassy surface, and a breeze ruffled the girls' hair. From somewhere came the plaintive cry of a bird.

"This is beautiful, Gerrick," said Natalie. "Is this where you played as a boy?"

"Oh, we went all over," he replied. "There's an old branch of the Erie Canal around here, just like back in Phrygia, and we liked to row on that too."

"You and your brother?"

"No, me and—" he paused abruptly. "Well, yeah, sometimes Mitch and me."

"And this furniture shop, it's been your family's business since you were a kid?"

"Longer than that," Mr. McKenna answered. "My great-grandfather opened the shop. My dad prided himself on using the same methods his grandpa did, and now Mitch does the same thing."

"Did you ever think of working there, in the shop?" Bridget asked.

"Oh, I did work there, when I was growing up. But I never thought of doing it for a living. Mitch was a natural. I was never so good with my hands." He rested one of the oars on the side of the canoe and held up one hand with the fingers spread apart, as if trying to figure out the reason for its lack of carpentry skill. "I've got scars all over from hammering and sawing myself. I'd probably be left with two stumps by now if I'd spent more time in the family business." Natalie laughed, and Mr. McKenna picked up the oar again. He looked serious and didn't join in Natalie's laughter. "It's a good life, though. Hard because owning a business means giving up a lot of security. There were times my dad thought he couldn't pull it through. One time I remember in particular, he about sold out to some entrepreneur from New York City. But . . . he was always around, you know? He spent a lot of time with us. Working in the shop with us or taking us out fishing or whatever. He never told us to get lost, even when we were too young—or in my case, too clumsy—to be of any real help." Throughout this speech, he had been gazing off into the trees around the pond, but now he looked at his daughters, meeting each set of eyes in turn. "I would have liked to have been more like that."

* * *

Dusk had fallen by the time they packed the canoe back into the shed and climbed up through the trees toward the house. They ate dinner with Mitch and Annie and then, tired and well fed, got into the car for the long drive home, or so Bridget thought. Lydia insisted on one more stop.

"C'mon, Dad, you know we have to visit Richard and Laura."

"It's late, Lydia," Mr. McKenna responded, "and I didn't call them to let them know we'd be in town. They may not even be home."

"But if they are, and they find out we were here, you know they'll be hurt that we didn't stop and see them."

"Yeah, Dad," Charly seconded Lydia's request. "We can't leave without at least saying hi to them."

"Who are Richard and Laura?" Bridget asked.

"Our great-aunt and uncle," Lydia replied.

"Oh, you mean our grandfather's brother and sister?"

"No," said Lydia, leaving it at that. No one else offered to explain further. Mr. McKenna was still intent on avoiding the visit altogether.

"It's rude to drop in on people, Lydia," he said.

"Gerry, if they're family," Natalie argued, "it does seem like you could stop and say hello. We don't have to stay long."

"Yeah, Dad, c'mon," Charly pressed.

"You promised to give me the full tour," Natalie reminded him. "If you've got more relatives hanging around here for me to meet, then let's meet them."

"They're not my relatives," Mr. McKenna said.

Bridget and Natalie both stared at him blankly.

"Oh, all right," he said finally, slowing the car and

making a U-turn. He drove them back to the outskirts of town and parked at the curb in front of a modest ranch-style home with a light on in the big front window.

"Looks like they're home," Lydia said, flinging the car door open and leaping out of her seat. She ran up the sidewalk to the porch and rang the doorbell before the others had all extricated themselves from their seat belts. As they followed in Lydia's wake, the front door opened and a plump woman stood silhouetted in the rectangle of light from the living room. She waited until everyone had joined Lydia on the porch and then said, "Come in, come in! I didn't know you were in town." She moved aside to let them past her into the room, which was comfortably if shabbily furnished with armchairs and overflowing bookcases. All of the several end tables bore a lamp and at least one open book.

"Sit down anywhere you can find a place," she invited warmly. "Just shove those books aside if you need to. Richard," she called toward the kitchen, "come on out, it's Gerrick and the girls." She beamed around at them all, apparently glad to welcome her drop-in visitors, and then her eyes rested on Bridget and her smile faded. "And who is this," she asked quietly, moving slowly in Bridget's direction. "Is it . . . it can't be . . . is it Bridget?"

"Yes, ma'am," Bridget answered. She had settled herself in one of the armchairs, but she got to her feet now. The woman held out both her hands, and Bridget raised her own and let the woman clasp them.

"Bridget, our Bridget, I never thought . . . and you're the image of her, you are, just like I said you would be."

Mr. McKenna decided it was time to make proper introductions. "Bridget, this is your mother's aunt, Laura. Laura, Bridget came back to live with us after the accident. And this is my friend, Natalie."

But Laura wasn't interested in Natalie. "Richard," she called again to the kitchen, "come and see Bridget."

Richard hobbled into the room, moving unsteadily with the aid of a cane. "Bridget?" he echoed. "Bridget is here?"

The two old people marveled over her. "Isn't she the image of Christy?" Laura said.

"It's amazing," Richard agreed.

"Oh, poor Bridget," Laura gushed suddenly, taking Bridget in her arms. "I'm sorry, so sorry, this summer must have been horrible for you."

"When we heard about Christy," Richard said quietly, "we just couldn't believe it. Even after so many years without seeing her, we just couldn't imagine . . ." He paused, not knowing how to continue.

"We couldn't imagine a world without her in it," Laura finished. She released Bridget but held on to her hands again. "It must have been so much worse for you."

Overwhelmed and confused, Bridget shook her head. "I don't understand," she said. "Who are you talking about? Who is Christy?"

Laura's face mirrored Bridget's own confusion for an instant but quickly cleared. "Oh, of course, you didn't hear her called that. I know when she got older she preferred to go by Margaret. Your mother, of course. I'm talking about your mother."

"My mother went by Christy?"

"Yes, when she was a girl. When she was growing up here. It's her middle name, you know: Christine."

"My mother grew up here?"

"Yes, her folks lived just down the street. Of course, they passed away quite a while ago, before Christy went out to California. But this is where she met your father, didn't you know?"

Bridget shook her head again. "There's so much I don't know. And more and more all the time." She thought of the envelope in her treasure box at home, the label "C & C." She had never heard her mother referred to as Christy before, but of course that must be what one of the Cs stood for. And the other?

"Laura—Aunt Laura," Bridget began, "there's so much . . ." *So much I want to ask you,* she meant to say. But suddenly she felt acutely aware of her father's presence. She didn't want to talk in front of him. She wanted to whisk Laura off somewhere private and listen for hours as the old woman expounded on the mystery that was Bridget's mother.

"Bridget," Mr. McKenna said softly. "Laura, Richard, we have to be going. It's late. We just stopped in to say hello."

Bridget turned to face him. "Just stopped in to say hello," she repeated, "as if I wouldn't have any questions?"

Mr. McKenna's countenance darkened, but he said quite gently, "We'll come another time. For now . . ."

Lydia, who didn't like the attention the couple were showering on Bridget, jumped up from her seat. "Yeah, let's go. It's late."

Bridget lingered for a few moments longer, but eventually Mr. McKenna succeeded in herding them all back out toward the car.

"It was nice meeting you," Natalie said as she passed through the front door.

Laura, whose eyes had remained fixed on Bridget, glanced at Natalie in surprise.

"Oh, yes, of course," she responded hastily. "Nice meeting you." She stood in the doorway watching them, with Richard leaning on his cane behind her, even after they had all gotten into the car and started down the street. Bridget could see the little rectangle of light from the doorway until all the lights merged together into a blur behind them and the darkness of the highway engulfed them.

s e v e n t e e n

The next morning at breakfast, Bridget tried to question Mr. McKenna, but he refused to talk about the events of the previous day. The meal passed mostly in silence, and as soon as it was over, Bridget's father shut himself in his office. He even failed to gather them for family scripture study, which didn't seem to disappoint anyone. He emerged only in time to accompany them all to church, and after the service he sent them home alone so that he could stay for meetings.

After lunch, Bridget went up to her room and opened her treasure box. She held the manila envelope and wondered how many answers it might contain. She wished she could ask someone to read the letters for her and then report any pertinent information. Who was C? she wanted to know. If her mother had gone by Christy as a girl, it must be someone she had met when she was young. So, was it Bridget's father? She inspected the handwritten label. Maybe one of the C's was actually a G. But the writing was neat and clear. It was hard to imagine that she had mistaken one of the letters.

Eventually she put the envelope back without reading anything, as she had so many times before. She hoped her father would prove more talkative later, and maybe she could get some answers from him then.

But the next day's mail brought something that put all other thoughts out of her mind. Mrs. Prescott had a letter for her when she arrived home from school.

"I better give this to you right away," Mrs. Prescott said as soon as Bridget came in the door. "I've been watching for you to get home. I knew you'd be anxious to see this." She pulled an envelope out of her apron pocket and handed it to Bridget, who trembled as she took it. The return address said Stanford. She stared at it, suddenly too frightened to find out what it said. How could such an important verdict come in such a simple format? It looked no more impressive than a credit card offer or an electric bill, and yet it held the answer to her future. No, not even just that, to the past too. Because if it said that she was accepted, then all her efforts had meant something, and she could let go of all the frustration about coming to this backward high school and the stress of dealing with Mrs. Keller, whose expectations she couldn't understand, much less meet. All that wouldn't matter anymore because she would know for sure that next year she could go home. And she would go home with honor, the way she wanted to.

Only what if it said she wasn't accepted?

She didn't even want to think about that possibility, but it *was* a possibility, and she had to face that now. It could be a moment away, the end of all her plans. It wouldn't take long to destroy them. Only as long as it took to open the envelope.

It felt thin in her hands. What was it that people said about thin envelopes? She tried not to think about it. She felt Mrs. Prescott watching her and knew that she needed to be alone.

"I think I'll go for a walk," she said. Mrs. Prescott nodded.

Once outside, she turned north without thinking about it and retraced the route she had taken on her first morning in Phrygia. Friday's snow had all melted away now, but today the sky hung heavy and gray, threatening another storm. When she reached the canal, she left the road and sloshed through muddy grass to the bank. Here she had sat on that first morning, resolving to take matters into her own hands. Had she succeeded? She had meant to get answers to her questions, but the questions had piled up and the answers seemed out of reach. More than anything, she wanted to leave this place and go home to familiar things. She looked down at the envelope. She couldn't drag this out anymore—she just had to do it. She ripped into the paper and tore out the letter inside. It was a single printed sheet, no brochures or housing applications . . . but maybe that stuff came later. She fumbled clumsily as she unfolded the letter. An eternity seemed to pass as she struggled to get it where she could read it. And then, in the briefest of moments, she had her answer.

She wasn't going home.

They wouldn't take her. They didn't know how desperate she was, how hard she had worked . . . Oh, now she was being stupid. That stuff didn't matter. If she wasn't good enough, she wasn't good enough, that was all there was to it.

She had started crying without realizing it. The scene before her blurred, the tree branches running together like a giant net. If only she had worked harder. But how—how could she have?

If only Mrs. Keller had been more reasonable, then the last set of grades sent to Stanford would have been perfect, all A's. What did that woman want? How many times did Bridget have to tell her that she wasn't her mother? Her mother—there was the crux of the matter. How could she have condemned Bridget to spend her senior year here? How could she have sent her daughter's life plunging off course as recklessly as the car that had killed her? All for some stupid boyfriend whose name she wouldn't have remembered in a few weeks time if . . . if she had lived. If she had lived—oh, if she had lived—that would have made all the difference.

"Mama," Bridget groaned, her chest tightening in a sob. "Mama, why? Why, why, *why*?" She cried with abandon, not caring if some passerby chanced to hear her. What did it matter? What did anything matter anymore? And then she heard a voice say, "Bridget?"

She sucked in air quickly and choked, coughing and spluttering, but even as she struggled to catch her breath she whipped around angrily, ready to shout at whoever had addressed her. She had come here to be alone, she needed to be alone. Why was someone bothering her now?

Jeff took a hesitant step toward her and said again, "Bridget?"

"What are you doing here?" She flung the question like an accusation. "Don't tell me you're still searching for that stupid beetle!"

He glanced down at his shoes, poking at a clump of grass with one toe. "No, no bugs this time." He met her eyes sheepishly. "I saw you leave your house with an envelope, and you looked so anxious that I thought it might be the one . . . you know . . ."

"And so you *followed* me?"

"Well, no, not exactly. I just thought I'd wait around for you to get back so I could hear the news, and then you didn't come back, so I thought I'd walk and meet you along the way, and then I heard you—"

"How did you know I'd come here, anyway?"

"I didn't know for sure, I only thought maybe."

Bridget turned away and wiped at her tears. "I don't really want to talk right now."

"I know. I'm sorry."

"I want to be alone."

"I know."

"So, go away!" she ordered. She heard the sucking sound of displaced mud as he raised his feet to go, and when she turned back she saw him retreating into the trees. "Jeff," she called after him. "Wait!"

He stopped and looked at her inquisitively, and she gaped back at him, her mouth open in a silent cry.

"I'm not sure I want to be alone after all," she confessed finally. The sobs that she had stifled still shivered through her chest. He walked back to her, and this time he came to her and put his arms around her. She rested her cheek against his shoulder.

"A shoulder to cry on," she muttered, laughing stiffly and hiccuping.

"Right. Might as well make use of it."

She felt tears leaking out again, quietly this time. A pain seeped through her whole body. "It's just—" she began, her voice quavering, "it's all I ever wanted."

"I know."

"I don't know if I can stand it."

Jeff was quiet for a moment, and then he said, "You can, because there are people who want you here, who will be relieved not to lose you."

"No, no, no," she cried. "I have to go home. Somehow. I'll go to another school in California." But the future seemed bleak anyway. It wouldn't be the same, going home to attend a school she had chosen at the last minute.

"Bridget," Jeff said. "Bridget, everything will be okay." He rubbed one hand up and down her back to soothe her. "Bridget, maybe you *are* home."

She tore away from him. "No, no, you're wrong!"

"Bridget, I . . ." he was staring at her intently. She had never seen him look like that before. "Bridget, I've wanted to tell you . . ."

"What?"

He shifted his weight uncomfortably. "Look, this is probably the wrong time. I don't expect you to say anything back, I just wanted you to know . . . people will be glad if you stick around. *I'll* be glad . . ."

"That's sweet of you, Jeff, but—"

"Bridget, I love you."

"Shut up!" screamed another voice. "Shut up! Shut up! Stop it!"

Both Bridget and Jeff spun around, startled, and saw Lydia standing a little way off, her fists pumping in the air.

"Lydia," Bridget exclaimed, "what are *you* doing here?"

"I wanted to talk to Jeff, and I saw him walking out here. But you make him lie; you're a big liar!" She ran to Bridget and shoved her. Jeff grasped her around the waist and pulled her back.

"Lydia, calm down, it's all right."

"No, it's not," she screamed, her arms flailing. "She makes you tell lies, you don't love her, nobody does. Mother didn't love her best, she didn't choose her because she wanted her!"

"What are you talking about?" Bridget shouted over her sister's screams. "You're not making any sense!"

"Mother didn't love you best, she only took you because she decided at the last minute, when she already had you in the car, and she drove off and she had you with her, but she didn't want you, she didn't want you any more than she wanted us!"

Bridget had thought her sister was just rambling, but now she began to pay attention. "What are you talking about?" she said again. "What are you saying?"

"When Mom decided to leave, she just took you, she just left. She didn't stop to think. If she had thought, she wouldn't have left us that way." Lydia began to cry. "She wouldn't have left us. And Jeff doesn't love you," she mumbled through her tears. "No, you can't have everyone. You can't have everyone."

"Jeff, what is she saying?" Bridget demanded, but he was staring at Lydia with a mixture of fear and tenderness.

"Lydia, you don't have a crush on me, do you? Not on me, the bug guy."

Lydia began to cry harder.

"Jeff!" Bridget yelled. "What is she talking about?"

Jeff looked up at her. "Don't you know, Bridget?"

"No, I don't know! I don't know what you're all talking about, what you're keeping from me!" A new set of tears, this time from frustration, swelled up and spilled onto her cheeks.

"When your mom left, she didn't tell anyone." Jeff let the words tumble out swiftly, as if he had been keeping them in for a long time and couldn't manage it anymore. "She just picked you up from school and disappeared. She drove by the turnoff for home and went to California instead. It took her three days to get around to calling your dad to let him know where the two of you were. Don't you remember any of that?"

Bridget opened her mouth to tell him that he had it all wrong, but the breath had gone out of her.

"Bridget, you're back home now after ten years, you're home where you were supposed to be all along. Why can't you just stop fighting it and let people care about you!"

"No," Bridget croaked, her voice still refusing to function normally. "You don't know what you're talking about. My mother didn't . . . she wasn't . . ."

"Mother didn't really want you," Lydia sobbed. "She wanted me, she wanted me."

"My mother didn't kidnap me!"

"They had the police after you, searching. There was no note, nothing. They thought something awful had happened."

"Stop it, Jeff, that's enough!" Bridget clamped her hands over her ears, desperate to shut out his voice.

"But no," Jeff went on, "there hadn't been an accident, no blood, no death, your mother had just neglected to inform her husband that she was leaving him, that's all, and that she was taking you with her!"

"She didn't want to take Bridget," Lydia cried again.

"Hush, Lydia," Jeff said, his voice gentle again. "She didn't know *what* she wanted. She wasn't thinking."

"Don't talk about my mother that way!" Bridget commanded. "You don't know anything about it, you were seven years old!"

"So were you. Don't you remember? Don't you remember any of it? You do, but you don't want to. You want to remember what your mother told you."

"My mother never told me anything but the truth."

"Oh, yeah? What did she tell you about your father, that he didn't want you anymore, that he was a jerk and you were both well rid of him?"

"Nothing!" Bridget shouted. "She told me nothing about my father! She didn't lie, no, no, she didn't—" But she couldn't say anymore. Suddenly she was crying as hard as Lydia. She remembered what Melanie had said about the presents her father had chosen for her. Had her mother really kept them from her? Had she intercepted any and all communication from Bridget's father? No, it couldn't be true. It hurt too much.

It couldn't be true, but then what was the real explanation? Her mind raced, filling her head with thoughts and images she didn't want there. She tried to shut them out, but they kept on coming, memories of her mother, of both her parents, and things that weren't memories at all but that played out just as vividly. She saw her father coming home to an empty house, calling for his wife, who should have been there, and hearing only his own voice. She saw the worry on his face when she hadn't returned hours later, when he phoned her friends and found that none of them had seen her. She felt his panic as the hours turned into days with no clues, only emptiness. And Lydia, old enough to understand a little of what was going on . . . how had it been for her to know that her mother and sister had disappeared? Even worse, to know that her mother had left her voluntarily and let her suffer those three days when she could have stopped it, when she could simply have turned the car around or even picked up the phone to say, "I'm safe. I'm safe, and I love you."

A wave of sickness swept over Bridget. She had admired her mother for so long, and all the time Margaret had been this selfish person, a person whose little children didn't matter to her. What Lydia said was probably true—it was only by chance that she even took Bridget with her—and she probably regretted it too, when she couldn't flit off to parties and other events at a moment's notice. . . . But she did that anyway, Bridget remembered. *She left me alone anyway.* She thought of the dream that she had had on her first night in Phrygia, of the scared nine-year-old girl huddled on the sofa in her mother's town house yearning for morning to come. That memory, she knew, was true enough, that fear was real enough. But her mother hadn't cared. Her book had already been a best seller by then; surely she didn't really have to go to that book signing in L.A. Or she could have rescheduled it for some weekend when Suzanne's family could take Bridget in. But that might have been inconvenient. Why should she put herself out? She wasn't that kind of person, Bridget saw now. She didn't care what her children went through. She hadn't loved Lydia enough, and she hadn't loved Bridget either, and she had hardly even known Charly.

She didn't love me, Bridget thought. *She didn't want me. She didn't want any of us.*

She turned away from Jeff and Lydia and hurled herself up the bank toward the road. Breaking through the trees, she ran without checking for traffic, ran as hard as she could, her breath tearing in and out. She had to get to

Melanie. Melanie would know what had really happened; she could tell her that none of this was true, that this nightmare wasn't real.

"Melanie," she yelled from half a block away. "Melanie, Melanie, I have to talk to you!" She ran to the door and pounded on it. "Melanie!" What if she wasn't home? What if she had gone off to do errands? But no, the door opened, and Melanie stood there with flour up to her elbows and on her cheeks, looking alarmed.

"Bridget, what is it? What's happened?"

Bridget wanted to tell her everything at once, but instead she leaned against Melanie and sobbed. Melanie patted her clumsily with what felt like the side of her arm, probably because she didn't want to get flour all over Bridget. As if it mattered!

"Bridget, sweetheart, come and sit down at the table and tell me all about it," Melanie coaxed. "Come on, come and sit down." Bridget allowed herself to be led into the room and settled into a chair. Melanie turned to the sink to wash up. "When I heard you calling," she explained, "I just dropped everything, so excuse the mess." She dried quickly on a dishtowel and then came to sit next to Bridget. "Now tell me, what is it? What's happened? Is everyone all right?"

Bridget nodded.

"No one is hurt?"

Bridget shook her head no.

"Thank goodness for that. But then what can it be? What's upset you like this?"

Bridget didn't know if her voice would work, but it just had to, she had to know the truth. "Melanie," she began, struggling to get herself under control. "Melanie, my mother—did she . . . was she . . ."

"Yes? What is it?" Melanie prompted.

"Is it true? Did she kidnap me? Did she take off without

telling anyone? I know it couldn't have happened like that. She and Dad got a divorce, it was all legal."

Melanie looked away. She didn't answer immediately.

"Melanie? Tell me! Tell me the truth. What happened?"

"What do you remember?" Melanie asked carefully.

"I don't know. I don't know anymore." *That day in my car, I just turned and sped away.* The words of the song she had written for the talent show last spring came back to her, running through her mind with new meaning. *The land flowed by so fast, no stopping, no home place, no love, no warmth, no place to stay.* But those were just some made-up lyrics, she told herself. Hadn't she said all along that they didn't mean anything?

"She picked me up from school—" Bridget faltered. "Just like every other day. And my sisters weren't with her."

"No," Melanie affirmed. "She'd been running errands that afternoon, so she'd left them with me."

"You had them?"

"Yes. Lydia was in kindergarten then, but she went half days, so she was already home from school. Your mother had dropped her and Charly off with me. I was expecting her back around 3:30, after she picked you up. But she—"

"She never came," Bridget finished dully. She felt as if all the emotion had left her, as if she had died inside. "She passed the turnoff for home and went to California instead," she said, repeating Jeff's words. "And she never meant to take me with her."

"I don't know what she meant," Melanie countered. "Her decision to leave was sudden, but I don't think it was as impulsive as people believe. I think she had had it in her mind for a long time. I think she had planned things out, not knowing if she would really act on the plan or when she would do it. She could have dropped you off somewhere if she didn't want to take you, or she could have waited for the next day, when you and Lydia were both in school and Charly was with me. She knew you were old enough that you could deal with the life she could give you. She couldn't have taken care of Lydia and Charly as well; they were too young. So it wasn't an accident that she left them behind."

"I thought she did it for their sake, because she knew she wouldn't have much money."

"Well," Melanie considered, "I think that's true."

"She could have had enough money if she'd wanted it. She could have had alimony, child support . . ."

"But she didn't," Melanie said. "She wouldn't take anything from your father. She wanted a clean break. She was finished with this part of her life."

"I was sure it was all his fault, that he had driven her away with his stupid rules. That's what his life is all about. But she . . . she . . ."

"She didn't like rules," Melanie filled in the blanks. "It was hard for her here. Being in the Church was hard for her. To her credit, she did try."

"She did? She did go to church? Lydia said so, but I didn't know."

"Yes, she went every week when she lived here. And more than that, she served in every position they asked her to. She brought meals to sick members and shut-ins, and she stayed late at church events to help clean up. She did it all, but her heart wasn't in it."

"Why did she do it then?"

"I suppose it all went along with the life she was trying to create here, the life she ended up walking out on."

"What do you mean?"

"She wasn't raised as a Mormon, you know, but she joined the Church because it was so important to your father. He wanted to be married in the temple. So it was always something foreign to her, something she had given in to for Gerrick's sake, and she resented that. She loved him, but she wanted to love him separately from his religion. She didn't understand that his beliefs are part of what makes him the man that he is, the kind of man that she would love. It didn't work to break him into pieces and love certain pieces without loving the others. So of course she was unhappy. Who can blame her, really?"

I can, Bridget thought. "I could tell people here didn't like her," she said out loud. "But I didn't understand why. I thought they were just closed-minded, or that my father had brainwashed them because my mother wasn't around to tell her side of the story. But all the time they knew this about her. They knew—"

"They knew that she wasn't perfect," Melanie said. "You're used to people who only knew her as a famous novelist. People who thought she was larger than life."

I *thought she was larger than life*. How could Bridget not have seen through her before? The ugliness of what her mother had done haunted her. "Not perfect?" she said to Melanie. "That's putting it mildly. How could she do that? How could she abandon—" She stuck on that word. Hadn't Mrs. Stewart at the bookstore used the word "abandon," and Bridget had disliked her for it. "How could she not tell someone where she was going?"

"Maybe she thought Gerrick would find a way to bring her back if she didn't put some distance between them. Maybe she didn't trust her own resolve. I don't know. None of us do, so it isn't worth thinking about."

"But they had the police out searching for missing persons!"

"Yes, it was a scary time. We thought we were all safe in this little town, and suddenly we didn't feel safe anymore," Melanie remembered. "It was such a relief to find out that you were both okay."

Bridget shook her head. "It doesn't make any sense!"

"What part of it?"

"Why did she marry my father in the first place?"

Melanie shrugged. "Well, she'd loved him since she was a little girl."

"And then she married him and had kids and had to deal with real life, and then she decided she didn't love him anymore," Bridget surmised.

"No, I think she loved him still. I don't think she ever stopped."

"How can you say that?"

"Because even after she left she thought about him."

"How do you know?" Bridget questioned. "She never talked about him."

"Maybe not, but she wrote about him."

"What? What are you talking about?"

"Don't you know? Colin the superhero? He's your father."

Bridget stared at her. "What? No, I don't think so. You're wrong."

"Colin is your father's middle name. It's what your mother called him. She thought 'Gerrick' was too stuffy. And the adventures she wrote about—those were real. Or at least, as the titles of the books say, they were 'mostly true.'"

Bridget burst out of her chair and began to pace back and forth. She couldn't sit still any longer, couldn't hold all this new information without exploding. "My father—Colin the superhero? My father is nothing like Colin!"

He could row like Colin, though, and his father owned his own business, just like Colin's father. Well, that didn't mean anything. Those were common enough traits. And Colin had a friend named Kristy, just like her father, but it wasn't even spelled the same. Her mother's middle name was spelled with a C, not a K. Then she thought of the conversation she had overheard between her father and Natalie on the drive home from Oberrath College. According to her father, her mother had left him because he had "grown up." She realized now that Colin would never have grown up. In the book Margaret was working on when she died, Colin was in high school, but Margaret had sworn that she wasn't going to write anymore Colin books after that one. She wasn't interested in Colin's life as an adult. But of course, her main audience was children so that only made sense.

"This is all crazy," Bridget exclaimed. "It can't be right. And my mother—I can't believe my mother was . . . was so . . ."

Melanie came to her and folded her into a hug. When she let her go, she said, "Bridget, I don't want to sound like a broken record. But you should open up a corner of your mind where your mother isn't a villain."

"How can you defend her when you knew her, when you saw what she did?"

"She was human, Bridget. She was fallible. But there was more to her than the mistakes she made. All her goodness—you saw that. Don't forget it now, okay?"

Bridget shook her head. "I don't know what to think. I don't know where to go . . ."

"You don't need to go anywhere. You've come home now." Melanie put a hand on Bridget's shoulder. "You're home."

* * *

That night Bridget awoke to the sound of Lydia crying. She tried to shut out the noise and go back to sleep, but her sister's mourning seemed to tremble through her own body. She lay in her bed listening to Lydia's grief until she couldn't stand it anymore. She got up and padded downstairs. She found Charly sitting cross-legged on her bed, staring helplessly at Lydia, who shook with the intensity of her sadness.

Bridget eased herself down onto Lydia's bed and placed

a hand on her sister's back. Lydia started under the touch and then jumped away as if burned.

"D-d-don't you t-t-touch me," she hissed, the sobs tearing at her through the words. "Go away!"

"Lydia," Bridget said. "I'm so sorry. I'm so sorry for what happened to you."

"She d-d-didn't l-l-love you b-b-best," Lydia spluttered, burying her face in her pillow. "No, no, she d-d-didn't!"

"You're right," Bridget replied. "She didn't. She loved you. She left you here because she knew Dad could take better care of you than she could. She knew you'd be better off here."

"She w-w-wanted m-m-me," Lydia moaned. The words came out muffled from the depths of the pillow.

"Of course she did," Bridget soothed, reaching again for her sister's back and rubbing gently. This time Lydia didn't recoil. "That's why she wrote to you all the time. She missed you so much. She loved you."

Lydia cried for a long time, and Bridget sat stroking her back, waiting for the grief to spend itself out. Finally, the sobs began to die down, and after a while Lydia lay quiet and trembling with her face still hidden. "She didn't," Lydia whimpered.

"What?" asked Bridget. "I didn't hear you."

"She didn't love me," Lydia repeated in a small voice.

"Tell her, Bridget," Charly prodded, coming over to stand next to Lydia's bed. "Tell her she's wrong. Bridget—" Charly gasped, "you're crying too!"

Bridget leaned over Lydia, pressing her cheek against the girl's dark hair. "I love you, Lydia," she whispered. She reached out and grasped Charly's hand. "I love you, Charly. I love you both."

Charly began crying softly. *That makes three of us,* thought Bridget, and she held onto her sisters until the tears had washed the sharpness of the pain away.

e i g h t e e n

The next day at school Bridget tried unsuccessfully to concentrate, but the day passed by in a haze. As she left the building alone, having let Jeff know that she needed some space, she couldn't remember what any of her teachers had talked about. She saw Jeff heading toward home with Lydia and hoped that the two of them would reach an understanding of some sort. She began walking slowly, not in any hurry to arrive home herself. A few snowflakes floated into her vision. The storm that had hung over the town since yesterday was ready to break loose. She felt no excitement about the snow this time. She couldn't imagine ever getting excited again.

A car pulled up next to her. "Bridget," called a familiar voice. She stopped walking but stared at her feet. This was all she needed. "Bridget, get in please. It's cold. You're not even dressed for this weather."

She turned her head to meet her father's eyes. "I'm just never dressed right for you, am I?"

"Bridget, I'm sorry."

Her eyes widened. "What did you say?" It hadn't even come out sounding pompous. It had sounded, well, genuine.

"I said I'm sorry. Please get in the car. We need to talk."

She obeyed this time, rolling up the window quickly and welcoming the warm air blowing from the vents.

"Melanie told me what happened yesterday. I'm sorry

you had to find out about things the way you did." He pulled the car away from the curb but didn't turn it toward home.

"Did she also tell you I didn't get in to Stanford? I know you won't be sorry about that."

"I *am* sorry," he contradicted. "I'm sorry that something happened to make you sad. I'm sorry that you're suffering."

Bridget gazed over at him, wondering if those words had really come from her father. Her first few weeks in New York, he hadn't even seemed like a real person; he was a set of rules, a schedule, a stopwatch ticking away disapprovingly. But lately, she had caught glimpses of a human being underneath. "I just wanted to go home," she told him now. "I wanted it so much."

"And you wanted to be good enough," he added. "I understand that. It's what I always wanted too. You thought if Stanford accepted you, that's what it would mean: that you were okay, that you were enough. I thought if Christy— your mother, that is—if she loved me, that meant that I was good enough, and when she stopped loving me, it meant I was broken."

Bridget was still watching him, but he kept his eyes focused on the road. "Are you Colin?" she asked.

"I was once," he replied.

"What do you mean?"

"That used to be me," he said. "Apparently I changed."

"You grew up."

"I don't know. Maybe it was more than that. Maybe I really did change. I didn't do things right when we were first married. I wanted to provide all the good things in life, so I worked hard, and when Christy complained that she never saw me, I didn't listen. I didn't hear what she was trying to tell me. I just worked harder. I thought that was the right thing to do, but now I see it was a mistake."

"But it's still what you do," Bridget informed him. "You're never home."

"I know. I keep making the same mistakes." He glanced over at her. "It scares me, to tell you the truth. I want to change, but I don't know how. I worry that I'm not being a good father to Lydia and Charly, and to you, but all I can think to do is work. It terrifies me to think of marrying Natalie because I'm afraid it will all fall apart again. She's very much like Christy, in lots of ways."

"But she already knows the grown-up you. That's who she fell in love with."

"I'm afraid she just puts up with me. Sooner or later she'll come to her senses and realize that she deserves better."

Bridget couldn't believe her father was saying this. Maybe he couldn't believe it either, that he was letting her see his real self this way, because he sounded a bit stiff again when he said, "Maybe we should head home now."

"Okay."

They rode in silence until he turned onto their street, and then he volunteered suddenly, "Do you know my favorite memory of your mother? It was when I was in junior high. I was running for student government, class president or something, and I had to give a speech. Well, I froze up completely. I stood up there in front of the whole school, and all I could think about was what an idiot I must look like. Especially to *her*. I wished she had been home sick or something. But she saved me. She came up behind me and squeezed my hand, and that awakened me. It was like magic."

"I know that moment," Bridget told him. "I've read about it."

He pulled the car into the driveway and turned off the engine. "That's right," he mused, looking over at her. "It's in the books, isn't it?"

"Yes, it is."

"You know what's always been a mystery to me? And maybe you can help me with this."

"What is it?"

"How did she know what it was like to be me?"

Bridget shook her head. "I don't know. That was her genius."

"It was her magic."

They both reached for the door handles, but once Bridget had climbed out of the car, her father spoke to her again.

"Bridget," he called to her across the roof of the car. She looked at him through a thickening slurry of snowflakes.

"Yeah?"

"What are you going to do tonight? Maybe we should all go out for pizza. It's been a long time since we did that."

"That's a good idea," she said. "Only let's not stay out too long. I've got some college applications to work on."

He nodded. "All California schools?"

"No, not all," she admitted. "I figure it doesn't hurt to apply to Oberrath."

"No, it doesn't hurt. That's true." They headed inside, shaking the snow from their clothing in the little foyer between the doors.

"I wasn't completely honest with you when you asked me about my future plans," Bridget declared as she stomped to loosen a piece of wet snow that clung to her shoe. "I know what I want to go into. I didn't tell you because . . . well, I don't know. But I've always wanted to be a lawyer."

Her father's eyes twinkled. "Really?"

"Yeah."

"Lydia's always wanted to be a writer."

"I know."

"Just promise me one thing," her father requested.

"What's that?"

"Be smarter than I was. Than I am. Don't work too hard. There's more to life than school and work."

Bridget smiled. "Like pizza?"

"Yes," he replied. "Like pizza."

n i n e t e e n

Bridget finished her college applications as quickly as possible and then tried not to think much about the coming year. She still longed for California, but she wasn't sure she could bear going home now. It wouldn't be the same going back to attend some school other than Stanford, but even more than that, the new knowledge she had about her mother had tainted her memories of the place. When she imagined San Francisco now, their familiar street, their town house, she felt repulsed. She didn't want to think about her mother at all.

She kept to herself a lot as Christmas approached. She had avoided Jeff as much as possible, embarrassed by the emotion they had both shown. She didn't know how to respond to his declaration of love. Probably he didn't mean it anyway. It was easiest to believe that.

Lydia ignored her as much as possible, which at least brought peace to the house. Matt ignored her too, and Bridget was content with that. She spent time with Charly now and then, once to build a snowman on a Saturday afternoon, a few times to go downtown or into Rochester for Christmas shopping. Overall, life seemed bland but bearable, and she worked hard to focus on the present moment and leave the future to take care of itself.

One evening Mrs. Stewart from the bookstore phoned and asked to speak to Bridget.

"I have a request to make," Mrs. Stewart said when

Bridget picked up the receiver. "If you don't want to do it, I understand, but I at least wanted to ask."

"Okay." Bridget had no idea what to expect.

"I don't know if you remember, but when you came into the store this fall I told you that your mother's publisher had been pushing me to host some kind of event where people could come and ask questions about your mother."

She paused, and Bridget said, "Yes?"

"Well, I didn't want to do it. I thought it was exploitation. But the publisher is still pushing for it, and I started to think maybe there was a way to do it tastefully and respectfully. What do you think? How would your mother have felt about it?"

"I think she would have loved the attention," Bridget responded truthfully.

"Well, what I wanted to ask you is, would you be willing to come and speak about her? And then answer questions? You're the one who should do it. You knew her best."

Bridget hesitated, then said slowly, "Mrs. Stewart, I'm sorry, but I just don't think I could talk about her."

"I understand," Mrs. Stewart said quickly. "I probably shouldn't have asked. It must still be very painful."

"I'm sorry," Bridget said again.

"Not at all. Don't give it another thought."

"What was that about?" Mr. McKenna asked when she hung up the phone.

"It was Mrs. Stewart from the bookstore."

"What did she want?"

"She wanted me to come and speak about my mother and answer people's questions. The publisher wants her to have something like that as a promotional event."

Mr. McKenna looked thoughtful. "Hmm," he said. "Sounds like Christy's kind of thing."

"Yeah," Bridget agreed. "That's what I said."

"Are you going to do it then?"

"No, I can't. I can't talk about her."

"You knew her best."

"There were some very important things I didn't know about her," Bridget pointed out. "Now that I do know, I don't want to talk about her ever again. She disgusts me. She doesn't deserve the adoration of all those fans. Maybe I could tell them that, peel a little of the fake gold off her reputation."

"Bridget, don't be bitter," her father counseled. "You loved her and trusted her for seventeen years. Don't throw that away because of the events of a few days."

"I can't go there and talk about her books like she was some wonderful person."

"Then go and talk about them like she was a talented but human person."

"I don't get it," Bridget said. "Suddenly everyone's so ready to forgive her."

"Well," Mr. McKenna replied, "we've had ten years. I guess we should give you a little more time."

It snowed the next morning and again over the next few weeks, with big fluffy flakes that piled up swiftly. By the time school let out for the Christmas holidays, the town lay blanketed under two or three feet of snow. "Oh, this is perfect, just perfect!" Charly had enthused with every new snowfall. "A perfect, white, white Christmas!"

Charly and Lydia were relieved and excited for the vacation from school, but Bridget worried what she would do with herself. She didn't want to sit around with too much time to think. She considered going over to visit Jeff and trying to make things right with him, but she couldn't imagine what to say. She was upstairs in her room reading a book from her father's library when the doorbell rang on the afternoon of Christmas Eve. She didn't pay much attention; she knew either Lydia or Mrs. Prescott was downstairs to answer it. Soon a familiar voice sounded in the downstairs hallway, and Bridget's stomach lurched uncomfortably. She hadn't gone to Jeff, but he had come to her.

"Bridget!" Mrs. Prescott called. "Come on downstairs, honey, you've got a visitor." Bridget didn't move at first. Could she pretend to be asleep? She shoved the book aside and rested her cheek against her bedspread, closing her eyes tight like a child trying to shut out the world. She could hear Mrs. Prescott coming up the stairs to fetch her. The woman's tread seemed more energetic than usual. Maybe those brussels sprout breakfasts were paying off.

"Bridget," Jeff said softly from the doorway.

She sat up quickly, startled to hear his voice so close. "I'm s-s-sorry," she stuttered, "I didn't expect you. I thought Mrs. Prescott—"

"She said her legs were too tired to walk up two flights, so she just sent me up."

"Oh." There seemed to be nothing more to say.

"I've missed you the past little while," he told her.

She met his eyes and admitted, "I've missed you too."

"Look, I never meant . . . I didn't want to ruin our friendship. I shouldn't have said what I did. Can you try to forget it? Just block it out."

"I guess you think I'm pretty good at that," she joked, but it wasn't funny and they both ended up staring at their shoes.

"Just forget it and let's start where we left off before all this happened," he pleaded.

Was that possible? she considered. Was it even what she wanted? "Well, are you saying . . . ?" She let the question hang unfinished in the air.

"What? All I'm saying is that I want to be friends," he declared, shuffling his feet and stuffing his hands in his jacket pockets. "That's it. No strings attached. I'm not asking for anything more."

"Ah."

"Ah? What is that supposed to mean? Come on, Bridget, you've got to be clear with me, you know I'm not as good with people as I am with bugs."

"I was just wondering," Bridget began, feeling shy but curious, "just, you know, are you telling me you didn't mean what you said?"

Jeff looked mortified. He shifted uncomfortably from one foot to the other and then back again. "Um, well, uh . . ."

Bridget felt inexplicably disappointed. "Okay, I guess you didn't mean it. It's all right," she said flatly.

"No, I . . ." He finally stopped scrutinizing his shoes and looked at her. "The truth is, I did mean it. But I promise I won't let it get in the way of things if, you know . . . I still want to be friends."

"Jeff," said Bridget, sliding off the bed and coming over to where he still stood in the doorway. "The thing is, I love you too."

"What?" he gasped.

"Don't be so shocked. You've been a good friend, my best friend. Why shouldn't I love you?"

His face fell. "Like a friend, you mean."

"You know, I think language can really get in the way of relationships," she complained. "Of course we're friends, but that doesn't mean . . ."

"It doesn't have to mean . . ."

"It isn't about being *just* friends . . ."

He moved a step toward her and bent close to her, and she let him. She let him kiss her. For a moment, an instant, all the things that had troubled her melted away, leaving only the warmth of being with someone she cared about and who cared about her too.

"Oh, my stars!" cried Mrs. Prescott from the hallway. "Oh, heavens to Betsy!" Jeff turned and stepped sideways so that both he and Bridget could see Mrs. Prescott through the open doorway. "I never should have done it, what was I thinking?" she fretted.

"Done what?" Bridget asked.

"Sent a boy—a *boy*—up to your room. What was I thinking? Oh, when your father hears about this—but I never meant for him to *stay* up here! Why didn't you both come down to the living room?"

Bridget giggled. "Mrs. Prescott, calm down. There's nothing to be so upset about. We'll go downstairs now."

"Nothing to be upset about? But you were in your room . . . oh, my stars, you were in your room *kissing.*"

Bridget glanced over at Jeff and saw that he was red from the roots of his hair to his shirt collar.

"My father *is* kind of uptight about boys," she said.

"Is your father home right now?" Jeff asked.

"No."

"Then maybe we should all go downstairs and forget this ever happened."

Safely installed in the living room, Bridget whispered, "You don't really want to forget everything, do you?"

"What? What are you talking about? I think you're going to have to remind me." He winked at her. "You know, jog my memory."

* * *

That evening when the family gathered around the lit Christmas tree, Bridget snuggled contentedly into one of the armchairs. It felt good to have things right between her and Jeff again, and it seemed only natural that their friendship should develop into something more. She watched her father sorting through the packages under the tree to find one for each of the girls to open early. The grownup Colin—she still could hardly believe it. Only—once in a while—it didn't seem so far-fetched. Like tonight when he had said he'd forgotten something and had run upstairs, returning a moment later wearing a Santa hat.

As the evening drifted on, she sat thinking about friendship and about Colin, how he had fallen in love with his best friend too, and they had married and had children and . . .

And Colin had rules for them the live by, because he was a Mormon, and Jeff was a Mormon too, and Christy wasn't and Bridget wasn't, and the whole thing had fallen apart. . . .

Pleading exhaustion, she left the living room early and went upstairs. This time when she opened her treasure box and pulled out the manila envelope, she didn't put it back without reading what was inside. She took out every letter and read every word, all the expressions of endearment between Colin and Christy, all the jokes, the details of everyday life, the messages that meant, even when they didn't say it, "I miss you and I love you." She shouldn't have been afraid of these letters; they were sweet and tender and innocent. They had been written while the two were at college in different cities, before marriage and children, before Bridget's mother had driven off into the sunset.

"Christy, how could you?" Bridget · whispered. She thought of her beautiful mother, imagined her sitting in front of the vanity demonstrating the proper application of lipstick. The memory made Bridget smile. *When all else fails*, she thought, *apply lipstick.*

Who had Margaret Lacey been? she wondered. What had she felt in those final days before she turned her back on New York forever? Had she been as selfish as Bridget had imagined, making the decision carelessly? Had she been unsure of herself, unsure of her future? Had she felt desperate, lonely, isolated among people she didn't understand? No, her mother was never unruffled. Or at least, she never let people see her that way. But when she wrote, she knew how it felt. She knew what it was like to be afraid. She had understood the insides of other people, the invisible places that they didn't show to everyone. How had she done it? What had been in her own heart? What were the secrets that she kept?

* * *

The day after Christmas, Bridget called Mrs. Stewart. "I've decided I'll come and talk about my mother—if you still want me to, that is."

"Are you sure? You don't have to, you know. I'll tell the publisher to shove it."

Bridget smiled at the woman's choice of words. "It's okay. I want to do it."

"Wonderful," said Mrs. Stewart. "That's just wonderful news."

She wanted to tell her father about her decision, but he had shut himself in his office. She waited around for him to come out until she couldn't stand it any longer. Then she went up to the door and knocked. She thought it was one of the boldest things she had ever done in her life.

Silence reigned on the other side of the door, but as she raised her fist to knock again, the door opened.

"Oh, uh, Bridget," said her father, looking startled. "What is it?"

"Am I disturbing you?"

"Well—no, of course not. Come in." He opened the door wider and stepped aside to let her pass. She expected to see legal documents spread out across his desk, but the desk was clear except for a single open book in the center.

"Individual scripture study?" she asked, recognizing the book.

"Yes," he said. "I know, I should be out there with you girls instead of in here, and we should be reading as a family. I just can't get everyone excited about that."

Bridget nodded sympathetically but said nothing, not wanting to encourage more family scripture reading.

"I guess you think I'm pretty bad at this stuff," her father said.

"What?" Bridget asked, surprised.

"I try to make you girls do all the right things, but I don't live up to my own standards. I know you think I've been unreasonable at times."

Bridget couldn't help smiling. "*Well*," she began.

Her father smiled back at her. "That's okay, you can give me a list of my shortcomings later."

Bridget laughed. "After I've had more time to think about it?"

"You've had plenty of time already, I should think."

"But I guess maybe . . . I mean, I think I understand some things now. Anyway, I came in to tell you that I'm going to do the event at the bookstore. I'm going to go and talk about Mom."

He nodded. "You're the only one who should do it."

"I'm not sure how well it'll go. I'm not great at speaking in front of crowds."

Her father shook his head. "Neither am I."

She thought of Colin's speech before the school. "I'll just do the best I can," she said.

"That's all we can do."

She opened the door again to leave, but before she shut it behind her, she said, "Dad?"

"Yes?"

"I know that's what you're doing—the best you can."

Her father gazed at her for a long time without speaking. Finally he said, "Thank you, Bridget."

She nodded and left him alone with his scriptures.

She found Lydia loitering in the hallway, perhaps waiting for her own chance to speak to Mr. McKenna. Bridget took a deep breath and asked, as cheerfully as possible, "Did you need to see Dad?"

"No," Lydia replied.

"Oh, okay." Bridget made a move to pass her, but Lydia stepped in front of her.

"I wanted to ask you something," Lydia said.

"Okay." Bridget braced herself for whatever was about to come next.

"Are you going to do it?"

"Do what?" Bridget asked, confused.

"You know. Are you going to talk about Mother at the bookstore? Is that what the phone conversation was about?"

Bridget hadn't realized that Lydia had been listening. But after all, it wasn't a secret. "Oh," she said. "Yes. Yes, I am."

"Well—" Lydia looked down at her feet, tracing an invisible pattern with her toe. "Um, would it be all right if I came?"

Bridget gaped at her for a moment but then made an effort to mirror Lydia's nonchalant manner.

"Yeah, that would be fine. Just fine."

Lydia looked up and gave Bridget a half smile. "Cool," she said, sounding like Charly.

* * *

Mrs. Stewart scheduled the event for early February. Winter still lay in thick drifts over the little town, but Mrs. Stewart fixed the store up to look cozy and served hot chocolate and spiced cider to the guests until she ran out of both drinks and space. The people who couldn't fit in the store to hear Bridget milled around outside, perhaps hoping for a chance to speak to her afterward.

Mrs. Stewart had asked her to prepare a short speech to give before she opened the floor for questions, so Bridget began by describing her mother as she knew her. It had been difficult writing her thoughts, but in the end she had found something important that she wanted to say.

"My mother was a real person," she told her audience. It was a little overwhelming to look out over them all and not even have a guitar to hold on to, but she needed to do this. "It may be hard for you to imagine if you've just read her books, but she did all the things normal people do. She went grocery shopping. She did laundry. She took out the trash. She always said those things were real life, and she didn't want to be above that. She made mistakes too, just like we all do. I even remember one time that she wore a shade of lipstick that didn't match her complexion at all." Bridget smiled, and a soft wave of laughter rippled through the crowd.

"She taught me a lot of important lessons. One thing she even taught me after she died. I've learned more about her over the last few months, and I understand now that her life didn't turn out the way she planned it. She fell in love with her childhood friend and married him, but it wasn't like playing house. It was hard work. And so she gave up on that life. But she didn't throw it away completely. She took the best parts of it, and she built her future out of those. She used her past experiences to inspire her writing. She maybe thought her past choices had been a mistake, but she couldn't have written what she did if not for her experiences. I think we can all learn from that because lots of times life doesn't turn out the way we plan." Bridget thought about her own future, the one that didn't have Stanford in it. The disappointment still ached. "But we can take what happens to us and make the very best out of it. And sometimes that best is better than we could ever have imagined. I know it was for my mother."

After her speech was over, Bridget answered questions for nearly two hours, until Mrs. Stewart finally stood up and announced that they had to bring things to a close.

"That went really well, Bridget," Mrs. Stewart told her

later when the store had begun to clear out. "Thank you for speaking. You did it just right."

Bridget didn't tell her that she was still trying to make herself believe all the things she had said, that she was still trying to find a balance between holding her mother on a pedestal and hating her for what she had done. She thought she might have to work at that for the rest of her life.

t w e n t y

In the spring, several things happened in quick succession. The last of the snow disappeared after one day of heavy rain, Bridget received an acceptance letter from Oberrath College and an offer for a full-ride scholarship there, Mrs. Keller returned one of Bridget's essays marked with an A and the comment "Better than the last Colin novel," and her father invited the missionaries over for dinner again. All in all, it was a busy week.

"Where are you from, Elder Snyder?" Bridget asked one of the missionaries over a meal of steak and green bean casserole.

"I'm from Idaho," he told her.

"Oh. A potato farmer?"

"No, I lived too far south for that. A dairy farmer."

"Oh. And how about you, Elder Grover?"

"I'm from Smithfield, Utah. Have you ever heard of it?"

"Never," Bridget admitted.

"You're missing out," Elder Grover declared soberly.

After dinner, they all went into the living room and the missionaries began talking about their feelings about God. Bridget reflected that they sounded a lot like Jeff, and when they talked about God as a Father, they really seemed to think of him that way.

"Bridget," said Elder Snyder, "what are your feelings about Heavenly Father? Do you believe that He exists?"

"I don't know," she said honestly. "When I was growing

up in California, it seemed like if there was a God, He wasn't very much like a father. Or at least, He was a very stern father whose main job was to punish people. My mother and I mostly stayed away from religion."

"I understand," Elder Snyder replied.

"Yeah," said Elder Grover. "That's the impression that a lot of people get. But I know that our Heavenly Father, although He does have to be stern sometimes, He's also very loving. He gives us rules—commandments—to help us become our best selves. He knows each of us personally. He knows you, and you can get to know Him, just like you know your earthly father."

After the missionaries had gone, Mr. McKenna pulled Bridget aside and asked her what she had thought about the things they said.

"They're both very nice," she hedged. "And they seem sincere."

"Yes. They believe in what they're saying."

"But—"

Her father's face fell. "But what?"

"I don't know. This is all still foreign to me. And the main thing is . . ."

"Yes?" her father prompted. "Go on."

"Do I have to join the Church in order to be part of this family? That's what my mother did, and it didn't work out very well for her."

Mr. McKenna looked startled. He took a step away from Bridget and began pacing back and forth.

"I'm not saying I wouldn't ever join," Bridget explained. "Maybe it's all true, I don't know. But I need to know that it isn't a requirement. That you'll still love me even if I'm not part of the Church. I don't ever want to join without having my heart in it, the way she did."

Mr. McKenna paused in his pacing, his back to Bridget. "I told you I keep making the same mistakes," he said, just barely loud enough for her to hear. "I hoped it would be simple to have Christy join, but you're right, it didn't work out too well." He turned slowly and looked at her. "Of course it's not a requirement."

"Good," said Bridget, relieved. "Thank you. I'll think things over, I promise. But I need some time."

He nodded. "Of course."

She watched him retreat into his office and wondered if it were possible, as the missionary had promised, to get to know her Heavenly Father as she had her earthly father. After all, she had started out thinking that Mr. McKenna was very stern, that he was all about punishment, or at least disapproval, but now she recognized that that wasn't his true character at all.

The next night when Jeff came over to pick Bridget up for a date, Mr. McKenna came out of his office to speak to them. "Ten-thirty," he proclaimed as Jeff helped Bridget put on her coat.

"But, Dad," Bridget objected, "it's a Friday night. How about eleven?"

Mr. McKenna folded his arms across his chest. "Eleven? I suppose that isn't too unreasonable. But I'm going to hold you to that." He eyed Jeff formidably. "Young man, I've told you both eleven, and I hope you'll help my daughter keep track of time because I do *not* mean 11:01."

"Yes, sir," Jeff responded meekly.

"Rules, rules," Bridget muttered.

Her father raised an eyebrow. "What was that?"

"Nothing," Bridget lied.

"I'm not an old man yet, Bridget. My hearing is fine. I'm not sure yours is, though. Don't you remember what the missionaries said? Rules from fathers are there to help you become your best self."

There, she thought, that was the man she knew, the one who would actually compare himself with God. But she had seen enough of him now to know that he wasn't as pompous as he sometimes seemed. She smiled at him sweetly and said, "Aren't you late for your date with Natalie? You better get going. Are you giving her the ring tonight?"

The change in his expression was humorous. From towering patriarch, he was reduced to jittery teenage boy. "Um, yes, over dinner at the French restaurant she likes."

"Sounds great, Dad," Bridget said, meaning it. "See you at eleven, then. I trust you'll be home on time?"

He narrowed his eyes. "Hmm, I think we'd better make it midnight."

Jeff and Bridget exchanged smiles. "Okay, no problem. And thanks again for the digital watch. Best Christmas present ever!"

She laughed as she and Jeff walked through the double doors into the crispness of a spring evening.

"You know," she remarked, linking her arm through Jeff's, "it's not so bad, really, having a curfew. I mean, I never used to have any rules, but it's kind of like having someone watching out for you, right? Caring that you stay safe."

"I guess you could look at it that way," Jeff agreed.

"And in the end," she said, "it's nice to come home."

about the author

Anative of Preston, Idaho, Amber Esplin studied French and history at Brigham Young University before spending a year in the Bay Area in California and then going to graduate school at the College of William and Mary in Williamsburg, Virginia. She began writing her first novel, *Leaving Eden*, after assisting a professor with a research project involving orphan children sent from England to America as apprentices. Upon completing the graduate program, Amber moved to a northern Virginia suburb of Washington, D.C., where she worked as a copy editor for microbiology journals. She now does freelance copy editing from her home in Midvale, Utah.

She began writing poems and short stories as a child and credits her eighth-grade English teacher, Mrs. Lewis, with encouraging her to pursue writing. In addition to writing, Amber enjoys running, playing the piano, and hang gliding. *The Long Journey Home* is her second novel.